T0374574

REGENESIS

REGENESIS

New Beginnings

D. R. KIN

PARTRIDGE
A Penguin Random House Company

To order additional copies of this book, contact
Toll Free 800 101 2657 (Singapore)
Toll Free 1 800 81 7340 (Malaysia)
orders.singapore@partridgepublishing.com

www.partridgepublishing.com/singapore

Contents

PART 1   FATE

Chapter 1   An Exceptional Flight 3
Chapter 2   The Good Doctor 11
Chapter 3   Finding Inner Strength 16
Chapter 4   Her Illness 25
Chapter 5   Discovering Eric Shi 34
Chapter 6   Strength in Time of Need 43
Chapter 7   Recollections 48
Chapter 8   Eric's Secret Past 52
Chapter 9   Connected 64
Chapter 10   Alex's Conviction 69

PART 2   GREEN ENERGY

Chapter 11   A Worthwhile Idea? 77
Chapter 12   The Mother of All Decisions.................................... 82
Chapter 13   Regenesis Is Born 90
Chapter 14   A Pair of Opposites 94
Chapter 15   Alex's Massive Change in Direction 100
Chapter 16   Defining the Team 106

Chapter 17   China 110
Chapter 18   Moving Forward 115
Chapter 19   Thirty Years Too Long................................... 119
Chapter 20   Sleeping with the Devil or Devils....................... 123
Chapter 21   Turbine Woes 133
Chapter 22   Satisfaction All Around.................................. 137
Chapter 23   To the Ocean 141
Chapter 24   The Last Piece of the Puzzle............................ 147
Chapter 25   The First of Its Kind.................................... 153
Chapter 26   The Floating Research Ship 157
Chapter 27   Rendezvous.. 165
Chapter 28   The Final Day 174
Chapter 29   Sabotage 180
Chapter 30   Chaos and Death 187
Chapter 31   World News... 195

PART 3   A LIFE TO SAVE

Chapter 32   Reconciliation...207
Chapter 33   A Secret No More 212
Chapter 34   An Illness without a Cure 218
Chapter 35   A Search Begins 230
Chapter 36   A Time for Reconciliation................................237
Chapter 37   Discovery..247
Chapter 38   The Answer 258
Chapter 39   The Ultimate Test....................................... 265
Chapter 40   A Dangerous Move 274
Chapter 41   A Continued Secret......................................285
Chapter 42   Regenesis: New Beginnings 288

PART 1

FATE

CHAPTER 1

AN EXCEPTIONAL FLIGHT

The plane suddenly shuddered, and Alex quickly held onto the glass of water on his tray table. The fasten seatbelt sign came on.

The intercom suddenly came alive. "This is the captain. We're experiencing turbulence at the moment. Please fasten your seatbelts. We should pass this turbulent air in about ten minutes. Our flight should be smooth the rest of the way to Penang. I hope you'll continue to enjoy your flight."

Alex focused his attention back on his notebook. The title of the slide showing was "Current Molecular Therapies for Lung Cancer." He had to finish writing his slides for his lecture next week at the annual Malaysian oncology meeting in Penang, Malaysia. Alex was already tired. He had attended a rushed three-day meeting in Switzerland to discuss a new lung cancer drug trial. These days, trials were international, in order to recruit fast and obtain results fast.

He moved in his seat, sensing the ache in his back and buttocks. It was already several hours into the flight. Economy class was a bit cramped. Luckily he was near the end of preparing for his lecture and soon could get some sleep.

He stretched out his arms and legs and noticed the flight attendant walking toward the front. He admired her slender form with nice curves. These days you didn't always get to admire the flight attendants, as beauty and looks seemed less a criterion to be a flight attendant.

He closed his notebook as the plane shuddered again. He decided to take a short break and shut his eyes, waiting for the turbulence to pass.

Alex woke as he felt someone shaking his arm and calling his name. He struggled for a moment. The pretty flight attendant he had noticed earlier was looking straight at him. The cabin lights were fully on. He put on his glasses and glanced at his watch. He had been sleeping for more than an hour. He looked at the flight attendant, who still had her hand on his arm. They were trembling. Her pretty face was serious, without her usual smile. Her eyes were wide open, her mouth pinched closed.

Alex immediately focused his thoughts and realized this was not the usual wakeup call you get from a flight attendant. He glanced at her nametag and asked, "Miriam, is there a problem?"

She said calmly, "Dr. Liang, a passenger has taken ill. Can you please come and help?"

Alex unbuckled his seatbelt and got up. His legs were numb from his cramped aisle seat. He nearly tripped as he hurriedly followed her to the front. He noticed many passengers' eyes following him as he rushed forward.

As they reached the first-class cabin, there was a commotion. A few passengers were in the aisle, obstructing the view.

"Please clear the way and take your seats. We're coming through," Miriam said loudly as she guided Alex forward.

A fat man was lying face-up in the aisle. The man was lying flat out, and his color was not good. He was heaving and trying very hard to draw a breath. An attendant at his side was comforting him and checking his pulse.

"What happened? How long has he been like this?" he asked the attendant.

"A few minutes. We had just finished serving dinner. His wife screamed, and we found him like this on his seat. We got him to the aisle shortly before you arrived."

Alex felt the man's pulse. It was weak. This man was semiconscious, and his breathing was labored. Alex put his ear to the man's chest. He could just hear a stridor as he breathed.

Alex knelt and swept his fingers into the man's mouth. There was no time for gloves. He shuddered at the thought, as he was a bit obsessed with cleanliness, but left his fingers in the man's mouth. There was nothing big in there; only a few particles of rice. By now another flight attendant had brought the Ambu bag, a handheld pump, and an oxygen mask. Alex had observed that the man's chest was not rising. He tried to ventilate him with the Ambu bag and mask but to no avail. Air was not going in. The man's chest wouldn't rise.

The man must have choked on his food. He quickly did a Heimlich maneuver, thrusting his palms upward just below the man's sternum. The man's belly was huge and wobbled like jelly.

With an energetic thrust moving sideways rather than inward, he seemed to only displace the fat sideward. His efforts seemed ineffective, and nothing was displaced from the man's throat. The airway was still blocked. The man's color was now very bad. He was turning a darker blue. He had stopped trying to breathe. Three minutes had now passed. The man looked lifeless. There was no pulse now.

This man will be dead in seconds, Alex thought.

"Knife," Alex said with great urgency. *Oh god,* he thought. *They only have plastic ones.* He allowed himself a brief smile when he realized first-class passengers got better cutlery, such as this large one with gold-plated ends. But it was too big.

"A smaller one with a sharp end," he said hurriedly. A smaller knife instantly appeared.

He knew what he was about to do was a procedure he had run through his mind at least a hundred times in his younger days, when he worked in an emergency department, but he had never done it before. Alex was about to make a cricothyroid puncture. He had to do it now or the big man would die.

He groped in his breast pocket and then his trouser pocket. Not there. Of course the ballpoint pen was in his jacket pocket, and that was safely stowed overhead.

"Give me a ballpoint pen quickly," he said without looking up. He had to watch the man for any clue of any changes. A pen was slipped into his hand. He opened it up and threw out the spring and ink inside. He only needed the hollow metal as a tube.

Maintaining full attention on the man, he located the cricothyroid area in the middle of the man's neck. He stabbed the cricothyroid area with the knife. It wasn't easy as the knife wasn't as sharp as it needed to be. It took some effort. Alex hoped he had not fractured the small bones of the man's throat. He had no choice and hoped for the best. Then he slipped the half of the pen into the hole he had created. If he was correct, he would be able to blow air into the man's lungs now. He blew into the pen and the man's chest rose. What a relief!

"Start CPR. Chest compressions now," he instructed the flight attendant. Alex blew into the hollowed pen between chest compressions. A minute passed, and he could now feel a faint pulse. The lights made it hard to see if color had returned.

"Stop." Alex instructed the flight attendant to cease chest compression, as the pulse was stronger. The man started to breathe, but it was still inadequate. Alex was too breathless to continue and instructed another flight attendant to continue blowing into the hollowed pen.

How was he going to give the man oxygen? There was no way he could fashion a connector fast enough to use the Ambu bag to ventilate the man. His mind was racing, searching for an answer as he looked around. The Ambu bag was useless, as it wouldn't connect. He looked into the opened emergency box and noticed a nasal prong set. He tore it open. He quickly put it on the flight attendant who was breathing into the man. He looked bewildered.

Alex said, "Breathe in through your nostrils and breathe out into the hollowed pen. This way your oxygen will increase. Your exhaled breath will have more oxygen. He will get more."

The flight attendant nodded and continued.

After another five minutes, the man started to breathe more normally but with much effort as the hole of the ballpoint pen was small, only less than two millimeters in diameter. He was waking up and began to struggle. It would be difficult to sustain him like this.

Alex looked up and asked, "How long before we land?"

Miriam, the flight attendant answered, "The captain has already started an emergency landing. I'll go and check."

A minute later she returned, saying, "We should land in about thirty minutes." At that moment, the plane started to descend.

The captain spoke over the PA system. "This is the captain. We have a medical emergency with one of our passengers. We've been cleared to land in Mumbai and are now making our descent. Crew, please prepare for landing."

Alex noticed there was no hint of panic or fear in his voice. *Looks like we're in safe hands,* he thought, *but half an hour is too long. This man will not last like this.*

Alex said loudly, "Another ballpoint pen, please!" But the few that were quickly gathered were not useful.

He got up, said, "I'll be right back," and ran to his seat. His pen was in his jacket in the overhead bin. He grabbed his Parker pen, made of a light silver alloy.

As he ran back, he dismantled the pen and only held the metal refill and the hollow part. By inserting the refill through the narrow tip of the hollow pen, and twisting it forcefully, he widened the hole to three to four millimeters in diameter. Alex knew it would widen. In the past, he had widened the tip similarly when he dropped and dented the pen's tip. Any bigger and it might not fit the hole in the man's neck. He knelt beside the man.

"When we're ready, stop blowing and remove the pen. I'll put in another larger one. It has to be done swiftly or I might not be able to insert it again. The hole closes fast once you pull out the pen."

The flight attendant nodded.

"Okay. On the count of three, remove the pen. One, two, three!"

The flight attendant pulled out the tube in one movement. Alex successfully pushed in the larger tube. Within fifteen seconds, the man's breathing was less labored. Now they could stop giving him mouth-to-pen ventilation. Alex put an oxygen mask over the hollow ballpoint pen tube and asked the flight attendant to hold it in place.

Alex knelt back on his haunches. He felt the strain in his legs and back. He took a deep breath and looked up. Besides the two crew members who were helping here, there were Miriam and another senior flight attendant.

The flight attendant said, "Thank you. I don't know of anyone with the courage and skill to do what you did." Tears of relief swelling in her eyes, as well as eyebrows frowning in disbelief after witnessing a nearly impossible rescue.

Miriam gave him a brief smile while still trembling in anxiety or fear. The rest of the crew were busy preparing to land.

Alex bowed his head and said a silent prayer. He hoped he would never again be called to do this. He knew the man was not yet out of danger, and much remained to be done, but it could only be done on the ground and in a hospital. Many complications could have occurred or might still. Something seemed still to be blocking the man's throat. Alex was lucky he managed to bypass the obstruction with the procedure. The bleeding from the wound he'd created might have been trickling blood down to the man's lungs. He could drown in his own blood. The knife had been pretty blunt, and the force he'd had to use might have fractured the cartilage around the windpipe, meaning if he survived, the man might have to live with a permanent hole in his neck in order to breathe. Infection might occur soon. Brain injury might have already set in, as it took some time to revive this man.

He was jolted out of his thoughts as the landing gear was engaged. They would soon touch down.

As Alex feared, the man began to struggle. Alex wondered if it was an epileptic fit. Now was the time to get more details. "Anyone know this man? What exactly happened? Does he have fits?"

Miriam said, pointing to a tall, slim Asian lady standing close by, "This is his wife."

She was in tears, her face in a deep frown, her mouth tightly pinched. She shook her head and said in a stuttering, soft voice between sniffing back her tears, demonstrating by holding her own neck with her hands. "No, he doesn't have fits. I think he choked on his food. He was eating as usual but suddenly stopped, grabbing his neck."

Alex said, "He should be all right. We need to keep him calm. We don't have any injections to relieve his pain. I need your help." Alex sensed her fear and anxiety and had to help her cope. Deep inside, he wasn't at all sure it would all be right.

He quickly led her to his side, indicating to her to whisper in his ear. "Please keep talking to him about anything. I'm sure your voice will soothe him."

Alex gave instructions as he knelt next to the man, thinking he would also need to talk to him. "Please hold him down. You hold his legs. Miriam, hold his left side and arm. And you, Sir, his right."

The wife whispered in Hokkien, a Chinese dialect, "Eric, I'm here. You'll be fine. Stay calm. Think of us and our children. You'll get through this, and we'll all be together."

Alex felt relieved as she was doing fine without his help. She continued to whisper to Eric.

Miriam said, "An ambulance and a paramedic team are standing by at the airport, and the nearest hospital has been alerted."

Alex thought, *They had better damned well be. If he dies, I might be in a lot of trouble. Doctors are always being accused of not doing it right or not doing enough—not to mention being blamed for complications.*

For the remaining minutes, which felt like hours to Alex, it was like time stood still. Everything seemed to move in slow motion: the plane landing with the usual bump, the slight jolt that accompanied the reverse roar of the engines, and the brakes giving another jolt before the plane slowed. This time the plane moved faster to the gate. With his adrenaline rush nearly finished, Alex felt the energy draining fast. As they reached the gate, he once again cast an observing look at his midair patient. The semiconscious man's color was a more acceptable pallor, much less blue. His breathing was regular although labored. He was not struggling as much as his wife continued to comfort him with words. Alex could feel that his pulse was regular and strong.

When the doors of the airplane flew open, the paramedic team rushed in and took over. Alex, slumped to one side, was ignored, as all attention was focused on Eric, the patient.

Eric's wife found a moment to touch Alex lightly on the shoulder and said, 'Thank you,' before she disappeared through the gate and tunnel behind her husband and the team.

CHAPTER 2

THE GOOD DOCTOR

Alex was drained of nearly every ounce of his energy. He sat there in the first-class cabin for what felt like an eternity. He closed his eyes, reflecting on what had happened.

"Can I get you something?" someone asked calmly.

Alex opened his eyes and realized it was Miriam speaking to him. Her voice was certainly different. It was more relaxed and gentle. She seemed to have overcome her fears rather fast. No more tremors.

Alex smiled at her. "A cup of hot tea would be nice."

Miriam said with a smile, "One nice tea coming up," and disappeared.

Alex was still sitting on the floor. He could see the passengers leaving the plane from an angle. They didn't notice him, as his view was partially blocked by the crew at the door. He turned and looked forward and saw the captain coming out of the cockpit. As Alex stood up, feeling all his muscles ache and a sense of light-headedness, his tea arrived.

Miriam, now smiling, turned to the captain. "This is Dr. Liang, the savior."

"It's a real honor and pleasure to meet you," the captain said. "I'm Captain Jeff Richards. Please call me Jeff. I'm not sure what you did, but you sure impressed my crew. A real thank you." The

11

captain took Alex's hand and shook it. They spoke briefly before the captain left to attend to matters with the emergency landing. "Call me anytime if you are in need. Once again, thank you."

By the time Alex finished his tea, everyone except him, Miriam and a few crew members, had left. Miriam led Alex to the first-class lounge. A few passengers on the flight recognized Alex and gave signs of approval. Some gave thumbs up. Others nodded, smiled, or mouthed a thank you. By Alex's tired and weary look, they probably sensed Alex wanted to be alone and didn't come forward to talk to him.

He was alone with his thoughts after Miriam left to get back to her work. He found his way to the restrooms and splashed his face with water. Then he went to a toilet cubicle, kicked the lid down, and sat.

With his head in his hands, Alex sat in the cubicle in the airport in Mumbai for the longest time ever. Alex's thoughts and feelings ran a gamut of emotions. Now alone, his deepest emotions surfaced. His hands shook. He had trouble focusing his blurry vision. His heartbeat quickened, and he felt like throwing up—and the next moment, the bread and cheese he had eaten floated in the toilet bowl.

Once his panic attack passed, he was exhausted once again. He felt cold and rubbed his hands together. He closed his eyes and fell asleep, lying his head on the toilet bowl seat, sitting on the floor. He had already been near exhaustion when he'd boarded the plane after a series of long meetings.

An hour later he woke, startled by a loud announcement. He smiled warily to himself as he realized he was on the toilet floor— something he would never ordinarily do, as he was a bit obsessive with cleanliness.

He picked himself up, smoothed his shirt as much as he could, and tucked it in. He washed his face and looked at his fifty-five-year-old face in the mirror. A flashback of the recent event reminded him where he was: Mumbai, India. He ran his fingers through his neatly cut short black hair. His slender, tall build and clean-shaven look made him appear much younger. He was frequently mistaken as being fifteen years younger. But he could no longer hide the bulging tummy that betrayed his age.

As he composed himself and his thoughts, he realized there might be consequences of his actions on the plane. He smiled. Should he be like some of his fellow doctors, who refused to use the salutation of doctor when booking airline tickets? He could have avoided the event if no one knew he was a doctor. However, he might have saved the man. *No, if I didn't help, I'd probably regret it for the rest of my life,* he thought.

He walked out of the toilet and approached the counter.

The attendant asked, "How can I be of help, Dr. Liang?"

"I was hoping you could tell me when my flight will leave."

"Certainly; let me check" she said while typing on her keyboard. "Here it is. Re-boarding in about two hours. Anything else? Can I get you a drink?"

"Could I speak to someone from the airlines and the captain? He did say I can call on him anytime," Alex requested.

"Most certainly. I'll make the arrangements. Please take a seat, have refreshments. And thank you for saving that man's life. Miriam asked me to make sure you are taken care of," she said.

That's very kind of Miriam. I must remember to write to commend them on their kindness and professionalism. Not only Miriam, but the rest of the crew, he thought.

A few moments passed and a tall Sikh man with a turban walked toward Alex. Alex noticed the man walking with an air of confidence with big strides, chin up, a big smile on his face.

"Greetings, Dr. Liang. I'm Mr. Mohan, assistant manager of operations. Captain Richards will be here soon. How can I be of help?"

"Thank you for coming. Well, I'm not sure how to tell you. I'm an oncologist and certainly not any emergency specialist. I'm not even sure what I did is acceptable and without criticism. I'm concerned about possible consequences."

At that moment, Captain Richards arrived. "Greetings again, Dr. Liang. Once again a pleasure to meet you. How can we help?"

"As I was saying to Mr. Mohan, I'm concerned about possible consequences of my actions on the plane. I'm not an emergency specialist. Although I did what I thought had to be done, I certainly cannot be certain it's beyond criticism.

"Do you remember the incident about the Chinese doctor who got into a lot of media trouble when he assisted a passenger on an American Airlines flight about six months ago? He had to put a tube into the chest of a passenger who'd had a pneumothorax, a collapsed lung," Alex related.

"But if I remember correctly, there was an investigation and no wrongdoing was found. There were no charges brought against him, although there were complications," Captain Richards recalled.

"True, but it was four months of investigations and then a hearing. The media was in a frenzy, twisting the facts—in the beginning, accusing him of not having a valid practice, and then claiming the medical complications that occurred had been avoidable and he'd been negligent. The airline played an observer role instead of coming out in support of the doctor."

Captain Richards thought for a moment and said, "Point taken. How can we help then?"

"I'd like to request my name be withheld from the media and the incident be handled in total confidentiality. I do not want my practice to be harmed. My patients would also suffer," Alex requested.

After some thought and discussion between the captain and Mr. Mohan, Mr. Mohan said, "I think it's the airline's policy not to disclose passenger information unless requested by the police or authorities. We should have no problem withholding your identity. I'm sure we can arrange that."

Mr. Mohan seemed a reasonable man and not superficial. Alex thought he probably really meant what he said. "I'm relieved. I hope nothing comes of it. I certainly want to put this behind me. Captain Richards, I hope you can put in a word to your crew not to mention my name to anyone unofficially too. I hope they will understand."

"I think that is easy enough to do, but I can't be 100 percent sure they will comply. I've already ensured that you have a seat in first class on the remaining of your journey. You'll get the privacy you requested," Captain Richards said with a big smile, showing off the usual corporate professionalism.

"At least they'll try. And you're very thoughtful to have arranged for the seat. Thank you," Alex said with a sense of relief that he had accomplished what he'd set out to achieve by meeting them.

As the two men prepared to leave, Alex turned to Mr. Mohan and asked, "Could I make one more request?"

"Please ask. But I may need clearance from my superiors," he said with a slight frown, probably wondering what other request there could be.

"Could you pass on my business card to the wife and tell her she can contact me anytime? I'd like to keep abreast of her husband's condition and progress."

"But of course. That's very generous of you to want to follow through. Very good of you," Mr. Mohan said with a relief on his face.

Alex smiled as he realized Mr. Mohan was probably thinking Alex wanted a reward of some kind.

The two men left, leaving Alex with a half hour to try to relax before boarding.

CHAPTER 3

FINDING INNER STRENGTH

Eric's wife continued to feel her body tremble as she followed her husband through the gate and passageway, half-running, half-walking to keep up with the paramedics rushing to the waiting ambulance at the airport.

She couldn't run any faster. Her weary body just couldn't keep up. She felt her heart racing, her slim legs aching, and her lungs panting as she pushed on with every ounce of her limited energy. As she reached the ambulance, they had already gotten her husband inside. They were setting an IV line as she entered. The door of the ambulance slammed shut, and they were off with sirens blazing.

Her husband had an oxygen mask over his face. The paramedic injected a sedative. He was very professional. "Ma'am, I'm Vijay. We're giving your husband a mild sedative and analgesic to help him relax and to reduce the pain. We'll be at the hospital in about twenty minutes. We'll get there as fast as possible. A police rider is clearing the way."

She heard him but was too out of breath herself to say anything. She nodded in approval and felt she might need resuscitation.

As the ambulance arrived, she had caught her breath and was in less pain. Her legs were rubbery but the aches were gone. Her color was better. She had to keep calm for Eric. She must.

The ambulance backed into the entrance and the sirens stopped as the vehicle halted. The door opened. Two medics in white coats were on hand with a doctor.

"One, two, three," Vijay said and they lifted the stretcher out of the ambulance and wheeled him away. The doctor was busy checking his pulse and listening to Eric's lungs, and they disappeared round a corner into the casualty area.

As she climbed down from the ambulance, which was too high for her to jump, a helping hand steadied her. She looked up and saw a friendly face.

"I'm Staff Nurse Santikumari. You can call me Shanti. I'll look after you, ma'am. You look very tired. Can I get you a wheelchair?" Shanti asked in a typical Indian accent. She sported a worried look on her round face, her bright eyes lighting up.

"Thank you, but no. Please take me to Eric," she said, a fleeting thought of the numerous times she'd had to sit on a wheelchair before. She shuddered.

"I'm sorry, ma'am. He has been wheeled straight into the operating theatre. He should be fine. I'll take you to our waiting room."

Please, please keep Eric safe. We all need him. I need him, she prayed in her mind with her eyes closed, while clenching her fists, as if it would make her energy swell and make her prayers answered as she waited in the waiting room. The staff nurse was still sitting there with her. She felt less lonely with Shanti there. She felt Shanti's hands on hers.

When she opened her eyes, a young woman in her early twenties wearing a dark-blue uniform stood in front of her, as if waiting for her to do something.

"Ma'am, I need your help to register your husband. Ma'am?"

"Yes, of course," she replied.

"I need your husband's and your passports, ma'am."

As she reached for her Louis Vuitton leather handbag, she had flashes of the crisis on the plane. She thought, *Why did Eric have to rush eating? He always does that. I have repeatedly cautioned him to slow down. I warned him he would choke—and it actually happened. He nearly choked to death!*

Fleeting images of Alex cutting into Eric's neck sent cold shivers down her spine and tears to her eyes. Dried tears already lined both cheeks. "No, Eric will be fine. He has to be!" She psyched herself and brought all her inner strength out. This time she had to be there for Eric, as he had been for her so much, unreservedly so, for the last four years.

"Here they are," she said as she found the passports in her handbag. She looked on as she wrote Eric's full name, Eric Shi Yang Chang. She wrote sixty years for age. She scribbled his passport number. She filled in Taiwanese for citizenship. In the next-of-kin column, she wrote Shi Mei Lin, forty-five years for age.

"Ma'am, can I have your credit card please?"

Mei Lin brought out her platinum preferred Visa card and said, "I hope this will be enough. Please make sure the very best care is given to Eric. We'll pay any amount needed." She suddenly realized she was not in Taiwan and no one would know who they were. They were just passengers from another country.

"Of course, Ma'am, certainly," the girl said.

Two long hours had already passed since Eric was brought into the hospital. Shanti had to leave to attend to other matters. Mei Lin was now alone in the waiting room. She could only focus on the tiled floor as she rocked and shook in her chair. She felt cold and numb. She didn't know if it was day or night. All she could do was focus on the lines that edged the square tiles, as if Eric's survival depended on her total concentration on those lines.

A pair of elasticized shoe covers suddenly broke into the pattern. She looked up. A man in green scrubs stood before her.

"Ma'am, I'm Dr. Ravichandran. Your husband is out of surgery and is in his room. Can you follow me, please? I'll show you to his room."

Soon, Mei Lin found herself in a cubical in the post-surgery recovery area just outside the surgical theatres. She had put on a green coat for cleanliness.

Eric was in his bed with his eyes shut. He was breathing normally. Tubes ran down his arms. Monitors, constantly bleeping, showed his steady vital signs.

She turned to the doctor with an enquiring look.

"We removed a piece of meat from your husband's throat," he said in heavily accented but clearly understandable English. "It had obviously choked him. The emergency procedure saved his life."

"Will he be fine? I'm worried about brain damage," Mei Lin said.

The doctor shook his head and said, "He should be okay, but we'll have to observe him for the next few days. Since his vital signs and responses are good, I believe he will fully recover."

She sighed in relief as he continued. "We'll have to monitor him for infections. You probably understand the procedure done wasn't under sterile conditions. But in such situations, it rarely is. We've given him powerful antibiotics. Luckily there was no bleeding. Also, miraculously, the incision the doctor made didn't damage any critical structures. I don't think there will be any long-term damage to your husband."

"Thank you, thank you, thank you," Mei Lin said, with all her heart. Her prayers for the last hours were answered. A sense of relief overcame her. She trembled and her legs gave way.

The burly doctor caught her, and after a moment, she regained her composure.

"Thank you again. Please do anything and everything possible. Please understand I do not know the rules or procedures in your country. I'm assuming we have to pay for all his treatment. Please rest assured we can afford all the care he needs."

"Erm, you can discuss that with the clerical staff when the time comes. I assure you we'll do our very best. I'll make sure he has round-the-clock care he needs," Dr. Ravichandran said, a bit taken aback by her frankness. "In a few hours, we shall move him to a high-dependence private suite. He will have twenty-four-hour monitoring and a personal nurse. There will be an attached room for you to use."

Dr. Ravichandran left, leaving her alone behind the curtain with Eric. Mei Lin could not remember a time when she felt more alone or helpless. She had always been capable and had always been a great help to Eric. Until her illness she never had to turn to Eric for help. She had always managed, and what she did not know she learned. But they had never been challenged like this. Now she found herself without any medical resources of her own to call upon. She was dependent on the people who had saved Eric's life. All she could do was be there for him. Having suddenly remembered their children, Mei Lin tiptoed out of the cubical, as if any noise would wake Eric, who clearly was sedated.

"Can I make a call on my cell phone?" she enquired.

"No problem, ma'am," was the reply.

She quickly called. "Kai Ching?" His cute, high-pitched voice always lit her up. He was rather mature in his thinking at eight years old and had a curious mind, like his father. "Mummy here. How are all of you?"

"Hi, Mum. I just woke up. Daddy didn't answer his phone. I was going to call you instead but fell asleep," Kai Ching replied.

"Sorry, I was rather occupied. We're in India now. There was an emergency on the plane and we had to make an emergency stop. Did you finish your homework?"

"Yes, Mum," he said in an annoyed tone. She always asked him every time she called. "Where is Daddy?"

"Daddy is asleep. I'll tell him to call you soon ya," Mei Lin replied. She could sense his disappointment and said, "We'll get you a nice colorful Indian suit tomorrow."

"Yahoo!" he shouted.

At least she managed to keep him happy. "Is ta-chi there?" she continued with a calm voice she felt was not hers.

She heard the boy shout excitedly for his older sister.

"Hi, Mum," his sister said sleepily. "It's late. Anything?" she asked, slightly annoyed. Just like any teenager, she was a bit rebellious.

"Is Kai Ching still there?" Mei Lin asked.

"No," she replied curtly.

"Something serious has happened. We're now in India. Daddy is in the hospital," Mei Lin said.

"Huh? Daddy's in the hospital?" she replied with a sense of urgency. "Is he okay? What happened?"

"Daddy choked on his food on the plane and lost consciousness. He is very lucky, as he was revived quickly. He is okay now and in the hospital resting," Mei Lin explained, not wanting to go into the gory details with her daughter. "The doctors here are excellent, and he is in good hands."

"I'm so, so sorry. I hope Daddy will be okay. He has to be," she replied with an urgent and tremulous tone.

"Daddy's okay. Don't worry, Kai Lean. He will be okay. I'm with Daddy now. He is asleep and resting. You have to be strong and look after Kai Ching while we're in India. Don't tell Kai Ching what's happening. He only knows we're in India because of an emergency. I don't know how long we'll be here."

"Okay, I will."

Mei Lin could hear her voice between short sobs. She knew her daughter was softhearted and caring. She loved her daddy very much.

Mei Lin heard a grunt coming from Eric's curtained cubical. Eric must be waking up. "I've got to go. Daddy needs me now. Please take care of yourself and your brother. Bye-bye."

She rushed over to Eric. He seemed to be trying to wake up and moved a little while making a few grunts. She held his hand and squeezed gently, wanting him to know she was there for him.

A nurse was checking on him. She smiled at Mei Lin and nodded, indicating all was well. Mei Lin leaned close to her husband's ear and spoke quietly to him. She told him she would soon have to leave for a little while but that she would be back soon. She told him the children were fine and that they sent their love and that the children were keen to see their parents again.

She touched Eric to reassure him and gave him a kiss on the forehead. Then she ran her hand across his hair as she always did to soothe the children when they were ill. She felt a slight constriction in her chest and knew she loved Eric very much and that she could not bear the thought of losing him. She stayed at his side for another half-hour and then jolted herself out of her trance-like state and got up.

Mei Lin said to the nurse, "This is my cell phone number. Please call me if there are any changes. Please look after him."

"I will, Mrs. Shi," the nurse replied.

Mei Lin knew a few encouraging words to the caregivers would go along way to help Eric. At least she could do that little bit. She felt a weight on her chest as she left Eric. She kept glancing back as she walked away. Now that Eric was unavailable, she would need to keep things afloat for him. She mentally put together a list of things she had to do for Eric.

She went to the front desk of the hospital and politely said, "I'd like to see your CEO, please."

The thin Indian lady in the saree was a bit startled and had a worried tone in her voice as she asked, "May I ask why?"

"Don't worry. I'm not here to complain. I need a personal favor from him. Could you please call him for me?"

"I'll try. He might have left, ma'am," she said while already dialing a number.

A quick conversation in Tamil ensued. Mei Lin didn't understand a word but the tone seemed okay.

The receptionist hung up and said, "You are in luck, ma'am. His late-afternoon meeting just finished. Dr. Ashok will be in his office soon. Mr. Rajbans will show you the way." She signaled the attendant to guide Mrs. Shi.

Soon she was waiting in Dr. Ashok's office. He walked in quietly and she looked up. He was a small man, shorter than she was.

Slightly plump with a nice round midriff. Bespectacled and sporting a small moustache.

He smiled and greeted her. "Mrs. Shi, let me express how sorry we are that your husband is unwell. I assure you he is in the best of hands. Please, come into my office." With that he guided her inside. "Now what can I do for you?"

"Thank you for seeing me. I'll be brief. I don't think you are aware that Mr. Shi is a well-known businessman in Taiwan. He has many businesses. Things could go very wrong if the media is involved. I'd like your cooperation to keep his condition private. I understand your hospital probably already adheres to strict codes of ethics and privacy for patients."

"I'm sorry, but I'm not aware of Mr. Shi's status. Are you talking about the Shi Corporation? The rumored corporation that has been investing in pharmaceuticals?"

"Yes. You seemed well informed," Mei Lin said in surprise.

"Ah, I'm interested in pharmaceuticals. I have a small share in a company in which the Shi Corporation has invested," he replied. "It's an honor to meet you, unfortunately in unusual circumstances. I assure you complete privacy will be given to you and your husband. I'll get my assistant manager to only look after Mr. Shi and your needs and nothing else. In that way, I can guarantee your complete privacy."

Mrs. Shi was rather amused that Mr. Shi's reputation was known in India. She really didn't see that coming. She was nevertheless thankful for Dr. Ashok's help and left his office feeling good. She had finished the first task on her mental list.

She headed for the entrance of the hospital to catch a taxi back to the airport to get their luggage. As she walked past a tall Indian man dressed in a white-long sleeved shirt and matching white trousers sitting near the entrance, she recognized her bags. He was dozing off and jerked himself awake.

Mei Lin stopped and turned. He had recognized her and quickly got up to introduce himself, "I'm Mr. Mohan, assistant manager. I'm sorry I fell asleep waiting for you. I brought your luggage. I didn't want to disturb you while you were with your husband. I hope he is recovering well."

Mei Lin said, "That's very kind of you. I haven't seen you before. How did you recognize me?"

"Oh. I was there when you rushed after your husband. I can recognize you even by your dress, ma'am," Mr. Mohan said.

Indeed, Mei Lin was wearing a beautiful black cheongsam with a gold and red dragon on its front, which fit her slim tall figure. *Aren't I obvious in a crowd?* she thought. "Okay. Thank you," she replied.

"We've booked you into a suite in a nearby five-star hotel, the Mumbai International, complements of the airline. Let me show you to your hotel," he said with his left hand outstretched, showing the way to the waiting limousine.

The journey to the hotel was relatively short, as she hoped it would be. It was indeed a five-star hotel, with a grand entrance. A turbaned bellman opened the door as the limousine pulled up.

With her bags unloaded, she turned to Mr. Mohan. "Thank you for your kindness and hospitality."

Mr. Mohan shook her outstretched hand and said, "Good night, ma'am. It's my pleasure to be of service." Just as he was about to turn and leave, he remembered he had a task to do for the kind doctor and turned around, saying, "I nearly forgot. I have to give you his card." Mr. Mohan handed Alex's card to her. "The good doctor wanted you to have this. He said to call if you need him. He also wanted to know how Mr. Shi's condition would turn out. He is a good man."

As she walked into the hotel, she wondered why Mr. Mohan seemed to stress that the doctor was a good person. She was a little puzzled but brushed the thought aside, as she had other things on her list to do tonight.

CHAPTER 4

HER ILLNESS

The bellhop led her up to her room. Another pushed her luggage on a cart. She couldn't help noticing the fine craftsmanship in the décor of the hotel as she walked through. There were classic Maharashtra furnishings, fit for a king and queen's residence.

She was in the shower moments after the two men were tipped and left. As she showered, she touched the four-inch scar over the right side of her chest. Every time she did that, she would think, *Thank God. I'll be fine.* She felt her waif-like body, with hardly an ounce of fat, was as much a result of disciplined eating and exercise as it was the visible evidence of her health. Her slim muscles were weak, so different from the days she was an athlete in school. She could run the two hundred meters with hardly an effort then. Not now. She touched her skin, feeling its slight roughness, especially around her neck and upper chest. The rash had been with her now for a few months, a gentle reminder of the medication she was on. As she dried herself, she tried to avoid glancing at the mirrored wall. Four years and so much had changed. She had aged, her skin no longer taunt, her rash clearly visible without her cheongsam. She shuddered at her own appearance and quickly robed.

Refreshed after a half-hour shower and padding about in a bathrobe while her short wet hair dripped, Mei Lin picked up the business cards. She perused Alex's with some interest. Until then she'd known nothing of the man who had saved her husband's life—not his name, his country, or the medicine he practiced.

She read Alex's card. "Dr. Alex Liang SY, Consultant Medical Oncologist, MBBS (Mal), FRCP (UK), Fellow in Oncology (Mal), The Straits International Hospital," and in brackets, "Oncology Division." An e-mail address and telephone numbers was listed at the bottom corner. The name sounded familiar. *Where have I heard it before?* she thought.

Mei Lin then lay on the bed, completely exhausted but very troubled. Unable to shut her eyes for the brief rest she needed, her thoughts strayed.

Flashes of her husband being resuscitated crept into her mind. Then she could picture herself near collapse as she chased after them to the ambulance. She just didn't have the energy. With part of her left lung having been removed, she wasn't able to cope with running. When she was in the ambulance, she wanted to help, hold Eric's hand, talk to him. But she couldn't even help herself. She nearly passed out in the ambulance from lack of oxygen. She refused to let the paramedics know, as she wanted Eric to have absolute attention. She thought of death then. Although the last few years she had been facing death, this was different. She was nearly there this time. Tears swelled in her eyes as she prayed, "God, why are you testing us so much? Now two of us have nearly died. Eric has been so good to me. Please don't let harm come to him. I'm ready if you have to choose one of us. I'm ready." She was crying, overwhelmed with a sense of despair and helplessness.

Unconsciously, she touched her scar again and ran her hand over two other small scars next to it. The scars served to remind her to treasure life. Her memories of the last few years flooded back as if they only happened yesterday.

"What's that?" she'd asked as she pointed to a white spot as large as a nickel on her chest X-ray. She had just finished her yearly routine medical examination.

"We're not exactly sure. It can be a simple infection, like tuberculosis, or an old scar from a previous infection. Worst-case scenario would be an inactive tumor," her general practitioner said. "It's probably nothing to worry about." He added in another breath, "But for completeness, I'll ask my good friend to see you."

She detected a little hesitancy in his voice, and the "but" clearly underlined there was a problem. *He doesn't want to scare me,* she thought, with a slight tinge of fear.

The next week she underwent a series of tests. At the end, she was alone waiting for her results. Eric was in China discussing a business deal with Ching, one of his closest business partners. She fidgeted with the edge of her beautiful, red, flowing cheongsam. The silky feel always brought a sense of calm when she rubbed her smooth hands on it.

A half-hour passed and still her doctor had not appeared. She looked around and caught sight of a poster on his office wall. It read, "Lung cancer—the most common form of cancer. Be aware, beware, get a checkup. It's curable" A smiling, medium-built Chinese lady was seated in the background, in focus, with two young teens sitting beside her. A slightly elder man stood behind her, holding her hand, which was flexed back on her own shoulder.

I hope I don't have that, Mei Lin thought as the door opened. "Dr. Yue, how are the tests?" she quickly asked.

Smiling as usual with a poker face, not betraying any news yet, he said, "Have a seat." He sat at the edge of his table, seemingly wanting to be close to her as he broke the news, "I'm afraid the tests are positive for cancer. But it's only in the earliest stage. With surgery, we're fairly certain we can cure you."

"How early is it? Please be truthful to me. I need to know," she quickly blurted. Her voice was anxious. Her heart was pounding as she waited for his reply.

"It's the truth. It's very early. At this first stage, we have more than an 80 percent chance of a cure," was the reply.

"Are you sure?" she asked with disbelief. "Are you sure it's cancer? Are you sure you can cure me?"

She left the clinic alone in a sort of daze. She walked initially and then ran to her Audi in the car park. Tears flowing, her breath halted, trying to hold back further tears, she slipped into her car. As she crossed the junction, her mind drifted into prayer, "Please …"

Suddenly an extremely loud horn sounded, and she turned to the sound coming from her left. A car was coming straight at her, its brakes screeching, swerving left and right. In a split second, she was passed the junction, her foot still on the accelerator. The other car just missed hers by inches and came to a complete stop in the middle of the junction. She slammed on the brakes, realizing she had just run the traffic light, and in the process banged her head on the steering wheel.

"Hey, you! You can't drive—don't drive. You drunk, bitch?" the driver screamed as he ran over to her car and tried to open her door in anger.

She turned to him in a daze, her eyes puffy and filled with tears that ruined her mascara. She saw a blurry image of the man as she peeped through her tears. She whispered a sorry.

The man seemingly calmed down, probably realizing she was a real mess. He said, "Hey, lady. Be careful. You don't want to hurt anyone. You're in no condition to drive."

"Yes, yes. You're right," she said, realizing she shouldn't have gone alone to see her doctor.

"Open the door. I'll drive you to the side," he said, "Do you want me to call someone to pick you up?"

"Yes, yes."

A few moments later, a limousine arrived. "Ma'am, you okay?" her driver asked. He helped her up and got her home in the limousine.

At home, she was paralyzed with fear. She laid in bed until Eric arrived home. She was a mess. Her maid had helped her dress a small cut over her forehead. She didn't even realize she had injured herself.

Eric had an expression of a man possessed when he rushed into their bedroom. "Mei Lin, what …" His voice trailed off. "Are you okay? I'm calling the doctor!" He already had his cell phone out and started to press the tiny buttons, which were a bit too small for his chubby hands.

"No. Don't call. I just came from the doctor."

Eric stopped and stared at her.

"I didn't tell you I was going to see a specialist after my routine checkup," she explained. "I didn't want you to worry about me when it could just be nothing. But it's not nothing. It's cancer," she said and started crying again.

Eric's cell phone fell to the floor and shattered as it hit the sharp edge of the bedside marble table. Neither of them was bothered about it. They were hugging each other.

A moment later, their two children ran into their room, wanting to welcome daddy home from his trip. They fell silent, looking at their parents in an embrace, with tears flowing continuously in almost total silence.

Realizing they were there, Mei Lin outstretched her hand to them. They ran the few steps and joined in the hug. "We're a family. I'm blessed," she said to herself in a whisper, "I'll be fine."

She felt Eric's hold on her tighten further, realizing he heard her whisper. His warmth flowed into her, and a sense of calmness slowly returned.

A week later, she was recovering from surgery. The best surgeon in Taiwan had operated on her. From her bed two days after surgery, she asked, "How am I, Doctor?"

"Good news. We can confirm we indeed reached the tumor early. All of it has been removed. We had to remove half of your right lung to be 100 percent sure we removed it all."

"Does that mean it's over? I don't need the dreadful chemotherapy or radiation?" she asked, reflecting on what she had read over the week.

"No, not at all. You'll be fine. There is less than 10 percent chance it will come back. So we don't need any additional treatment," he said with an air of confidence.

"Thank you," she remarked, holding onto his hands. She turned to Eric, who appeared to be mumbling something. She caught the words "thank you" and realized he was giving thanks in prayer. She squeezed his hand and they smiled at each other. When she turned, the doctor had already quietly slipped out to give them the moments they needed to absorb the good news.

Since then, she had been very careful with her health. She ate more greens, exercised, and practised yoga. A sense of calmness became her norm. Eric seemingly approved. But despite her advice, he wouldn't change his ways. She knew that in front of her he would try to abstain from the unhealthy fatty, sugar-laden foods he loved but didn't abstain from when she wasn't around. He just loved his food.

Eight months before the fateful flight, she was again in prayer. She was in church, having just completed her appointment at the clinic. "God," she prayed, kneeling in front of the altar, "thank you for the last five years of good life. Thank you for all the blessings you have given my family and me. I know when it is time, I'll be ready." Her calmness came from the five years of yoga and prayer. She had just completed her twentieth checkup and thought nothing could go wrong anymore. The fear of cancer had almost completely disappeared.

Yet God had thrown another challenge. Strangely, Eric was not with her again. His flight was cancelled, and he could not arrive in time to be with her for the checkup. She had lied to him that she had postponed it until he returned.

As she left the church, a text message alerted her. *Ah. Eric has got an earlier flight. He will be back tonight.*

At dinner, the kids were chatty. Kai Ching was asking Daddy to relate his trip to Switzerland. He wanted to know how winter was there. They had winter in Taiwan, but the pictures he had seen of Switzerland were amazing. "I want to go there, Daddy! When I grow up, I want to be like you, traveling around the world. Can I?"

"When you grow up, you can come with me," he said with a big smile on his chubby, round face with triple chins.

Mei Lin observed her husband and kids, sharing their laughter and joy.

Eric glanced at Mei Lin, and a little frown creased his forehead.

Mei Lin gently shook her head, indicating she was okay. She would wait until after dinner.

"Both of you to my study. Presents there on my table." Eric patted Kai Lean and gave her a look, indicating she should bring her brother along.

Mei Lin knew she could not hide it from Eric. He already knew something was up, even though she was so much calmer than the first time.

She reached out and held his hand as the children ran out of the dining room. He stared at her, waiting for her to speak.

She wanted to speak but felt a lump in her throat. Her heart pounded. It was nearly thirty seconds before she was calm again and spoke. "I was with the doctor today. Dr. Yue says the cancer is back. They found a spot on the X-ray today and continued with a scan. It has spread."

She paused as Eric's grip tightened. His facial expression certainly didn't reveal his emotions, she thought, and continued. "He says there is a treatment available, and after that I should be fine for a couple of years. It's in my lungs and bones."

They had been through it all. This time it was different. "Cure" was not a word Dr. Yue had used. This time she was told she had a couple years' more. That really resonated in their minds.

"I'd need to start medication soon. He says within a few weeks would be fine. Let's take the kids and have a holiday. They deserve that at the very least. We're a family."

After their brief holiday, she started her treatment, a series of monthly injections and a new medication called Tarceva. She had seen that on the poster in Dr. Yue's clinic, the very same clinic with the poster with the word "cure." Tarceva didn't cure ... but it didn't really say it did. It was just named on the edge of the poster. *How misleading,* she thought.

*

"Dr. Yue, how is Mei Lin?," Eric asked. It had been six months since Mei Lin's treatment. He was now alone in the clinic. He needed to know the complete picture of Mei Lin's health. He was very composed, as if this was a business deal. He didn't know how else to handle it.

"She has responded well to the treatment. Today's checkup is really remarkable. There is no sign of the cancer on her PET scan. It's the best news possible," he answered.

"She's cured?" Eric asked with a hint of hope in his voice.

"Erm, not really. The medication is powerful but not that powerful. Cancer cells are so small. Even the best scans in the world cannot see the minimal traces of cancer."

"Then there is no cure for Mei Lin?" Eric remarked, the tinge of hope now lost.

"Well, she should have a few years of quality life. Advances are rapid and a breakthrough will come," Dr. Yue said with an air of confidence, trying to hide the white lie.

Eric had been keeping abreast with lung cancer since Mei Lin's cancer was discovered. He knew there was nothing new on the horizon. With a word of thanks, he left. He would continue his quest for Mei Lin's cure. He would never stop. He couldn't give up. He needed her forever. He would never give up hope. He was going to Switzerland again in a few months, and he would take her along on all his trips and, at the same time, consult with the best doctors.

*

Mei Lin was full of life in Switzerland. She shopped, toured, and had great fun with Eric. This was the first holiday they'd had in nearly a year.

She looked at Eric in bed one night. The light shining through the silky, nearly transparent curtains lit up Eric's face. His hair was neatly cut on the sides. He was balding, and the shine was smooth over the top of his head. She stroked his hair on the sides of his head. He stirred and let out a snore. His tummy rose with each breath and gentle snore. When he lay on his side, his snore was gentle. When he lay on his back, his snore would wake an elephant. Looking at him so peaceful in sleep, she only wished that when her time came, he would handle it well.

She shook him a bit, and he surprisingly woke almost instantly.

"Are you feeling unwell? I can call the doctor," Eric said, his eyes wide open.

"No, silly," she said with a smile. "You remember the trip we wanted to make almost three years ago? We wanted to return to Penang to visit my sister there. I think we should make the trip on the way back. A detour would be nice. I just want to be basking in the sun there for a while."

"Of course, Lin. Certainly. Why the suddenness of it? You feeling okay?"

"Just want to. Nothing else. I'm fine," was her reply. "I'm good."

"Okay, tomorrow I'll call Dr. Yue and get the name of the doctor he arranged for us in case of emergency three years ago. I think I lost his contact info."

"No. No. You shall not do any such thing. I'm fine. Don't remind me. I want to feel well, not sick," Mei Lin said.

"If you insist, I won't. But don't sunbathe. You're on medication. Your rash will get worse," came the quick reply, recalling Dr. Yue's caution about sun exposure.

She knew he would call anyway but kept it to himself. He would do anything for her whether she agreed or not, as long as it was right for her.

"Night, night," she whispered, snuggling closer to him, hugging his large, soft frame, and they fell asleep in each other's arms.

CHAPTER 5

DISCOVERING ERIC SHI

A lex boarded the plane after calling home. He left a message with the maid that he would be delayed almost a day. He could not reach his wife on her cell. She wasn't answering. It was probably buried in her handbag again or on vibration mode, he thought.

First class was more comfortable than he had imagined, he thought shortly before falling into a deep sleep. This journey was totally uneventful.

Soon he was in a taxi on his way home. He still had the lingering feeling of discomfort having rescued the fat man. Who was he? He couldn't help worrying, as he knew they were rich. He spotted a Mont Blanc and Rolex on him. Even the shaving lotion he must have used smelled of pure quality. She had a Louis Vuitton bag and exquisitely cut diamonds for earrings, necklace, and bracelet. He knew quality when he saw it. His wife was a socialite.

He needed to find out more about this couple. Who were they? Would they bring trouble to him? *For my sake, he'd better recover,* he thought.

In the taxi, he called Ramesh, his lawyer and childhood friend. He had plenty of connections, including some not-so-respectable ones. He should be able to get some information for Alex.

He glanced at his watch. It was already nine in the evening. He would try his luck and call him. Hopefully he was not occupied by one of his many girlfriends.

"Hello, my buddy. How are things, Ah Liang?" Ramesh asked.

"Not so fine, actually. Ramesh, I need your help. I just got back from Mumbai."

"Mumbai? You in Mumbai. Ha. I go to Mumbai, not you. You are such a bloody clean freak, you wouldn't consider it," Ramesh remarked with disbelief. Ramesh knew about Alex's somewhat-mild obsession with cleanliness.

"Well, I had no choice. It was an emergency landing," Alex explained.

"Okay. Go on. I'm all ears."

Alex explained as simply as he could about the midair crisis and rescue. He was worried about possible litigation. He needed to at least know who the fat rich man was.

After much thought, Ramesh said, "Bro, I'll find out as much as I can. Leave it to me. I'll handle it."

When the taxi pulled up at the gates to his house, he had to press the buzzer and announce himself before the automatic gates slowly swung open. He could have summoned the chauffeur to meet him at the airport but decided he should not vary his routine, which was to take a taxi. Anything out of the ordinary might raise questions from his wife, none of which he was prepared to answer.

A maid opened the front door.

"Is ma'am home?" he asked.

"No. Ma'am is out at a wedding dinner. She said you were supposed to go with her. She did get your text that your flight was delayed though. So ma'am went alone, sir," she answered. "I'll take your luggage, sir."

"Thank you. Just put them in my study. I'll sort them out later," he instructed. He headed to the master room for a long hot shower. He had been waiting for this shower for nearly a day.

Meanwhile, Ramesh was busy calling his contacts. Ramesh was an interesting friend indeed. They were close buddies in school. While Alex studied hard in school, Ramesh found ways to avoid studying. Yet the sort of street-smart kid made it. He had the gift of the gab and used it fully to his advantage at work and at play.

He just loved women. "What red-blooded man wouldn't?" he retorted when asked at a reunion. "You are just cowards. See a lady, get hot—but dare not. Ha. Chickens."

Of course the wives were not around.

The list of flight attendants he'd dated was too long even for him to remember. But they all loved him. He never promised anything except pure fun in the bedroom and a nice dinner or drink.

After about ten phone calls, he finally reached someone who might know something. "Ah, Demi, I heard you just arrived from Switzerland. Want to have dinner tonight?"

"Aw, I'm tired, Ramesh," she replied, "It's been a really long flight. We had to stop in Mumbai. I just finished an extra report. Too much work as a senior flight attendant. Have to write reports for everything."

"Then you are still at the airport? Poor, poor thing." Ramesh knew he got his catch for the night. "I can come straight to the airport to get you for a nice dinner."

"Well …" She paused. "Okay. I don't have to fly or work for the next three days. You promise me to be my date for three days."

Ramesh laughed and agreed. He had a date with her. Now he was hers for three days. They all fancy me, he thought.

"I'm full," Demi remarked. She had only eaten a salad. Some flight attendants were like models, always wanting to maintain their figure.

Don't worry. You'll get lots of exercise tonight, Ramesh thought with a smile.

"Did I tell you we landed in Mumbai?" she asked. Before Ramesh could answer, she continued. "I was in first class as usual as chief flight attendant. Suddenly, Mrs. Shi screamed and her husband was near unconscious, grabbing his own neck. I froze. I feel so silly now. The other flight attendants had rushed to help him. I just froze. Can you believe it? Me, frozen? It was a minute or two before I came around. One of the passengers, a doctor I think, came forward and helped. He was really cool. Barking instructions and everyone followed. Ha. Just like in the army."

Ramesh thought, *That's my bro.*

"You wouldn't believe it. He sliced open the man's neck. Blood everywhere. Then he stuck a pen in his neck. A pen. At that moment I had to sit down, as I nearly fainted at the sight of blood."

Ramesh smiled a bit. He knew she liked to exaggerate.

"He nearly killed the poor man. I don't think he really knew what he was doing. He was like a boy scout, having fun cutting up a rat or something like that. Anyway, he was saved. We had to land in Mumbai. The paramedics did a good job and resuscitated him and brought him out quickly. I was of no help and only observed. At least I can write a report about it. Miriam was great. I envy her. She even had the presence of mind to hand the poor man's wife her handbag before they left for the ambulance. She must have guessed their documents were inside."

Hmmm. If she believes what she told me, then her report will certainly not be good for Alex. He knew best as a lawyer that how people perceived things mattered, having had to listen to so many versions of stories in and out of court. He would have to consider protecting Alex if the need arose.

"What was the man's name again? I thought it sounded familiar," Ramesh asked, trying to fish more out of her.

"Oh. It's Mr. Shi. He flies fairly often in business class. I don't know why they flew first class this time. Come to think of it, it's the first time I met his wife. She is pretty but a bit too thin. She had a funny complexion."

Ramesh cut into her thoughts, trying to keep her focus on the man. "Do you know who Mr. Shi is?"

"Yes I do, as a matter of fact. But you keep it a secret or I could lose my job. You know these days, privacy rules are so important. He is well known in Taiwan. He owns Shi Corporation. He even has, I think, a university in his name. He is kind though. Not like the many businessmen I have met. But he likes to eat. He finishes all his food. Not sure why though. Ours can't be all that nice," she continued, straying away again from the question.

Ramesh had what he needed and wanted to excuse himself. "It's getting late. Let me settle the bill and we can go." Ramesh got up, paid the bill, and indicated to her he was heading to the bathroom. He was already distracted by Demi. He could feel his urge for her. The sight of her half-exposed size D breasts shaking in front of him as she talked and half-enacted the story had made her closeness nearly intolerable. He needed to get her home and give her the first of the three best nights she would ever have.

"Hi, bro. Sorry to wake you. I think you want to know soonest, right?" Ramesh phoned Alex.

"I haven't slept yet. I slept well on the plane from being exhausted. Tell me the news," Alex said with some excitement and anxiety.

"The fat man's name is Mr. Eric Shi, of the Shi Corporation. I've heard of him. You can look him up on the Internet. But don't let the news out. Demi made me promise not to tell or she might get sacked."

"I certainly won't say anything. Thanks, Ramesh," Alex said and hung up. So he really is a big shot, as Alex suspected. He felt goose bumps just thinking of whose neck he had slit. *So who is this Mr. Shi?*

Alex typed Shi's name in a Google search. More than ten thousand hits. There were news reports of him and Shi Corporation. He went directly to the Shi Corporation site. The screen burst into a dynamic presentation of Shi Corporation. Alex sat transfixed by what he read.

Eric Shi, founder and majority shareholder of Shi Corporation, had become one of the few powerful business figures in Taiwan.

Starting at a young age in the 1980s, when the Internet boom was beginning, he hedged his bets there. From a small startup, Shi Corporation diversified into a service provider and then into hardware manufacturing. Soon it manufactured and supplied parts for medical equipment. Now it had ventured into many related and unrelated businesses. Of note, over the last several years the corporation had entered the pharmaceutical industry. He recognized the names of the pharmaceutical companies that were listed. Every one of them was in oncology, particularly lung cancer. Just two weeks ago, the corporation had bought an up-and-coming biotech company in Switzerland. Alex had done clinical research for this company. They were into lung cancer research. Thirty percent of Shi's Corporation assets were now pharmaceuticals. It seemed a bit odd to Alex. He knew some of the companies made similar medications for lung cancer treatment. Seldom would a company invest in competitive companies. It wasn't logical, as the market was already near saturation. If one company wins, another loses. *Was Mr. Shi returning from this investment on the flight?* he thought.

I'd have frozen if I was going to perform the procedure knowingly on him, he thought. *Maybe he was lucky that I didn't know who he was. If not, he might be dead for sure.* A cynical smile crept on his face as he considered that if he'd frozen, he wouldn't need to be worried. *No, I can't think that way. Every life is worth saving.*

He needed to know more about the man. He searched for pictures of Mr. Shi, and there were thousands of hits, but it would seem he was a more private man than Alex had thought he would be. The only nice family picture he came across was at a charity dinner organized for sick children. There was Mr. Shi in the middle, with an older man. This picture, probably taken a couple of years earlier, showed him to be less fat, though had a chubby look with almost all of his hair intact. He was flanked by his wife. She looked stunning and a bit taller than Mr. Shi. Two children were in front of them. They had to be his kids. A boy and a girl. They were surrounded by kids. The photo was taken in Shanghai. The caption indicated that the elder man was Mr. Ching, a business associate of Mr. Shi's in China.

Further browsing led him to an article about Mr. Shi, written by a legendary reporter. It took Alex an hour reading through the rare interview he gave the reporter and what the reporter had unearthed about Mr. and Mrs. Shi.

Mr. Shi grew up in a rural part of Taiwan. His father was a farmer. His mother was a clerk at a local post office. He got a scholarship and went on to the National University of Taiwan. Graduating with first-class honors in engineering, he worked with a multinational company before finding a niche market for computer programming. He went to successfully nurture his company to great heights, making a success for himself.

"What is your greatest achievement, Mr. Shi?" the reporter had asked.

The reply was fast. "The Shi Institute. I have always believed in Taiwan. We have vast talent. Unfortunately, with the wars and the already-strained relations with China, our talented Taiwanese had little opportunities. I believe education widens the mind and brings success to all who work to achieve their highest potential."

"But isn't it true that you created the institute to suit your own needs for your companies? Eighty percent of the top graduates go on to work for you."

"No, no. They are always given a choice to work for us or anyone else. But of course if they wish to work for us, we expect the very best from them. In fact, many choose to study at the institute, as we have probably less bias or discrimination. Thirty percent of our intake is from other countries. Rich and poor alike. I want opportunity for all."

The reporter commented that he felt Mr. Shi's passion for education was probably real but his companies benefited from it. Loyalty seemed to be an asset in Taiwanese companies. He observed that besides the sciences, the institute mandated a course for all students in traditional teachings of philosophy, especially Chinese philosophy. He remarked that Mr. Shi had hardly donated to charity and might not be the philanthropist he portrayed himself to be.

Is Mr. Shi good, bad, or in between? Probably in between, he thought.

There was a comment in reply to the article, written by some who penned his name as only Stephen. He wrote, "You are mistaken. I'm from the Shi Institute. I work for Mr. Shi. Mr. Shi has a vision of making Taiwanese equal to the rest of the world. Yet he believes without good virtues, we will not succeed. Being philanthropic does not mean giving away money. As Confucius taught, and quoted by many, teaching a man to fish is better than giving him a fish. Most of us from Shi's institute have rallied to his cause. Giving back to society is good, but there are many ways. I personally do not know if he gives to charities or not. If he does, he wouldn't let you know. Of that I'm sure. Do not let his image fool you, for behind that image, Mr. Shi is a great man."

Ah well, Alex thought with some comfort. *Guess all will work out as long as he doesn't die. If he does, I don't need to worry about him. I need to worry about his family ...* That thought made him think of Mrs. Shi.

Somehow the image of her compassionate face crying beside her husband, whispering in his ear was stuck in his memory. He soon turned his attention to searching for Mrs. Shi. Her maiden made was Hwang Mei Lin. She changed it after her marriage. *A bit strange for a Chinese woman to adopt this Western practice,* Alex thought.

Mrs. Shi had joined the Shi Corporation as a factory worker, took night classes, excelled in them, and soon worked her way to higher positions in the corporation. She graduated as a programmer and left the corporation in search of a better job. After a series of jobs, she returned to Shi Corporation.

Alex recollected the reporter's interview with Mr. Shi.

"How did you meet Mrs. Shi?" he asked.

"Ah, Lin. Well, she came for a job interview, and I was impressed with and curious about her CV."

"Why?" he asked, a little surprised.

"She was so frank with her resume. She actually wrote that she worked in one of our factories as a laborer. Most, if not all, would hide that fact and lace their past with flowery language disguising it. Then she left to join one of our competitors. She wanted to rejoin us. Reading her CV made me curious, and I wanted to meet the person."

"You interviewed her?"

"Yes. She was indeed different. She had that 'fire' in her. That attitude, that never-give-up attitude. She was passionate about her work."

"Was it love at first sight?"

"Maybe. No, I don't think so. But she caught my attention. She was smart and had a quick mind. She had that compassionate look about her. One that you feel very comfortable with. Okay, that's too much already. Let's talk about something else."

The reporter commented that this was the first time anyone had managed to get him to speak about his private life. Mr. and Mrs. Shi married three years after they met and she stopped working.

Alex could relate to the feelings Eric had for his wife. He had felt it just looking at her on the plane.

He heard the front door open and close. His wife had returned home. He looked at his watch. It was already one in the morning. He needed to work tomorrow. In the morning, he would ask his secretary to cancel his non-urgent cases. He needed a bit more rest. He had the uncomfortable feeling when his wife was around. He reflected on the opposite feeling he'd had when he'd observed Mrs. Shi, whispering comforting words to her husband.

Time for bed, he thought and walked out of his study.

CHAPTER 6

STRENGTH IN TIME OF NEED

M ei Lin suddenly woke with a jolt and looked at the clock. It was ten in the morning. She must have dozed off and slept the whole night. She was still in her bathrobe. The phone rang on and on. She wondered why the maid didn't answer, and grabbed it.

"Hello, is that Mrs. Shi? This is the nurse looking after your husband. He has woken up from his sedatives. I just wanted to let you know. He is fine," she said in her strong Indian accent.

Mei Lin could hardly understand her initially.

"Thank you. Thank goodness," she replied as she recollected her thoughts and realized she was in Mumbai, not Taipei.

"We will be seeing you shortly, yes?" the nurse asked.

"I'll be on my way soon."

She hurriedly got ready. She had rested and felt so much better. Her Eric was on the road to recovery. Soon they would return to Taiwan. Eric's phone was flashing a red light. She picked it up and unlocked it using his password. There were missed calls from Ching and Stephen. His secretary had also called.

The mental list of things Mei Lin had to do surfaced. She had to make a few urgent phone calls for Eric.

She used Eric's phone. "Hello, Mr. Shi," his secretary, Grace, said, thinking it was Eric calling, as his number probably appeared on her phone. "We have been trying to reach you. You have two meetings scheduled today. One already started. Stephen is waiting for you."

Mei Lin hesitated to answer.

"Hello, are you there, Mr. Shi?"

"Hi, Grace. This is Mei Lin." She paused.

"Oh. Mrs. Shi, sorry. I thought Mr. Shi was calling. How can I be of help?"

"It's okay. Eric has taken ill. You know he eats too much. He came down with food poisoning and needs to be in the hospital for a day or two. He's fine," Mei Lin lied.

"I'm so sorry, Mrs. Shi. Shall I let Stephen know and ask him to proceed?" his secretary enquired. She probably had not been in such a predicament before and did not really know what to do.

"I'm sure you know what to do. I cannot possibly be of help to Eric to run his business," Mei Lin replied.

"Yes, I'll ask Stephen if he wants to proceed without Eric. Please send Mr. Shi our best wishes and to get well soon. Oh, by the way, which hospital is he in?" she asked.

Now should she continue to lie? she thought, and answered, "We're actually in Mumbai. It happened on the plane, and they were kind enough to land here, as Eric was in some distress. He is fine and recovering now."

"Oh! I'm so sorry," she replied with slight astonishment in her voice.

Mei Lin couldn't be sure if she suspected something was amiss. Anyway, she wouldn't say otherwise in the company. Grace could be trusted.

"Don't worry. Eric will be back faster than you know it. He'll see you then."

That was one strike off the list. She would text Stephen instead of calling him, as he was in a meeting. She composed herself and typed. "Hi, Stephen, Mei Lin here. Sorry Eric couldn't take your calls. He has taken ill and is in the hospital. Please call me when you have a chance. Thank you." She still typed in full and not the short words and acronyms the younger generation was using. She was just old-school, wanting to be proper. She pressed send and waited for his reply.

A couple of minutes passed, and Eric's cell phone rang. Mr. Ching's name appeared on its screen. She took a deep breath and contemplated what she was going to say to him. Ching was a master in reading people. He could sense things in voices, faces, and mannerisms. She knew she could not fool Ching. He would catch on almost immediately.

"Good morning, Mr. Ching. How are you?"

"Good morning, Mrs. Shi. Where's Eric? In the shower?"

"Elder brother, I'm afraid I've some news. Eric has taken ill and is in the hospital. He can't speak to you right now."

"I'm so sorry. I'd come to Taiwan immediately if I could," he replied.

"We're actually in Mumbai," Mei Lin informed him and continued to relate the story in brief.

As she narrated, she realized Ching had hardly said a word, had only mumbled, "Hmm," now and then. He was probably listening intently as he always did. Ching never missed anything.

Finally, when she stopped, he said, "Mrs. Shi, Eric is a strong man. Full of character. Full of life. Full of perseverance. Full of energy. Full of inner strength. He will certainly recover. I'm sure of it. Tell him not to worry about business. The important thing is he recovers fully. Send my regards to him. Please call me anytime if you need me. And thank you for being honest with me. I'll keep the information to myself, as I know Eric probably wants to keep this quiet."

"Thank you, Mr. Ching, elder brother, for being so understanding" she replied in the usual polite way she greeted an elder.

Another task done. She wouldn't wait for Stephen. She needed to rush to the hospital. She was half angry with herself that she had slept so long. She only wanted a short half-hour nap and return to Eric's side. She felt a bit heavyhearted that she had let Eric down. She should have been with him last night.

Dressed in another cheongsam, she hurried to the hospital in the hotel's limousine. She was at Eric's side again. He was awake when she walked in. She smiled back when he smiled. She held his hands and lightly placed her head on his chest. He sniffed her hair. The scent was probably as nice as always. She didn't speak and just lay there looking at Eric. He seemed content, not in any fear. The silence was only punctuated with the soft bleep of the machine monitoring his vitals.

She was startled as her phone rang. Stephen was calling back. She smiled again at Eric, kissed him on his lips, and indicated that she had to take the call.

Outside Eric's room, she answered. "Hi, Stephen. Thanks for calling back."

Stephen said, "I'm sorry. I had my phone on silent mode, as I was in a meeting. Grace had filled me in. How's Eric? Is he really okay?"

"He's recovering. However, it didn't happen the way I told Grace. I think Eric would want things to be kept quiet." She paused when she heard Stephen gasp. "He's fine now and recovering. He choked and collapsed on the plane. He's lucky to be alive. We made an emergency landing and are in Mumbai," Mei Lin explained.

"Ta yee, I'll come over to Mumbai. I'll catch the next plane out."

"No need to rush. I need your help to reorganize his meetings. Somehow you have to keep it under wraps. We certainly don't want the media to know and have the shareholders lose confidence. Are you able to do that?"

"That shouldn't be a problem," he said as he thought hard. "Since you and Eric were away for almost three weeks, I'll say you and he are taking an extended holiday while Eric finishes negotiating his business there. I think that would be a good enough cover story. Can Eric take calls?"

"No. He can't speak. He is conscious and alert though. Maybe he can text instead. Put the word out that he has a sore throat and will text instead. I'll let Eric know."

Stephen replied, "Yes, that will do. I shall wrap up things here and be there soonest. Probably a day or so. Please take care. Send Eric my best wishes for his recovery. It shouldn't have happened to him."

She had nearly completed her tasks on the list. Now to call her daughter and let Eric communicate with the kids. *Thank goodness there is now the Internet,* she thought.

CHAPTER 7

RECOLLECTIONS

Eric spoke in a hoarse voice. "I've been here two weeks, Doc. Can I leave soon?"

"Yes, as a matter of fact, you can. We'll be doing a final scan today. If it's satisfactory, we'll discharge you tomorrow," the doctor said, giving Eric and Mei Lin a comforting smile.

They smiled and squeezed each other's hands upon hearing the good news.

"Doc, I want to thank you for taking care of me, and for being so kind to my wife. Will I get back my normal speech?"

"I think over time your voice will return to normal. I hope you are not the karaoke kind, though. If you are, you'd better not do that for at least a couple of months. I think it will return to normal. Just takes time," the doctor replied.

As the doctor left, Eric turned to Mei Lin and held both her hands as she laid her head on his large tummy. He knew she liked to do that. Even more at night, since the last two weeks. It was as if she wanted to feel him moving, giving her comfort knowing he was alive.

"I love you. Love you and the kids," he said, "You have been my pillar these weeks."

Mei Lin replied, "And you are mine for all these years. And even more so, these last few weeks. But Stephen has been guarding your business, not I."

"Ah, Stephen. Has he? He has been. He is family, isn't he? If I had a brother, I'd want it to be him. Did I tell you how I met him?" Eric recalled, just like the many times he had told Mei Lin. He knew Mei Lin had patience to hear him talk about Stephen.

"Stephen Lem was about twelve when I visited his school's science fair. At that young age, he was leading a group of students developing software. Although there were flaws in their program, it worked. He managed to use it to access my computer using a LAN connection. I was impressed. It was obvious he designed the program all by himself. His partners were just there for the show. Those days, the word hacking wasn't used yet. He had this flair for numbers and coding." Eric eyes had a glimmer while he spoke, stroking Mei Lin's hair as she moved her face over his tummy ever so slightly back and forth, acknowledging his touch.

"Stephen, ah, Stephen. He graduated from Shi's at the top of his class by a wide margin. His talent has been good for us. 'One Kill,' as we called him, really made an impact on the company. The antivirus software he created was beyond its years. Now of course, it's much, much more complicated. He really showed us his loyalty this week, didn't he?"

"Yup, he really did. You can trust him, Eric. I'm sure of it," Mei Lin said.

Alex continued, "He wrote in support of me when the only interview I allowed was portrayed without a balanced view. That's why I don't like to give interviews and will not ever again. They like to twist things."

At that point, a soft knock on their door revealed Stephen's face.

"Come on in, Stephen," Eric called out with a grin as Mei Lin sat up. "Speak of the devil and he appears!" Eric winced as he finished, feeling a slight sharp pain in his neck. He had called out too loud.

"You okay?" Stephen asked.

Eric waved in acknowledgement and nodded. "So how is business in Taiwan?"

"Looks fine. Your extended leave didn't cause any trouble. Dr. Ashok has been true to his word and managed to keep things very private. Ching sends his regards," Stephen replied while opening the bag he was carrying and brought out *char siew pau*. Eric's eyes lit up, and he could already taste the food in his mouth.

He said, "Where the heck did you get that? This is India, not Taiwan or China."

"Ah, I have my ways," he said and didn't elaborate.

As they ate, Mei Lin asked, "How's your mum?"

Stephen said, "She's fine. She sends her regards. Ah, I forgot. It's already been with me for over a week. How could I forget? She wanted me to give you and Eric these jade pendants. They have been blessed. She wants them to keep both of you safe." Stephen fished out two red velvet boxes from his jacket and passed them along.

The jade pendants were beautiful. They had the figurine of Guanyin, the goddess of mercy. It was the size of her thumb as she held it. Eric helped her put it on.

Eric said, "It's beautiful. It fits you nicely."

"Please send our regards to your mother. I still wonder why she refused to move into your new house. Staying in that small third-story apartment by herself," Mei Lin said.

"You know. Memories there with my late father. Friends around her. She was in my place on weekends. She already wants to return the moment she is in my apartment. She is fine where she stays. She loves it in her own space."

Eric had high hopes for Stephen. He had groomed him to be his most faithful business companion. These days, he would talk things over with Stephen before committing to a new business venture. Stephen had picked up the business side of companies fast. Eric was grateful, as he needed the time with Mei Lin. He could always count on Stephen.

"Stephen, can you help Mei Lin today with the necessary arrangements? We'll be leaving the hospital tomorrow. I think I'd like to fly home directly."

"Great. I knew you would be discharged soon. Mei Lin, don't let him eat on the plane, though," Stephen said jokingly.

When Stephen left, Eric asked, "Are you feeling okay? You look tired. Not keeping things from me?"

"No, I'm fine. The pills are still working."

"I've been thinking these nights. I can't keep my thoughts straight. I worry about you. I want the best for you. And now I'm in a hospital bed with you looking after me. It was not to be this way. I had always thought things happened for a reason. I can't see any reason. I can't imagine what it was for you to see me on the plane and in the hospital," Eric said, sharing his thoughts. "And I can feel your sudden jerks at night while sleeping. You must be having nightmares."

Mei Lin nodded.

Eric held her tight and they embraced.

CHAPTER 8

ERIC'S SECRET PAST

"And how do you feel now?" Eric's psychologist asked.

"It's two months already. I wake up less. Guess the two weeks of therapy with you may have helped. I feel some unreal feelings, something déjà vu-like. I find it hard to explain. Just feel like I'm not in my body but outside looking in. Do your other patients feel this?" Eric asked.

"Some do. But everyone is different. How do you feel about Mei Lin?"

"I love her a lot. She has always been my strength. Even when she is sick, she is strong. And that gives me strength. Especially how she handled it the second time. The relapse, I mean."

"Besides that?"

"What do you mean?"

"Guilt, anger?"

"Guilt or anger? I don't think so. More like despair. I can't lose her. And I feel helpless. Even more so when I was in Mumbai. Anger? Not towards her. To myself, maybe. Why did this have to happen to me? She watched the whole thing on the plane. Can you imagine what it was like? I know they hid the gory details from me when they explained what happened. As if it wasn't torture enough to have relapsed cancer and face death, she sees me possibly dying before her …" Eric's voice trailed while touching the scar on his neck.

Eric was observing his psychiatrist. He was almost motionless as he asked the questions, trying to get into his head. *How steady he is?* he wondered.

"This week, when we talked about your feelings about Mei Lin, I sensed you holding back a bit."

"Really?"

"Is Mei Lin your first love?"

Eric didn't want to reply. He looked at him, wondering whether to share or not. Maybe he really could help him tackle his deep emotions. "Actually, no. She is my last though."

"So who else has been in your life? Anyone you would like to mention?"

"There is one person …" Eric said, recalling his past.

Almost forty years ago, Eric was in the National University of Taiwan, in his second year of earning his engineering degree. Life was simple. Study. Eat. Sometimes party. Tackle a few girls.

Someone caught his eye at a party. His attention was immediately fixed on her when she walked in. She was slim, of medium height, with beautiful, almost porcelain white flawless skin. Her hair was stunningly black with a shiny glow, smooth and soft as silk. She wore no makeup yet her face glowed with energy. Her eyes were just the right size with stunning, thick black eyebrows. Her slightly pointed ears made her stand out. She spoke with a melodious, gentle, soft voice. It was love at first sight.

Before he could gather enough courage to walk over to her, Beng Seng approached her. His elation dropped like a bomb. His heart sank. Beng Seng, his roommate, was a suave character. He always got his catch. He boasted hundreds of flings with success and that no girl had managed to escape his charm. He had bedded them all. He got his catch, always.

Hours went by, and it was nearly two a.m. when he went home, a long walk back to his dormitory. Reaching his room, he saw the usual sign on the door: Come back later, signed Beng Seng. He must have gotten another girl tonight, Eric thought. As he turned to walk to the dormitory lounge to spend the night as he did so often when Beng Seng had company, he heard a faint muffled shout for help. That sounded like the girl he had admired. He froze and then put his ear to the door, wondering if he had imagined the call for help.

"No, no, please no. Help, help ..." He heard her voice again. There was no mistake. He tried the doorknob. It was locked. His emotions took over. He pictured his "love" being brutally assaulted. Eric only could see red.

Next moment, he was punching Beng Seng. He had smashed his fists into his belly, chest, and face. As he drained his energy, he came to his senses. Beng Seng was semiconscious, muttering, "Surrender, surrender."

Eric was panting, his whole body trembling with adrenaline. He would hear his heartbeat in his ears. He turned and realized the girl was in a corner of the room, holding her dress, which had been torn, exposing her chest. Her bra was torn and only held by a single strap. She was in shock. She wasn't crying; she just stared at him.

Eric continued to look around. The door was broken in. Her underwear on the floor was lit up by the hallway light. The lights in the room were not switched on. Noises were now coming toward the room. The students must have woken up from the ruckus.

He looked back at Beng Seng. His face was bloodied and bruised. Blood oozed from his mouth. He was starting to wake up.

"Beng, I'll kill you if you touch her again."

Beng Seng came to his senses, saw the madness in Eric's eyes, and nodded in total fear.

Eric was composed again. He got up, grabbed his long coat, and threw it around her. He helped her up and led her from the room. As he closed the door, two students half-asleep reached the room.

Eric said, "Go back to sleep. Nothing to see. Show's over."

One of them remarked, "Beng Seng again. Ah. Good night." They turned and walked away.

They were standing outside the dormitory as Eric buttoned the coat properly to hide her nudity. She was now crying softly, probably over her shock. They sat there until five am, when dawn broke. She had her face in her hands. Tears continued to trickle.

Finally Eric spoke. "Can I walk you back?"

"I live far. I'll get a taxi," she replied after a long moment of silence.

"Stay here. I'll just go in the corridor and use the phone."

An hour later, they were in front of her apartment. As she fiddled with her keys to open the door, Eric asked, "Anyone staying with you here?"

"No. My mate is away for two weeks."

"You'll be all right? Can I call your neighbor to come over?"

"No. No one must know."

"Huh?" Eric was surprised by her reply. "It's not your fault. Beng Seng is the one. I'll teach him a further lesson when I return."

"Please don't make this any worse. Come in and I'll explain."

Feeling a bit uncertain, he hesitated to go in.

"It's okay," she said, holding her door open. She held her head down, staring at the floor.

Eric walked in. Her apartment was nicely decorated and well furnished, unlike the usual student apartments they rented.

She sat on an elegant white sofa, continuing to look down at the floor, seemingly thinking of what to say. She had her hand clasped. Her legs were closed together. The sunlight shone through the slit between the curtains, lighting up her hair. She had the same radiant beauty about her that Eric had observed earlier.

Eric sat opposite her in silence, wondering what she was going to say.

"Thank you for saving me. I owe you my dignity. My family owes you our dignity." She fell silent for a minute before continuing. "He said he was going to give me a book to help me with my language. You must know I'm Japanese. I have been learning to speak Mandarin. I was hesitant. He told me his roommate was in and not to worry. I was foolish enough to believe him. He ... you just saved me in time. When you grabbed him and threw him to the floor, I just backed into the corner. I just couldn't move. I thought you had killed him. He wasn't moving for a while. Thank goodness he is not dead, although I wish it now."

"I just reacted. I really don't know what happened. I'm sorry I scared you. I promise you I'll return to teach him another lesson."

"No, no. You cannot. Please don't."

"Why?"

"I come from a prominent family in Japan. If anyone knows of this, it will bring shame to my family. I cannot let anyone know. My family sent me here to learn Mandarin and the Taiwanese culture. I'm being groomed to help my father in his business. Our businesses had expanded to reach Taiwan.

"He tried to … rape me. I was fighting him off when you helped. He did not do any real harm to me yet," she explained.

Eric listened attentively.

"Where are my manners? I'm Sukimi Hato." She introduced herself, looking up from the floor, trying to smile and holding back her tears.

Eric had heard of the name Hato. He had just read the news that Hato Industries had just signed a joint venture with a Taiwan company to start a ship-building company.

He was startled when she introduced herself, and said, "Oh." He realized the seriousness of the incident, and if the media caught hold of it, Taiwan and Japan's relationship might even be affected. He felt like holding her hands, but it was certainly not appropriate then. She was so much more composed now.

She should be okay, he thought.

Eric returned to his room, feeling angry again. He was going to confront Beng Seng and threaten to castrate him.

He opened the broken door but found the room empty. There were bloodstains on the carpet. He glanced at Beng Seng's side of the room. His things were gone.

Later, Eric enquired with the dormitory master and found he had moved to another dormitory. The dorm master asked Eric if the rumor about a fight was real. Eric just smiled and left.

"When are you leaving for Tokyo?" Eric asked Sukimi. "Will you miss me?"

"In three weeks. Of course I'll miss you. Always. Forever."

"Will your parents accept me?"

Sukimi fell silent. Eric knew the answer. Sukimi came from a prominent family. Traditions are a way of life. Self-sacrifice is sacred.

"We can keep in touch and continue to be best of friends," Eric said with a huge lump in his throat. "I can't believe nine months have passed so fast."

Sukimi had her head on his shoulder, and Eric was stroking her hair. They were perched on a rock overlooking the harbor. They loved to spend time here in the evenings just watching the ships pass by.

"I'll always treasure the time we've spent together. Our love is unbreakable. I'll always love you no matter what. You know that, don't you?" Eric said.

"Yes, I do. I'll miss you until the day I die," Sukimi replied.

"Don't talk like that. It's superstitious," Eric said and smiled. She was his only love.

As they enjoyed each other's company, an eagle swooped down and snatched another bird flying by. It suddenly reminded Eric of Beng Seng. He had meant to ask Sukimi about him these past few days.

"Sukimi, did you hear about Beng Seng's death?" he asked.

Sukimi stirred on his shoulder, not replying.

He continued. "It was in the papers. He was run over late at night a week ago after he had left a party. Apparently he died in the hospital."

She didn't reply, had just hung on tighter. He had wondered why. He had shuddered at the possibility that her family might have had something to do with it.

"Do you think of Sukimi?" his psychiatrist asked, bringing him back to the present.

"Yes, I do. As a matter of fact, every day or almost every day. I loved Sukimi and still do. We knew we could not continue after she returned to Japan, having completed her one-year overseas student exchange. Her family had already destined her to run the family business in the family tradition. A Taiwanese nobody would certainly complicate things and probably get her disowned. Or worse things may have happened."

"Do you two communicate?"

"We do. The occasional e-mail now. As time went by, we communicated less and less. I guess we got on with our different lives. We seldom talk about our feelings. More of how we're getting on, giving each other information about ourselves. She did e-mail me after the incident. I really don't know how she knew what had happened to me. But in business, one has his or her ways."

"What did she write?"

"It was rather cryptic as usual, in case someone sees our e-mails. She wrote that she heard a rumor about a certain Taiwanese businessman having a medical emergency on a plane from Switzerland. She hoped the man had recovered, as it was a terrible incident."

"Seems she cares for you."

"She does, doesn't she? I told her I heard 'he' was fine and had recovered well."

"Do you think your feelings for her have resurfaced and are affecting you?

"I'm not sure, but I've certainly thought more of her lately. We really had a beautiful time together. That year was the most exceptional year I've ever experienced and will never again have the chance."

"And you think of Mei Lin?"

"Mei Lin is beside me most of the time. Lin is different from Sukimi. We courted for a few years before we married. Hers was a slowly developing love. We shared each other and want each other, but not the same way. I'm much older than Mei Lin. She has beauty. She is caring, loves the family, and loves me. But it's just not the same."

"So you feel guilty now?"

"I guess facing death made me think. I do regret not trying to get Sukimi when I made it in business. By then she already had a fiancée arranged by her family. I couldn't make her life difficult, and I sensed she didn't want me to. I'm having mixed feelings these days. Waking up and then later thinking of so many things."

"Are you still having that nightmare?"

"Yes, almost every other night. When I wake, I can't sleep again for hours and have time to think."

"What is your nightmare like?"

"It was a bit blurry in the beginning. As it kept recurring, I remember that I was feeling the pain in my neck. Sharp pain. I couldn't move a muscle. It was dark. I couldn't see anything. Then my body was shaking. Convulsing, I think. Pain throughout my whole body. Muffled voices. Then suddenly light, and a lot of shouting, and I wake up. Sometimes it's different. I'm floating, seeing myself lying on the floor, all alone, with a hole in my neck. Blood on the white floor around me. I am looking around for someone. But no one was to be seen. I look back at myself and see a Chinese man raising his hand and then stab me in the neck again and again. I wake up in a cold sweat."

"Who were you looking for in your dream?"

"I'm not sure. Mei Lin, I presume."

"Hmmm. Not Sukimi?"

"I really don't know. I don't see anyone in my dream."

"You are indeed stressed," his psychiatrist remarked. "Are you aware Mei Lin is also having nightmares?"

"Yes, I know. That's why we came to you two weeks ago."

"Her nightmares are similar to yours, but less vivid. She also sees a Chinese man in her dreams. I think you and Mei Lin may have to confront your fears. Both of you are having symptoms of posttraumatic stress."

"What can I do?"

"From what I understand, the doctor who attended to you on the plane was Chinese. I think you may have to meet him."

"You really think so, Doctor? Subconsciously I think I've been trying to avoid that. I didn't even look at his business card in Mumbai when Mei Lin showed me. I just want to forget the whole thing."

"I do think you may have to meet the doctor. It could help."

"If you recommend it, I think I'll try. And do you think I should let Mei Lin know about Sukimi?"

"In time. Meet the doctor first," was his reply.

*

That night, Mei Lin found Alex's business card and passed it to Eric. He sat in his study staring at the card. He had not seen it and didn't ask the name of the doctor when he was in Mumbai. Eric's memory was sharp. The name immediately ran a bell.

He was the doctor Dr. Yue recommended if Mei Lin needed a doctor in Penang. They were supposed to visit Mei Lin's sister but hadn't made the trip then. Nor did they manage the second time. *What a coincidence,* Eric thought.

Eric looked at Mei Lin's puzzled face and said calmly, "That's the doctor."

"Which doctor?"

"The one Dr. Yue said we should see if we're in Penang."

"Oh," Mei Lin replied with some disbelief in her voice, "Are you sure?"

"Let me call Dr. Yue now and confirm."

Within minutes after Dr. Yue confirmed the doctor was Alex Liang, they were sitting quietly in Eric's study. It was such a coincidence. Eric wondered whether fate had a hand in his midair incident, while subconsciously stroking his Kuan Qin jade pendant, which hung from his neck. In Chinese tradition, Kuan Qin is the goddess of mercy—she is the protector. He was deep in thought, almost asking the gods for an answer as he continued to stroke the pendant.

*

Mei Lin studied Eric's face, with his forehead in a frown and his mouth moving as if he was going to say something. She was stroking her crucifix, hanging on a short chain around her neck. The same jade pendant on a longer chain hung between her breasts. Mei Lin was Catholic, whereas Eric was a Taoist/Buddhist. Each was thinking and possibly praying or asking the god or gods whether the coincidence was a sign.

"I think we should meet him—the doctor I mean," Mei Lin said. "I think we have to. Things may have happened for a reason."

Eric replied, "Yes, I think we should. The sooner, the better. I'll make the arrangements in the morning."

Later that night, Eric was alone in his study researching Alex. Who was this doctor? He searched the Internet. Alex Liang was working in a large private hospital in Penang. He has spent the last ten years doing clinical trials in lung cancer besides running a busy oncology practice with three partners. The website of his practice listed his credentials. He had graduated in the United Kingdom and then pursued further training in Australia before finally settled in Penang. A short write-up stated he was married with one child. His pastimes were listed as active in conservation and renewable energy.

He seems to have diverse interests, Eric thought. He searched more and saw many references to Alex's clinical trial research in lung cancer. He also came across a lecture he had given not too long ago to an organization in Malaysia supporting renewable energy. It had a video. He clicked on it.

"Energy is infinite," Alex said. Eric was staring at the face of the man who had rescued him from death. He looked composed, with an air of self-confidence; he had short hair, was balding a little, and had a medium build with reassuring eyes.

"It would seem abundant, and thus we should exploit it to the maximum. Without sufficient energy, we cannot have the lifestyle we have. Even with reduced requirements by having more efficient systems, like LED lights, the energy requirements continue to increase as many more people have access to better lifestyles. The demands of the modern era almost dictate that we need infinite power. So where do we go from here? The fossil fuel era is beginning to end. Now we have solar power, wind power, and tidal power. Nuclear power is great but, as we know, with much risk. The Chernobyl and more recently Fukushima Plant in Japan underscores the dangers of nuclear power.

"Humans will be humans. We strive to work less and get more done. Instead of cycling or walking, we need powered transport. No doubt the speed of transportation has increased exponentially, with bullet trains and jet planes crisscrossing the world.

"The population of the world has also increased over the last century to more than seven billion people.

"We continue to use fossil fuel and damage our environment. Billions of years it took to become fossils, and we depleted them in fewer than two centuries. Despite the call for renewable energy, few governments want to embrace it, as fossil fuel is cheaper. Our overreliance on it makes us unwilling to invest huge sums of money into modern renewable energy sources. I think the oceans have untapped potential to bridge the energy demands and the supply. We only have to figure out a way to harness the oceans' energy, and our problems may be solved. But we also need a method to store the energy indefinitely. Is that possible?"

The short video clips ended. Eric wasn't sure how he should see Alex. Is he the "almighty" doctor, a doctor with many talents, or the gung-ho doctor on the plane?

He would need to meet him face to face to read Alex well. Then Eric would make up his mind.

He would send Dr. Alex Liang an e-mail tomorrow.

CHAPTER 9

CONNECTED

"Mrs. Tang, we have good news for you today. Your lung cancer is gone. We can't see it anymore on today's scan. The oral medication has worked," Alex said with conviction.

"I couldn't sleep a wink last night. I prayed the whole night. Thank goodness."

"You can sleep tonight then. Just keep taking the tablets. Once daily. Do not forget," he stressed.

"Bye, Dr. Liang. I'll see you in a month," she said and then left.

She was his last patient for the day. He checked his e-mails as he did every day before going back. Ten new e-mails. Ha. His daughter, Katherine, replied to a message he sent. Been a few days since she e-mailed.

"Dear Daddy, How are you? I've been busy. Sorry I didn't reply your e-mail sooner. We could Viber or Skype you know. We seem to miss each other due to the time zones. I'm going to sleep. I have a long day tomorrow. I gather your clinic is busy as usual. Anything interesting going on? Thanks for sharing about your 'rescue' in midair. I do hope he is well—for him as well as for you, Dad. Things will always be fine. You'll see. I got to go now. Sleep beckons. Good night."

He smiled as he read her e-mail.

The fifth e-mail caught his attention. It was from ericshi@ shicorp.com. He froze. It took a good moment before his secretary opened the door, making a noise that startled him.

"Is there anything else, Dr. Liang? I need to leave a bit earlier today," she said.

"Go ahead. I'll leave in a while," Alex replied.

Over the past weeks, Alex's attention has been on his patients. He had already gotten over the fear of any lawsuit or repercussions. Ramesh had advised him to be patient and not worry, as the probabilities were that Eric Shi wouldn't pursue the matter.

Alex opened the e-mail and read it.

"Dear Dr. Alex Liang,

"Please allow me to introduce myself. I'm Eric Shi, of Shi Corporation. I'm the unfortunate person whom you resuscitated on the plane. I'm in your debt. I apologize for not contacting you earlier. I have made a full recovery.

"I'll be coming to Penang soon for a visit with my wife, whom you may have been introduced to on the plane. We would like to meet up with you. I do not wish to intrude. Please let us know when it will be convenient for you.

"Yours sincerely, Eric."

Alex felt happy reading the e-mail. Nothing untoward would happen. He was relieved. This was indeed good news.

He replied, "Thank you. I'm pleased to receive your e-mail. I just had to do what needed to be done on the plane. I hope you were not traumatized by the procedure. It should not be a problem to meet in Penang. I'm available for the next month. I look forward to meeting you and your wife."

That night, Alex went home feeling very good. He had saved a life worth saving. He planned to chat with Katherine.

*

"Is my dress all right?" Mei Lin asked.

"It is, Lin. Don't fret. It will be fine. The doctor prescribed this meeting. We'll be fine. And fate somehow has brought us all here in Penang. I'm curious to meet Alex," Eric said.

Eric had only two nightmares a week ago. This week was good. He didn't have any. Reaching out to Dr. Alex Liang probably did the trick. He had seen his face. He was no longer an unrecognizable "ghost," as in his dream. He felt good and much more rested than he had in weeks.

"This hotel is comfortable. Did you sleep well last night, Lin?"

"I slept for five hours. It's comfortable. The suite is nice. Glad to once again taste Penang's cuisine. Meeting up with my sis last night was very nice for us. Did you enjoy it?"

"I did. Luckily your sis didn't ask more about us canceling the last trip."

"Yes. She does not know."

The phone rang. Mei Lin answered and hung up. "He's here," she announced, "I've asked him to come over."

Eric opened the door almost at once when the doorbell rang. He was anxious and wanted to see Alex in person. "Good afternoon. You must be Dr. Liang."

"I am. You must be Mr. Shi. And you, Mrs. Shi. A good afternoon and welcome to Penang," Eric said while entering the suite, noticing Mrs. Shi in the background. The suite was large, Eric noted.

"I am Mrs. Shi indeed," Mei Lin replied, "Please have a seat."

They were comfortably seated on the sofa set facing each other. This was the lounge. Alex looked around. The beach could be seen outside the window. These were the beach-side suites, which were fewer than sixty-five feet from the beach.

He smiled when he saw Mei Lin's glance. "My apologies. I was just admiring your suite. It's nice." Alex tried to break the ice. "Have you been to Penang before?"

"I have a sister living here. We were actually coming here a few months ago. Fate has it that it had to be postponed to this week," Mei Lin replied.

Alex admired Mei Lin. She looked different from the lady he'd met on the plane. She was even better looking now. She was slim, wearing a blue cheongsam. A jade pendant hung down between her breasts. A cross on a gold chain was just around her neck, below the collar of her cheongsam. He noticed a slight rash over her neck, the same type of rash he had seen many times on his oncology patients. *It can't be,* he thought. Her short, neatly combed hair highlighted her facial features. She had nice, deep eyes, with a perfectly sculptured nose, and lips that seemed to continuously smile. He couldn't help feeling attracted to her, a feeling he had not felt for a very long time. Some how she made him catch his breath.

Eric said, "It's fate, it's it?"

Alex replied, "We make things happen. Like we're sitting here now."

Eric smiled. "Yes we are."

Alex focused his attention on Eric. Eric wore a tunic with a high round collar, similar to something Steve Jobs would have worn. *He must be hiding the scar beneath the high collar,* he thought. *He has lost some weight,* he noticed.

He remarked, "I think you look fitter now, Mr. Shi."

"Call me Eric. Indeed I have. Got to lose some weight and cut down on my food. Mei Lin ensures that I don't gobble up my food. Ha. No more choking."

They laughed together, lightening the atmosphere.

"Shall we have lunch?" Eric asked, leading the way to the dining room.

"I'm grateful to you. It's not easy to admit this sort of thing. I like to think that I can do anything and owe no one any debt. I am, after all, a businessman. Your act is why I'm still here. I had to meet you to overcome my fears. I feel comfortable with you, Alex. I can call you Alex, I hope. We can be friends," and Eric toasted with genuine emotion in his voice during lunch. "To a lifetime of friendship, long life, and trust,"

Alex raised his glass and acknowledged the toast. He seemed to be among friends now. He saw Eric glance at his wife, as if he wanted her to say something or wanted her permission to say something.

She shook her head ever so slightly to indicate a no. He wondered what it was all about. Was there something he wanted to say and she disagreed?

CHAPTER 10

ALEX'S CONVICTION

The next few months Eric and Alex became quite good friends. Eric introduced Stephen online to Alex. They communicated with e-mails and chatted on WhatsApp and Viber. Alex later realized Stephen was the person who wrote in supporting Eric when he was criticized by the journalist.

Over dinner, Alex introduced the Shis to his wife, Lai Peng, as friends from Taiwan. "I met them on a flight back from Europe. They have a sister here in Penang and we chatted. Now they are here on holiday."

"My pleasure to meet you, Mrs. Liang. You have a wonderful and kind husband," Eric said.

"Please to meet you, Mrs. Liang," Mei Lin greeted.

"Call me Lai Peng, please. Everyone calls me Lai Peng," she happily replied.

Lai Peng always noticed what her friends and people around her were wearing. She always was competitive in her fashion. *Mr. Shi has to be a very wealthy man. His Rolex would cost at least forty thousand US dollars,* she thought. *The jade he is wearing is beautiful and of the finest quality. His ring is solid gold with a huge diamond. Mrs. Shi's cheongsam is from the most prestigious designer store in Taiwan. Her matching jade pendant is similar in quality to her husband's. The shoes she is wearing would cost a fortune, designed by the finest in Hollywood. How on earth did Alex get to know them? Is there something he is not telling me?* she wondered.

"How long are you staying in Penang?" she asked.

"We're here until end of the week. We just want to spend some time here. We may just be looking for an apartment to buy or lease. We love the sunshine here, all year round. Mei Lin likes the beaches," Eric replied.

"Maybe I can be of help then," she hastily replied, sensing a chance to get to know Mei Lin. She could show her to her friends. Her status in society would immensely improve. She glanced at Alex and realized he was giving her a slight frown.

She continued. "Only if you are free. I don't want to impose."

Mei Lin replied, "I'll certainly take you up on your offer. We really need someone who can show us around. My sister has her hands full with her three children. She barely has time to even chat with me."

At that moment, her sister and family arrived, and Mei Lin greeted her. "Sis, come and meet Dr. Liang and his wife, Lai Peng."

Soon introduced, they continued with a sumptuous dinner. The children were entertained by their father. That left Mei Lin and her sister with Lai Peng.

"I'm going to leave you three here to chat. Alex and I will adjourn to the coffee bar area. You all have a nice time." Eric ushered Alex to the coffee bar.

"Finally, a chance to have a nice chat with you, Alex."

Alex smiled and called for coffee.

"Tell me, Alex. I'm curious. You have chatted with Stephen and me about renewable energy. You asked if we were involved with any renewable energy source. Any particular reason?" Eric asked.

"Not really," Alex replied. "You know I do have an opinion on renewable energy and have been championing it for a while. My hobby or sideline."

"Sure there is nothing more than that?"

"Sure," Alex replied unconvincingly.

Eric said, "I've looked into renewable energy for our factories and plants for the past few years. The problem we found is that the cost of setting up is too high. If we used solar energy, we wouldn't be able to recover our costs even after ten years. I'm sure you know that."

Alex nodded.

"We considered the fuel cell, but the energy comes from electricity, which in turn comes from either fossil fuel or hydroelectric power. We already do not have enough electricity from our hydro-dams. It's a no go as well. However, my factories and plants are using energy-efficient systems and processes. Stephen has even created a program to keep track of the changes and savings we will manage after we start."

Alex's attention was drawn in. He said, "But that will not solve the main issue. We need more energy every year. The growing population and improving lifestyles demand more energy. We had thought the Internet and electronic storage were going to reduce pollution and waste. Instead, the ease of the Internet and storage has created a need for more energy as irrelevant duplications of websites, and hoarding-style storage now seems uncontrollable."

"Agreed. We have other means. The Shi Corporation had started investing in alternative fuels, with planting crops for alcohol-based fuel."

"No, no. You can't do that. We don't even have enough land to plant crops to ensure the masses don't starve. I cannot agree." Alex was emotional when discussing his passionate "hobby."

"Well, we don't see any other way. Using bacteria or fungus to produce energy or using eels to harness electricity is still very far from reality."

Eric sensed Alex was now getting annoyed, and he tried to poke him a bit further. "We don't see any other way. No other feasible way, that is." Eric knew his stuff when it came to renewable energy.

Alex, clearly annoyed, said, "But no one wants to look at the ocean. The ocean holds the answer."

"We have tidal energy being harnessed. It's good but with plenty of problems. The sea won't give us the answer. The sun, maybe. Lava rocks and sodium potassium compounds to store solar energy is still far from any mass production."

"I'm not talking about tidal energy. I'm talking about deep-sea currents. There is so little research on it. I've pieced together an idea to make it work. Deep-sea currents are as sure as day. They only exist because of the sun. Sunlight warms up the oceans, causing the deep-sea currents, running up to the poles and back to the equator. It is in fact solar energy changed to sea currents. If we use turbines to harness the energy, it would be like the greatest conveyor belt pulling turbines to generate energy. Electricity. The sea current is the conveyor belt."

Eric quietly listened for the last few minutes as Alex blurted out his idea. "So that's what you have in mind? Didn't want to share it?"

Alex was taken aback. "Oh. I've been tricked." He laughed. "Never mind, my close secret is out."

They smiled at each other. Eric seemed to have found an equal in an intellectual debate.

Alex asked, "So what do you think? Can it work?"

"It's plausible. Have you worked out how the turbines would work? How to fetch the energy back to the shores? Deep sea is very far out in the ocean. Storms are standard. And it's not small scale at all."

Alex added, "I have some ideas for the turbine and also storage."

"Let me sleep on it and think it over. If I think it has merit, would you come over to Taiwan and meet my team?" Eric could smell Alex's excitement. He probably hasn't felt this excited in a while.

His eyes shone, and his smile widened into a grin as he said, "Of course. My only chance, probably."

Eric said, "Send me an e-mail detailing what we've discussed. Please feel free to share your ideas. I assure you I have no intention to steal them for myself."

As Eric left with Mei Lin to their hotel, he wondered if this was fate that brought them together for a reason. A higher calling.

Eric asked, "Lin, why do you not want to let Alex know about your condition? We need his help."

"No, not yet. You can see how happy he is chatting with you. I can also see the sparkle back in your eyes when you talk to him. Such happiness you had when you chatted. I saw the same sparkle when you courted me and when you talked about Stephen ages ago. I have not seen that sparkle since I became sick. I only see the sadness in your eyes. The eventual loneliness you fear. But since we met Alex, you have that sparkle again. I want you to be happy. I know you're already doing so much for me. The recent investments are for me, aren't they?"

Eric didn't reply. Having faced death himself so closely, it had changed him even more. He wasn't as sure of himself as he was before. "Okay, Lin. We'll tell Alex when and if we need to."

PART 2

GREEN ENERGY

CHAPTER 11

A WORTHWHILE IDEA?

"Do you think we have something here?" Eric asked those in his meeting room. He had shown them Alex's e-mail, which detailed his ideas.

"I called you together to decide if Alex really has ideas worth looking into. Last week we spoke, and he was pretty convincing. Kim, what are your thoughts?"

Eric trusted Kim, the director of Shi Institute. She had overseen many research projects and knew if they had merit.

"Frankly, I'm not sure. I'll need time to check on his ideas. They seem real enough. But will they work? I don't know."

"Stephen, how do you think?" Eric asked.

"Alex is serious. He's an amateur though. No experience. He's not an engineer. Ideas don't just become real. But I see your point. It's plausible to work."

"Hugh? Thoughts?" Eric asked Hugh Graham, an American, his senior advisor on renewable energy.

Hugh clearly outlined his thoughts. "Yes, Eric. I've read a bit on deep-sea currents and the technology to possibly harness its energy. There will be many obstacles. The energy is there for the taking. The questions are how and how much? For it to work, we need an efficient way to harness it. If the efficiency is below 50 percent, I don't think the numbers will add up. It will still be too expensive for today,"

Alex probed his advisor's intellect. "An estimate cost for production of less than, say, a million watts per day?"

"It's hard to say. There's no way we can estimate without running tests. Running costs may be as cheap as $1,000 per day, with a setup of half a billion dollars. Or it could be way above that. I really don't want to estimate."

"And what about you, Arsene?" Eric put the question to Arsene Widderman, a stout blond German who ran the European side of business. Arsene was a mechanical engineer by profession. Now he was chief of operations in Europe for Shi Corporation. He happened to be in Taiwan for a corporate meeting.

Arsene replied, "Looking at the idea, I'm excited. It's promising. You know I'm always an optimist. I do see something here. Energy is there, as Hugh said. I'd think it's time someone brought renewable energy up to date."

"Do we have an agreement to look at the idea?" Eric asked. He looked around and heads were nodding. "Okay, then. Stephen, could you arrange with Alex to come to Taiwan to meet up with us in the next week or two. Also, get a few professionals in the field to join us. Meanwhile, let's research up what Alex has let us know. I think he has not totally given us all his ideas. A meeting with him will give him the chance."

*

"Katherine, here!" Katherine heard Alex's shout in the airport arrival hall. There were so many people. She turned around looking for him.

"Hi, Dad!" Katherine saw her father and quickened her pace, dragging her two bags behind.

"Let me give you a hand," Alex said.

"Just one. You're not young, you know? You'll hurt your back," she remarked. "It's good to be back. Where's Mum?"

"She's catching up on things. She wanted to come, but then your flight got delayed and she couldn't make it. We'll meet her at home. The limo's waiting."

In the limousine, Katherine said, "Hey, Dad. Miss me? I'm sure you did. I'm glad to be back. Oh, Dad. Fill me in. The incredible stories you've been telling me online—I should write a book. You're flying to Taiwan next week?"

"I am, actually. I'm getting a bit excited about this. Maybe there will be something that will come of it. But, at the moment, it's just a whim."

"Aw, Dad. Come on. Have more faith. We'll be able to do this. You and me. I'll go with you. Give you support. You'll need all the support you can get." She grabbed his arm, closing in on him, blinking repeatedly in a manner he could not refuse.

"Okay. You can come along. But don't make a fool of yourself. Eric is a 'big' man."

"I won't, Daddy. I'll be so good. So good." Katherine really knew how to get what she wanted from him. "By the way, two friends will be arriving tomorrow. They want to join me but couldn't get plane tickets. They're my best friends. I've mentioned them to you, haven't I? Andre and Angelina. But they are not a couple. Angelina is going to meet up with her Internet boyfriend next week."

Katherine was always full of words. She loved to talk and didn't seem to tire from talking. She realized her father was quietly looking at her, smiling. She smiled and put her head on his shoulders. He was her pillar of strength. *Always has been and always will be,* she thought.

"Tell me your stories that happened in the past three or four months. I'd love to hear them again," she said. Her father's hand patted her head in acknowledgement.

"So tell me about yourself. What did you do last week? You haven't filled me in yet."

"Me? Ah. You know the usual—what lawyers do. Talk, talk, talk. And twist, twist, twist. Then write, write, write. Contractual law is boring."

"Come on. You enjoy it. You like the challenge, the debate, the twists and turns, hiding facts and mixing them up in your lawyer's jargon. I know you, *lah*," Alex said in the usual Malaysian slang, ending a sentence with *lah*.

Katherine smiled when she heard him say lah. It was good to be away from her busy schedule and talking in Malaysian slang. She had to avoid that when she spoke at work. Somehow, lah makes business conversations sound too relaxed and informal.

"Yeah—lah. Seriously, lah. It has been a bit boring of late. Work is there, but not as much. The contracts need to be so much more detailed these days. I can't talk about my cases, but in general, business is slow. I'm doing a Russian contract for an oil tycoon. I overheard one of their conversations in Russian. You know I'm into languages. They didn't know I understood them. Anyway, it seems they're spooked. The oil reserve they have been banking on is much smaller than they thought. How can there still be so much oil? We've already consumed trillions of gallons. I think the oil companies and governments are in a conspiracy. There has to be. They want to keep oil going as long as they can. I'm sure of it. They don't want something like solar energy or even nuclear energy to come in and take over before it all runs out. They want to milk us of every cent first!"

"Are you writing another book? You've been daydreaming again, haven't you?"

"No, no. I firmly believe there is some truth to what I'm saying. I can't give you specifics—a lawyer's oath and ethics. I do know they are not honest with the figures on oil reserves. Of that much I'm sure. Four years into my career and I can read rather clearly between the lines."

Alex's cell phone rang and interrupted their conversation. Stephen's name flashed. Katherine released her father's arm as he answered. "Hi, Stephen."

"Alex, I think you've already heard from Eric. Right?"

"Yes, I have. He said you'll fill me on the details," Alex replied.

"We'll be meeting next Friday evening. That will give us extra time if we need to stay late. Sorry. All of us have commitments and can only get together next Friday. Is that fine? But as Eric might have told you, we'll hear you out and see if we can move this forward. No promises though. Please don't get your hopes up."

"I understand,"

Katherine could sense an excitement in her father's voice as he stammered an answer. "I'll keep my feet on the ground. I think Friday is good. I do have to get my clinic settled before I leave."

Katherine tugged at her father's sleeve. "Tell him I'm going too."

"By the way, Katherine is here with me. I'm going to bring her along."

"Katherine?"

"Oh. Katherine is my daughter. She is with me these weeks from London. I need her to calm my nerves," he said with a smile.

She squeezed his arm in acknowledgement.

"Ha. Sure. I'm sure it will be fine," Stephen said approvingly.

"Okay. We'll see you in Taipei then."

Katherine was happy. She got what she wanted—accompanying her father to a meeting that might change their lives forever. Maybe even the rest of everyone's lives in the future. She knew her father well, and when he put his mind to something, he always succeeded. She would be there to push him.

CHAPTER 12

THE MOTHER OF ALL DECISIONS

Eric sat in his office looking out the window, waiting half an hour for the meeting to start. The view from the top of the Shi Corporation Tower was magnificent. It comforted him. He could see the Taipei 101 Tower in the distance. The mountains farther back made a great backdrop, with the sun setting behind them. He had seen this view a thousand times and still wanted to see it again.

He rubbed the jade pendant, reflecting on his decision to consider Alex's idea. "We can make things happen," Alex had said during their first meeting. It echoed in his mind. Had Eric read the situation correctly? To move on with this idea, he might not be giving his best to Mei Lin. He would have to concentrate on more things, which meant less time for her—most importantly, less time to focus on finding a cure for her. He would need to make a decision after the meeting.

"Mr. Shi, they're waiting for you in the meeting room. Shall I say you'll be there shortly?" his secretary asked.

"Thanks. Just say I'll be there in a minute."

She turned and walked to the meeting room, leaving Eric to gather his thoughts. He smoothed his turtleneck and straightened the jade pendant, took a deep breath, and smiled before walking to the meeting.

Eric walked in and saw Katherine at her father's side. "Hi, everyone. Welcome to Taipei. This is going to be an informal meeting. Let me introduce Ms. Kim, the director of Shi Institute. She will be leading the meeting. I'm sure in the last few minutes you have all introduced yourselves." Eric looked at the people in the room. Most were nodding. "Okay, Kim, all yours."

Kim started. "Welcome, everyone. Eric scheduled this meeting so we can listen to Dr. Alex Liang's idea or concept. He arrived today from Penang. Alex, the floor is yours."

Alex rose from his chair, feeling quite nervous. He glanced at Katherine and felt her grip on his arm, giving him support.

"Ahem. Thank you. I hope I'll not waste your time. I'll get straight into it.

"Almost all energy on Earth comes from the sun. The deep-sea currents are a result of the solar energy heating the water at the equator. The heated water flows to the poles of the earth cools and returns back to the equator. This results in deep-sea currents." Alex pointed to the projected slide on the wall behind him.

"This current is constant and never changes direction. We can predict the currents. Of course there are some changes with seasons and with the moon's gravity, but they are so minimal we don't realize them. The energy that can be harnessed is almost infinite.

"We need to harness this energy. Just harnessing a fraction of it may be enough to power the whole of Taiwan. Because the current is slow, at only a few miles per hour, I believe we underestimate its potential. We would associate energy with a Formula One racecar and not with a truck carrying bricks. The truck is slow but uses so much more energy to move. The sea currents are like the trucks—slow—but the energy there is tremendous. Currents have torn ships apart. They assist the normal migration of fish."

Alex stopped and looked around. There were eight people in the room besides Eric and Katherine, and they seemed genuinely interested.

"This is the design of the turbine I have pictured in my mind for the last few years," Eric said as he put up the next slide. "I have copies of the details in the folders I have prepared.

"The turbines are arranged in two parallel rows and joined in the middle. It will need to be very large. The cusps on the turbines will be huge, probably twice the size of a truck. The series of gears will magnify the oscillations and allow exponential increase in the revolutions in the attached electric generator.

"If the turbines and the generation of electricity succeeds, the distance to the shore is far too distant to be effective as the energy transmission will not be efficient.

"Any questions before I move on to the next part?" Alex asked, hoping to engage the audience.

"I am curious to know how the turbines will affect the marine life. Would they be injured when they hit the turbine? If too much energy is taken away, would the currents slow?"

Alex expected the challenge and was prepared. "That's the beauty of the turbine I've designed. It's not expected to move fast, just as fast as the current, at a few miles per hour. The cusps must be large to accommodate large creatures, such as dolphins, sharks, and whales. If creatures larger than the cusps are detected by sonar, the cusps will close and the turbine goes offline until they pass by. In this way, the cusps will be like large cups that can hold the creature until it turns at the end and allows it to continue its journey in the current stream."

Alex demonstrated with a cup held horizontally above the table, putting a piece of candy in the cup, moving it horizontally for about a foot, and then turning the cup quickly at the end, allowing the candy to spontaneously move out of the cup from its inertia.

Alex looked at Karim, who seemed to be in thought, his brow creased.

"As for the second question," Alex said, "I always wondered if the change in weather has anything to do with the increased energy in the currents as Earth's temperature increases. The typhoons and hurricanes seem to be stronger these days. If we release the energy from the currents, will it help the weather? I think the amount of energy we can tap into will be so fractional that it will not have any impact. Of course I'm speculating here without hard facts."

"The turbine alone in the ocean cannot possibly survive?" Stephen asked.

"True." Alex changed the slide. "It will have to be anchored to a platform, like an oil rig. I envision four turbines anchored to the platform. Of course the final number of turbines will depend on the configuration of the platform."

"You have given your concept quite a bit of thought," Stephen remarked.

Alex decided to move on and changed to another slide. "Now, having electricity generated, how are we going to transport it? I propose to store the electricity as hydrogen, as in fuel-cell technology. It's not new."

Kim asked, "The fuel-cell technology has been slow because of the potential danger it may cause."

"I think the dangers have been overstated. We use it for all the rockets we send into space. If we get it right, we can minimize the danger." Alex clicked on the next slide. "This is my design. We compartmentalize the storage of the hydrogen, putting nitrogen between compartments, eliminating oxygen. This way hydrogen will not combust if leaked. This will dilute the leaking hydrogen, and prevent an explosion," Alex explained.

He clicked on the second-to-last slide and continued. "This is the most important part of the whole concept. The efficiency to produce hydrogen by electrolysis is crucial. We have to achieve a high efficiency. Way above what conventional methods can do. If we cannot achieve that, it will still work but even more problems will need to be sorted out. Unwanted heat will need to be dissipated. The cost will increase. We'll need to consider more wear and tear costs."

The slide read "Electrolysis—Efficiency?"

He continued with the next slide, which simply read, "Meyer's hypothesis."

"Stanley Meyer's hypothesis is something we have to consider and maybe develop. I must admit this is the most important yet weakest link in the concept. I don't know if it will work. Meyer hypothesised that if he resonated or rapidly changed the amperage or voltage, he could increase the efficiency of electrolysis to near perfection. Unfortunately, few people think he has succeeded, and a majority feel his theory is a hoax."

Kim chimed in. "I've read Meyer's hypothesis. I didn't really believe it. I must say I've not experimented to see if it will work. It sounded a bit farfetched."

Alex didn't answer. He didn't know if it would work. He had thought Meyer's hypothesis was worth the gamble.

Alex looked around the room. These people were probably the brightest around. What were they thinking? He should have known his concepts wouldn't be accepted that easily. They were all silent. No indication they agreed. They all seemed to be deep in thought. Katherine was trying to give him a weak smile. He guessed Katherine also felt the audience was not impressed.

"Are you confident about your concept?" Eric asked after almost an eternity.

"As sure as I can be."

Kim stood beside Alex and asked the room for questions. "Yes, Jonathan?" Kim introduced him to Alex. "Jonathan is our research head in mechanical engineering,"

Jonathan said, "I can see your concept in my mind. The concept is easy and probably seems too simple to work. Sometimes that is why it will work. The ease of the concept is its beauty. But it will be a monumental task. The depth in which we would have to install the turbines would have to be close to two thousand feet deep. The material we'd need to design the turbines is another problem. It will need to withstand the pressure, temperature, and stresses. We'll also need to find a site where the current would be strongest yet not too fast. A sweet spot must be found in the stream where the current is strong, constant and with minimum turbulence. Too deep and near the seabed will cause turbulence. Too near the surface the current would not be strong. The site would be an area where the current converge thus compressing the energy it possess. Tapping it there would be ideal to yield maximum energy.

"Eric, the funding would be enormous. I think the main reason it has not been explored is because the size of the project will be so enormous it may be doomed to fail before we even start."

Alex felt his enthusiasm fall through the floor. He focused on Katherine as Jonathan completed his analysis. She looked straight at him, mouthing the words, "I believe in you." Her expression was strong, signaling him not to give in. He had to believe.

"I agree but what task is not enormous? If we break it into small pieces, the problems become small. I understand it will take time and a lot of research. Right now, it's belief that got me here today. I believe it will work. We make things happen. Things don't just happen for us."

Alex glanced at his watch. He had his timer on. It was nearly an hour already.

Eric looked at Alex, gave him a smile, and signaled to Kim to conclude.

"Thank you, Alex. We're impressed. We may take this further. I think Eric and all of us will need some time to think it over. But we're impressed."

"I'll meet up with you in your hotel later," Eric assured Alex as he and Katherine were leaving.

After they left, Eric took over from Kim. "Well, do we have something here to work on? Stephen? Kim?"

Stephen said, "The science is correct. We need to work out the details. Meyer's hypothesis is new to me."

"I don't see a problem there, although I have not heard of Meyer either. If Meyer believed in his hypothesis, he would jump at the chance to come aboard. If he doesn't, then it's just a hoax," Eric replied.

"The pieces are there. To put them all together will take some doing. But if everything falls in line, it should be promising," Kim answered.

Eric nodded in agreement. "The marine life would be preserved?" Eric asked, looking at Karim as if for assurance.

Karim said, "He has given a lot of thought to the design of the turbine. He may have just found the solution for the deep-sea-turbine concept."

"The cost will be enormous," Arsene said. "We would need land bases to develop the technology and then transfer it all to the platform Alex envisioned in the middle of the ocean."

"Give a figure. What are the chances it will work, Stephen?" Eric was digging deep into their thoughts.

Stephen answered, "I think it can work. Percentage? I don't know. Maybe a fifty-fifty chance."

Eric could not get any more out of them. He needed to decide. He concluded the meeting, thanking them. He had a lot to think about.

Stephen stayed on as the rest left. "Eric, I just want to say you should look at this with a business aspect and a scientific aspect," Stephen said.

"What do you mean?" Eric asked, almost sure of the answer he would receive.

"Well, are you looking at this because Alex saved your life? We have to be objective."

Eric didn't reply.

"If you decide to proceed, you'll have my unreserved support. I think it can work, but at a fifty-fifty chance, I'm unsure if we should proceed. You have made bigger decisions, and I'm sure you will again."

Eric nodded and walked back to his office.

The night view from his window gave a different perspective. The Taipei 101 Tower was fully lit and stood tall, alone. No other building was near its height. Eric was alone in his office.

This decision he had to make himself. He felt Alex's energy and excitement. He remembered feeling a similar enthusiasm when he was younger. Now past sixty, and with Mei Lin's illness, he was experiencing some form of depression, and his sparkle had almost been extinguished. Yet, as Mei Lin said, she saw the sparkle again. He had to decide tonight. No point dragging it on.

He knew Stephen meant well giving advice. He was clear in his mind. It wasn't that Alex had saved Eric and Eric was repaying a debt.

Eric clutched his jade pendant as if it would bring him closer to his gods. He was Taoist/Buddhist. He believed there had to be a reason he'd nearly died. There had to be a reason he'd met Alex.

How would it all come together?

He knew if he pursued this, it would take precious finances from his quest to cure his beloved wife. Was this the test? To be selfless for the betterment of humankind? He was alive, wasn't he? He felt he had no choice. He had to follow the path he felt had been lain before him.

He texted Alex. "I'm sorry I can't make it to your hotel. I'll come over tomorrow morning. I've made my decision. We'll proceed in stages. If each stage goes well, we'll go all the way. Good night to you and Katherine."

Eric left his office to share his decision with Mei Lin. He went home with a heavy heart, making a decision with so much uncertainty and so much to lose.

CHAPTER 13

REGENESIS IS BORN

"You look fabulous, Mrs. Shi," Alex said. His admiration for her was growing. But he would consciously hide it and continue not to address her as Mei Lin, leaving it more formal. "This is my daughter, Katherine, who is back for holidays. A month."

"Call me Mei Lin, please, Alex. Pleased to meet you, Katherine. How's the weather there? London, isn't it? Your father is proud of you. He mentions you often."

"The pleasure is all mine," Katherine replied, smiling warmly at the Shis.

Eric said, "Come, let's hurry to lunch. They have a flight to catch," ushering Alex and Katherine into the limousine.

Once they arrived at their location, Katherine remarked, "This place is magnificent. I feel I've gone back in time about a thousand years." She looked around, admiring the decor and furnishings, which were made to emulate the Ming Dynasty. Teakwood furniture was carved with the absolute finest detail. The mural depicted a war and was made in a way to look like an ancient scroll unfolding. The floor was solid wood. The building seemed held together with huge pillars made of teak. The lights were paper lanterns, but with bulbs inside.

"This dining hall has been designed to look like the hall of the Ming Palace in that century," Eric explained. He quickly changed the subject to the focus of the evening. "Now that a decision has been made, we have to make haste and try to complete each phase as fast as possible. We met this morning to make plans for the next few months."

Alex noticed the tone Eric was using. It wasn't the usual relaxed manner in which Eric usually spoke. He seemed more urgent and pressing.

"Stephen will send you the details of our plan by tonight. The details are quite important. We need to be sure of everything, as I firmly believe we have little time and only one shot at this. The scale of the whole thing is huge. Any delays or hiccups and we may not complete it."

Alex's excitement reached another scale. His heart pounded in his ears. Eric's words seemed to register in slow motion, and his mind raced on. Images of his past dream flashed in his mind. This was it. Alex glanced at Mei Lin as Eric continued to speak. She was silent but without her usual smile. Her eyes looked tired. Her shoulders hunched forward, different from her usual upright position. She seemed to be distant in thought.

"Your idea is worth a shot. If it can be done, I'll make it work. You have my word on that."

Katherine asked as Eric concluded, "It may be improper to ask, but the finance part of it will be enormous, I presume. How much will my father need to invest?"

That's my girl, Alex thought. *The lawyer in her guarding my interest. But right now, I'd give anything to see this through.*

Eric, a bit uncomfortable and clearly annoyed by the question, replied, "Actually, very little. A token amount. We'll have to set up a holding company to handle the whole project. Shares will be drawn up."

Alex reacted. "Katherine, I know Eric well enough. I want to see this through. I'd forgo any rights. I'll never have this chance again."

Eric assured him. "Don't worry about that. I'm not in this for the money. But if there is money in it, we'll share it equally. Your idea and concept. My team and work. Money will not be an issue."

Eric reached out his hand. Alex was taken aback, slow to react. Eric stretched it out a bit further. Alex took it, and they shook on it.

"A toast then," Mei Lin said. She seemed back to the present, Alex observed.

"To success!" Alex exclaimed, and the gold-edged, finest porcelain tea cups clinked together.

Now alone in the dining hall, Eric turned to Mei Lin. Alex and Katherine had left for the airport. "Do you think I made the right decision, Lin? We could lose everything. The business. Everything. I'll set up a trust just in case. That will ensure you and the kids will always be taken care of."

Mei Lin replied, with tears in her eyes, "This is an opportunity you can't pass up. If you succeed, the world we know will change. Since my illness, you have been there for me. You blamed yourself for my illness. Made all your factories and plants safe from pollution and toxic metals. Although you didn't share them with me, I can read your thoughts. My early years working in your plant have haunted you. But you are not to be blamed. Yet I don't know why we were led to this path. Maybe it's God's will and we've been chosen."

She unconsciously brushed her fingers over her crucifix. "There has to be meaning to these happenings. Alex and his ideas didn't materialize for no apparent reason. I trust God. And you do too. We've both been at death's door. Me twice, maybe three times. We know all the wealth we have cannot make us immortal. This is all meant to be. You have to do this."

Tears rolled down Mei Lin's cheeks. She was still looking down into the tea cup as if she could see the future in the few leaves at the bottom. She suddenly looked up at Eric, flashing a weary smile, and said, "Everything will be fine. You'll see. You and Alex will change the world!"

The future would be most challenging for all of them.

Alex was deep in thought on the plane back to Penang. It would be another few hours before touchdown. *Why was Eric so businesslike? Eric has not been like this before. And Mei Lin looked so sad. What is that they have not told me? Why was Eric interested in my ideas? No monetary interest. A businessman with no financial interest. Not guilt or debt to me, I hope. My dream may come true. I'm tired of treating patients with cancer. I have to believe in myself. Tackle the root cause of cancer. Pollution. Clean renewable energy will change cancer. Cancer rates should reduce. It will be a thousand times better than treating patients one by one. I can't refuse Eric's help.* Exhausted, Alex fell asleep.

Alex felt a tug on his sleeve. He slowly opened his eyes, and a sudden thought jarred him awake. *Phew,* he thought. *Thank goodness it's not another medical emergency.*

"Sorry I startled you," Katherine said.

With a sigh of relief, Alex dropped back into his seat and felt his muscles relax.

"Dad—hey, Dad. I just thought up a name for your idea. I have to share it with you. Does 'Regenesis' sound nice? It does, doesn't it? It's perfect."

Alex was really relieved. "Hmm, yes. It does fit nicely."

Katherine concluded, "Yes it does. Regenesis is born."

CHAPTER 14

A PAIR OF OPPOSITES

Katherine introduced her friends to her father. "This is Andre, and that is Angelina."

"Come in, please." Alex invited them into the living room. "Andre, have you been to Penang or Malaysia?"

"Dr. Liang, yes. I've been to Kuala Lumpur. Not Penang. I've toured this region before. Phuket, Bangkok, Jakarta, Hanoi. I think that's it."

"That's more than me. I've not been to Hanoi," Alex said with a laugh.

"I'd like to return. People are nice and less nosey, even though I'd stand out in the crowd."

"Yes, aren't they? Here's the tea," Alex said, as the servant, accompanied by Lai Peng, brought in the tea tray with a nice choice of local nyonya cakes.

"You all have met my wife?"

"Yes, we have. She fetched us at the airport and brought us to our hotel," Angelina answered.

"Sorry I was not there to welcome you all." Alex said.

"We were tired anyway from the long journey. Had a great sleep last night," Angelina continued. "Now that we're rested, we can visit all the places today and tomorrow."

As they had tea, Katherine explained. "Dad, Angelina has a boyfriend in Singapore. She's flying there the day after to meet him. She hasn't even met him in person but is deep in love!"

Alex looked a bit bewildered.

"They met on the Internet. He is the 'hulk' she is looking for."

Angelina raised her hand in a fist, as if threatening to punch Katherine. "Come on, Angelina. It's an open secret. You post it on your Facebook!"

Angelina faked a theatrical collapse on the sofa, and they all laughed.

Alex thought, *What is with the new generation? Why tell everyone what you are doing? Now Andre is taking pictures of the tea and cakes. He must be putting it on Facebook.*

Alex said, "What are you all going to do today?"

Katherine replied, "Let's see … today we'll visit the Kek Lok Si Temple, the Reclining Buddha Temple, the Indian Mosque, my school, Convent Light Street, and the Fort Cornwallis, using your limousine. Then we'll dine at the Eight Terrace Mansion. You'll get to taste real authentic Baba-Nyonya food, a mix between Chinese and Malay."

"I think Lai Peng and I will spend a quiet evening here and leave you all to your plans," Alex said, wanting to give them space.

After Andre escorted them to their room and left, Angelina said, "I'm sleepy. So tired after visiting all those places. How did you find this place, Kat? It's so quiet. Unique. I've never seen a hotel like this. It feels so modern yet it's in such old surroundings. I never expected such luxury." She sniffed the scented pillows lying on the king-size bed.

Katherine was on the sofa facing the bed. The television was flashing some news, its volume just loud enough to break the silence. "I know the owner. His son is a friend."

"Ha. Good to have friends in the right places. So how was your trip with your dad to Taiwan? Busy?"

Katherine avoided the specifics. "As usual, business for my father. I was there to give him support. Not that he needed it. More like I wanted to."

"You're close to your dad. I am too. I chat with mine almost every day. He pampers me. Can you believe it? I flew first class this time. I didn't know until we were at the airport that he'd upgraded me. Andre was a bit annoyed being left to economy on his own. You should have seen his face."

"What is it with you two? You don't get along, do you?"

Angelina shrugged. "Well, he is your friend. Not really mine. I'm your closest friend. I don't like the way he looks at me … like a lion waiting to pounce the first chance he gets. I'm glad I didn't sit next to him all those hours."

Katherine threw a pillow at her in reply.

"What do you see in him, Katherine?"

"He is handsome, isn't he? Anyway, I'm not really into him. Just a friend. Not too close."

"I think he's gay," Angelina said.

"Ha! That he is not. I've seen him few times with ladies. Never with a man."

"Frankly, we started out knowing each other in business. He accompanied his father to one of the meetings at my firm. He called me and we chatted."

"He dated you?"

"Not really. Well sort of. But we never had any chemistry. I think he has 'issues,'" Katherine reflected. "Not sure what they are. I can feel things, you know."

"Ah. You can. So what am I feeling now?"

"Hmmm. You're feeling itchy!" and she rushed over to her and tickled her everywhere.

The night was still young. Andre had been to these parts of the world many times. He would explore as he always did. It was midnight. It was time. He knew the girls were asleep by now. The clerk at the reception at check in had been discreet, as always. Knowing the unseen ways of the night, he dressed in a tight T-shirt and jeans. Clutching his cell phone, he opened the door to go down to the reception desk.

"I need some life tonight. Where?" he asked as he slipped a hundred Malaysian ringgit note across.

"Down the road on the left and you'll find The Club, a coffeehouse. Ask for 'Super Sam.'"

A short walk and he was at the coffeehouse. It was dimly lit. There was only a couple seated in the corner.

He approached the waiter and asked for Super Sam.

The waiter nodded and led him down the long corridor, opened the back door, and walked three houses down. He knocked twice, paused, and knocked another five times. It promptly opened. A muscular man with his potbelly spilling out of his shirt opened the door. Dragon tattoos were on both forearms. He grunted, and with a turn of his head, signaled Andre to go in. He was sizing up Andre as he walked in.

Soon Andre was in a barely furnished room that held just a few chairs. Andre was used to this and it didn't bother him. He knew they knew the clients were only interested in the merchandise and nothing else. He had to wait for about two minutes and was getting impatient.

Finally the door opened, and a middle-aged lady dressed in an awful, creased cheongsam that was too short for her aged body entered with a string of girls. Even without asking and seeing his type, they knew he only wanted young girls. All wore only G-strings. Many had tattoos, some just over their G-strings, obviously trying to hide scars from childbirth or abortions. All sported a small dragon and snake tattoo over their left breast. *Probably a mark of the triad group,* he thought.

Some smiled, others seemed totally disinterested. and a few seemed honestly frightened, trying to shield their breasts and privates with their hands.

He approached them and grabbed their breasts and felt their skin, trying to make his pick. He finished with the last and was not satisfied.

He passed $1,000 and whispered to the lady in charge. "Get me something nicer. Young, as young as possible. Untouched. Not these used ones."

She nodded and replied in broken English, "You pay, I get. One thousand no. Two thousand yes."

He knew they liked to negotiate. He would pay more if the merchandise was untouched and pretty. He nodded.

"Wait ten, twenty minute," she replied and led the girls away.

He had her tied up and gagged on his bed now. She was slim, with a nice pair of soft breasts. Her skin was smooth and perfumed. Her crotch was untouched, her pubic hair scented. He felt her tremble as he pushed himself into her. She let out muffled screams. She'd obviously been drugged when she was led into the room by the lady. He wasn't happy then. They promised to deliver her, and he would have her for the whole night. Unfortunately for her, the sedative would only last an hour. Now she was fully awake and could feel the terrible pain. With her every muffled scream, he pushed harder as it made him feel even more like an animal. He felt her warm blood trickling down his thighs as he trust forward. He would fully explore every inch of her. She would feel even more pain soon. He had the whole night with her. His imagination ran wild.

A knock at six in the morning and Andre, feeling a bit exhausted, opened the door. Two men walked in. Both were a bit taken aback by the sight. The girl was semiconscious, still gagged. Her hands were not tied anymore. Blood stained the sheets. Scratched and bite marks covered her body.

One of the men turned to Andre, wanting to confront him. Andre was much bigger than him. Andre showed his full height of six feet with a muscular body of a wrestler, and stared him down like a lion challenging another. A slight snarl and the Chinese man backed off.

Andre grabbed his wallet, took out a wad of hundred-dollar greenbacks, and passed them on, saying, "That should cover the damage. I'm sure you know."

After they left, he showered and would once again be the daytime "Dr. Jekyll." The evil Mr. Hyde would hide for another few days. No one must know. That was why he loved the East. They were more compromising. They feared the Russians.

Chapter 15

ALEX'S MASSIVE CHANGE IN DIRECTION

Alex was back in his practice the next morning. By late evening, he was about to finish his long day. He had to catch Dr. Alicia Moy, his partner, before she left.

"Alicia, would you mind waiting for me? We have something important to discuss," he said, half-opening her consultant clinic door and peeping in.

"Sure. I'm finished. Just paperwork for the next thirty minutes."

Alex returned to his room for his last patient.

"So are you ready for another test tomorrow?" Alex asked the young boy in front of him. "The test will be the same as the last one you did a month ago. We'll let you sleep, and when you wake up, everything will be fine."

The young boy was quiet. His mother chimed in. "He's frightened, Dr. Liang. How is his leukemia?"

"I think it's in remission. But we do need the marrow test tomorrow to confirm. It's vital we do that." Alex said.

"Honey, listen to the doctor. He knows best."

"What are you afraid of?" Alex asked him, waiting patiently for his answer.

"I'm worried I won't wake up."

"You already did it once."

"I fear I won't wake up after I've gone to sleep. I nearly couldn't wake up the last time. I was very woozy and had to force my eyes open. Doctor, have you had an operation before?"

Alex got close to the boy. The boy trusted him but was frightened. "Everyone is frightened. I've not had an operation. But I have experienced worse things."

"Really?" he asked in disbelief.

"When I was about your age, I loved to cycle everywhere. I grew up in a small town. I didn't like to study. I'd miss class and go out with my friends. But one day I got into real trouble.

"I had gone to the beach instead of going to school. I didn't like the teacher that morning. She was a fierce one and always liked to pinch me or twist my ears. I usually went to the beach with Ahmad, but that day, Ahmad didn't come along. I can't remember why. So I went alone."

The boy's mother was giving him a look. He understood and signaled to her with a few gentle nods, meaning it was all right. There was a lesson in his story, and he was not teaching him truancy.

"I loved the sound of the waves. It was early in the morning. The tide was out that day. I could walk out to the large boulder, which was about maybe sixty-five feet away. I waded up to about my waist to reach the boulder. I climbed up and stood up on it. I liked to do that. It felt nice looking down, seeing the little waves hit the boulder. It was not sunny. In fact, it was about to rain. Cloudy, you know.

"I laid back and watched the clouds. The sound of the waves was so nice, so peaceful that I wanted to sleep. I loved the cloud patterns in the sky. I could imagine a fairy, my teddy bear, and my little toy boat all up there. And I fell asleep. Guess what happened next?"

The boy thought hard and said, "The teacher found you and spanked you!"

"Ha-ha. Yes she did, but that came later. I woke up as the rain fell. I was still on this large boulder, but the tide had risen and the shore was now far away. The water was now deep and the waves strong.

"I was caught in a mess. If I waited, the water would be deeper. No one was around to hear me shout. If I tried swimming back, I wasn't sure I could make it. The water might be too deep. So I thought I could just slip down the boulder and test the depth. But I fell into the water. I was in real trouble. I couldn't feel the seabed. I couldn't stand up in the water. I had to swim back.

"So I gathered all my strength and swam. I got maybe fifteen feet, and just as I thought I could feel the seabed, the wave snatched me away from the shore. I was not as strong as I am now. I was being washed away. Soon I was drained of energy. I couldn't swim anymore and my head was underwater.

"I thought, *If I totally relax, I'll float upwards, as all things will float like my toy boat.* So I relaxed and started floating. Next thing I knew I was asleep."

Alex had the boy's full attention.

"A voice woke me. 'Wake up, wake up!' It got louder and louder until I woke up. I was on a small boat. The waves gently rocked me. My limbs were weak, but soon I had the strength to get up. And there was Ahmad's father, the fisherman. He had hauled me up as he was coming ashore after fishing. He saw me floating with my face up. Somehow I floated up and turned around. If not, I think I wouldn't be here talking to you. He took me back, got me changed, and got me to school. The rest you guessed. I got badly spanked!"

"Were you frightened?" the boy asked.

"Yes, frightened of being spanked!" and they had a good laugh.

"But seriously, I wasn't frightened when I was floating up to the surface. Somehow I knew I'd be fine. I'll tell you what. You be me. Imagine you are floating up, with your muscles relaxed, your eyes closed, hearing the waves, and focus on the clouds you saw when we go for the operation tomorrow. You'll fall asleep. I'll be there. I'll be Ahmad's dad and I'll wake you up. Everything will be fine tomorrow."

The boy was now excited, "You'll be there tomorrow? You promise you'll be there?"

"I promise. I'll be at your side when you wake up. I'll wake you up," Alex reaffirmed.

The boy left the room first. His mother followed but turned around at the door. "Was that a true story?" she asked.

Alex smiled and nodded. "Don't tell anyone." He wasn't sure if she had believed him.

His partner, Dr. Alicia Moy, was at the door as the clinic was about to close.

"Ha, your stories again. You make them up as you go along, don't you?"

Alex smirked but didn't answer. Sometimes they were made up. Sometimes they were true. Today's was true.

"Okay, let's get down to business. Alicia, have a seat."

"Wow, this sounds important. So what's this about? A VIP patient I mistreated again? They don't agree with me. You know I don't like to call them by their titles. Tan Sri, Dato, Your Majesty, Your Highness. They don't like me anyway," she complained as she sat down.

"No, it's not about you. It's about me."

"You? Okay, you've got my attention," Alicia sat up.

"I'm going to take a long sabbatical. It will be for a few months first. Then, if things work out, maybe two or three years."

"You want to take a sabbatical. You have not even taken more than two weeks' leave at once. Months of leave. You're burnt out or something? Are you feeling okay?" Alicia asked with absolute disbelief.

"I'm fine. Yes, actually I feel a bit burnt out. It's getting to me these days. Just too much work. I've contacted Sam—you remember Dr. Sam? He was my locum last year. He has been waiting for a chance to join us. I have not promised him a permanent job but have asked him to locum for me for three months."

"Are you okay? What will you do?"

"Ah, actually something I like. Research. Don't ask more. I've been sworn to secrecy," Alex told a white lie.

"I see," she said, still unconvinced.

"I'll be in Taiwan. They are good and have something going. Getting such an opportunity is unusual and I've taken it."

"Okay, I can accept that. When are you leaving?"

"In a week or two. Not fully confirmed. Let's get a drink, shall we?"

Alex closed his door, glanced from one end to the other. He would miss this place.

That night he sat quietly in his study. He enjoyed the peace he felt there. The room was a bit of a mess, with stacks of books and journals everywhere. But he liked it like that. It felt cozy. He gently moved his chair to the left and right, feeling it like the waves he felt in the sea. He recalled that day when he had nearly drowned. His buttocks were hurting. The teacher really could spank hard. His hands also hurt as they too were hit. He had been near death that day yet remained calm. He could have died, but he survived. That night so many years ago, he told himself he knew he was meant to be someone special. That gave him the drive to study. He took swimming lessons and became a champion school swimmer. It had all started from that day. And now he had arrived at this point in his life, a crossroads. A change of paths.

"Hey, Dad. Why you sitting in the dark?," Katherine asked.

"It's nothing. Just an old man thinking about his life. Getting old."

That same night in Singapore, Angelina was having a fun time with her mysterious new boyfriend. She'd had a full day with him, having arrived in the morning. He was more than she'd expected from his e-mails, texts, and photos.

In a corner of the Hilton's bar, she was deep in a passionate kiss with him. "I love your dark eyes, fair skin, and strong, muscular body. You should be on the cover of *Sports Illustrated*."

"Ha, my Middle-eastern, Chinese, and Portuguese ancestors made sure they kept the best parts and passed them down," he said laughingly.

Angelina knew she was caught in his charms. She felt like a fly going toward the "blue light" despite knowing it would be a trap, hitting the electrified net before dying in happiness.

"Let's go to my room and I'll show you how to play," he whispered as he led her to his room. She had no power to resist; she was totally possessed.

CHAPTER 16

DEFINING THE TEAM

"You mean Meyer is dead?" Kim asked.

"Yup. Died more than five years ago. It was reported as a stroke. Some dispute on the cause. There is a conspiracy theory that he was poisoned," Stephen answered.

"Any alternatives?" Eric asked, looking straight at Alex.

Alex wore a surprised expression. He probably hadn't known Meyer was dead. Alex was silent.

"I think there's a solution," said Stephen. "There are three people who took his hypothesis seriously. And as it happens, one of them is here in Shi Institute: Jack Colson. He has been with us for two years and works in theoretical physics. I've sent you and Kim his CV. I think he will come aboard. The other two are in Europe, but I haven't have time to research more on them."

"What do you think, Kim?" Eric asked.

"I've spoken to him before. He's bright. I think we should take him on," Kim said with approval.

"Let's bring him onboard. Jonathan, do you know him? Can you speak to him?"

"I will. I know him. Have good reports from the head of the department," Jonathan confirmed.

Eric glanced at Alex, who now seemed relieved that he missed the information about Meyer's death.

"Do we have what we need to start this off for now?" Eric asked.

"This floor in the research wing, where we are now, is good. It has high security and enough space for us to start. But it will not be enough to build models when we're in the second stage. It won't be sufficient," Kim replied.

"I'll leave you, Alex, and Stephen to work on the second stage. As we decided, the first stage will work the designs out on paper, check the science, do computer modeling, and work on materials to use, especially for the turbines and storage of hydrogen. Then we'll go into manufacturing the turbines, platform, and storage facility. The final stage will be the logistics of getting to the ocean site, which we'll have to identify in our first stage, and carry out live testing."

"What about financing?" Stephen asked.

"I'll look after that," Eric said, as he had already made plans. "Kim, you'll head the first phase, get the people we need to come onboard and plan how the second and third phases should be. We certainly will need to find a site for that.

"Stephen, your main task is to get the designs going, complete the computer modeling, and prepare us for the next phase.

"Jonathan, find the materials we need for the job.

"Karim, your task is to find the site for final live testing. I'm sure you know the ocean, including the ocean currents, better than all of us."

Eric had given them their assignments. They were ready to proceed.

"Let's give ourselves two months to complete this phase. We'll meet every week at this time. Any questions?"

Kim asked, "How are we going to transport the hydrogen from site to shore? And the platform?"

Eric turned to Alex as if asking for an answer.

Alex said, "I had thought of modifying an oil rig that will serve our purpose. A modified oil tanker can take on hydrogen after being fitted with the storage tanks."

Eric returned his gaze to Kim and could see her nodding. She asked, "And where are we going to find these two?"

Alex replied, "I have no idea. Borrow or lease them?"

Eric said, "I think I'll have to take care of that too. I'll sort out that part. Regenesis has begun."

With that, the first of many meetings ended.

It was almost a month into the first stage. Jack Colson had just returned from leave and joined them two days earlier.

"So how far did you get with Meyer?" Stephen asked.

"I worked out his principals. The high voltage and low-amp pulse currents he used to increase the electrolysis of water is interesting. I'll need a few weeks to test out his theories. I'm sure there is improvement in efficiency, but the increase is unlikely to be as high as he had described. I don't think it's possible to reach the efficiency levels he claims, which are near 100 percent,"

"You think you can do this?"

Jack replied with confidence. "I can try. If it's possible, I'll be able to."

"Let me know if you need anything else."

"Okay. I'd like to ask a few people who are very interested in helping."

"As long as security checks are okay, they're in."

"Thanks, Stephen," Jack said and left.

Stephen focused his attention on the three computer screens on his table. He needed to check the designs for the turbines. Somehow they weren't clicking for him yet. Some things didn't seem right. Alex was in charge of the turbine design, but he wasn't an engineer and wouldn't see the faults.

Elsewhere on the research floor, Jonathan was discussing with Kim the design for the storage of hydrogen.

"We can use anti-Newtonian fluid-saturated material to line the compartments. We'll use carbon fiber for the walls to lighten the weight," Jonathan explained.

Kim asked, "Can the carbon fiber withstand the pressure? And the weight if they are piled up?"

"I think the pressure is fine, but I'd not pile it up. Why would we need to pile it up?

"To maximize space, I presume."

"Hmmm. That would pose a problem if we do that. But I still think it's worthwhile to use carbon fiber instead of steel. Steel will be fifteen times heavier."

"Okay. Let's use carbon fiber and see how we can redesign the storage. We can ask Alex later again regarding his design. But does it make scientific sense to build it like he wants, with nitrogen?"

"It does actually. A clever design. It increases the space needed, as well as the weight. That's why I considered carbon fiber to lessen the overall weight."

"Interesting," Kim said as she looked at her watch. "I need to leave for another meeting. Continue the good work, Jonathan."

Kim was satisfied with the progress. They were on track to complete the first phase.

Chapter 17

CHINA

"Mr. Anderson?" the soft Chinese-accented voice behind him said. It belonged to a slight Chinese woman in a perfectly tailored black and red pants suit.

"Please follow me," she said and moved a little to show him the way. They took the elevator to the eighty-eighth floor. When the doors opened, he walked across a plush carpet toward the men standing by an object their bodies obscured.

"George," exclaimed the well-groomed, gray-haired, thin Chinese gentleman dressed in a Chinese traditional suit. He extended his hand. "I'm so glad to see you. I hope the flight was comfortable and that you have been well looked after."

"So good to see you too, Ching. Yes, as always. Your hospitality is flawless. Slept like a baby on the flight and slept the same in my bed last night," George said as they shook hands.

"Come and look at this, George," Ching said as he moved aside to reveal the obscured object. "My most recent acquisition. It's from the twelfth century, which as you know, was a prosperous time in China's long and often prosperous history."

George looked at the piece of wood heavily decorated with carvings of figures that looked purposeful and pictograms depicting a sailing ship, a Chinese junk to be precise. On the outer edges were carved objects he didn't recognize.

"Go on," George said after clearing his throat. "Tell me about it." George was conscious of the second gentleman in the room who had not been introduced, but he knew he had to be patient and polite. He knew in the Orient one could not use the informal, backslapping ways familiar in the states.

"I acquired this at Christie's last week," Ching continued. "It's a carving of a Chinese junk plying the waters of Southeast Asia. We traded heavily with what was called Nanyang and the Spice Islands in those days. We sold silk, as we still do, and chinaware, and we bought spices, which we sold here and traded across the silk route. Do you know what those items carved on the edges are?"

Anderson shook his head.

"Spices. Here's cinnamon, and this is pepper. This other one is nutmeg, and this other one is wood. Teak to be precise, if I'm not mistaken. We Chinese love teak. Good furniture is carved from teak, and the best houses have teak beams. Do you know how hard teak is? Even today it's cut the old-fashioned way. Chainsaws have been known to be blunted and even broken when sawing down a teakwood tree."

"What wood was used to carve this, and why make this carving?" Anderson asked, now a little intrigued.

"In Borneo, the state of Sarawak to be precise, the wood is a Borneo ironwood called Belian. It's a hardy wood but softer than teak. The provenance of the piece claims that this must have been part of a longer carving, possibly presented to the emperor to record the adventures of a great sailor. The commemoration of a great voyage from China to seek out treasures for trade in Nanyang appeals to me. I feel a kinship with this sailor, this adventurer. Unfortunately these days we Chinese collect everything, so I paid a small fortune for this. Too many bidders these days. Too many rich Chinese."

Ching was enjoying his joke and walked away to take a sip of tea while he let his guests admire the woodcarving.

"But I have forgotten my manners," he interjected as he suddenly returned. "George, this is Eric Shi. Eric is from Taiwan. A clever fellow, even if he is Taiwanese. Eric, this is George Anderson."

The two men shook hands and greetings as Ching continued. "As I've mentioned to you in an e-mail, Eric has an interesting project you might want in on. Eric needs your help. He has sent me the details, and my trusted engineers have discreetly looked into it. It has merit.

"Please excuse me for a few minutes. I have to attend to some matters. I shall be back in short while. I hope Eric can show you his project."

Eric said, "Thank you." He had been observing George the moment he entered the room. George was a stout man with a nice graying moustache and a friendly, smiling face. He was sporting a cowboy hat, a white shirt with blue embroidery, and a pair of denim jeans. He wore a large gold Rolex. His boots were well polished and gave a soft squeak when he walked. He was a real Texan.

Eric asked, "Shall we have a seat? I'd like to show you a short video that I put together to introduce our project,"

George smiled and relaxed on the couch.

Eric showed the video on his notebook.

Eric observed his George's body language and reaction as George watched the video, which showed, in animation, Alex's idea and designs, and the plan to move ahead in three phases, ending with the final live test. He seemed interested and sat up halfway through.

George asked, "Do you have the details of each phase, especially the platform in the ocean?"

"Yes, we have. I can send you the details via e-mail."

"I think I know why I've been asked to come here. You need my oil rigs, am I right?"

"As a matter of fact, yes. Ching knows you have the resources we need. We need a platform to anchor the turbines to and to house the storage of hydrogen and the production facility."

"So you need an oil rig and Ching thinks I'm the man."

"Yes."

"And Ching thinks I'll give you one?"

Eric hesitated and then replied, "He highly recommended you, saying you've never failed him. You also own the world's largest oil rig company, having more than 60 percent of the market. Do you have one we can use in short notice?" Eric felt George was direct, and a direct reply was best.

George smiled. "If it was not Eric Shi who was asking, I wouldn't. I do know of the Shi Institute and Shi Corporation. I employ a couple of good engineers from your institute. They work hard. What business would there be for me if I were to give you one?"

"I was hoping you would be happy with exclusive rights to all the platforms to be built for this purpose."

"And what must I do in return?"

"If you are generous, the platform and the modifications need to get to the project to work. Of course, if you want, we can offer shares in return for your investments."

Eric sensed George was going to go for it, and George was hesitating to see if he could get any further advantage out of this venture.

Eric continued. "If it works, it will change the whole energy supply in the world. Oil rigs might be the thing of the past. Imagine losing out on new technology that will be in place in the future." Eric had to tempt him further.

"I do see its potential. I'm concerned with the timing and whether it's economical as yet. Let me have the details, and I'll think it over. I'm sure if the science is correct, I'm in 100 percent."

Eric knew he had not finalized the deal as yet. Probably by e-mail and conversations over the Internet in the next week would be enough to make George want to commit.

Just then Ching returned. "I see smiling faces. You have struck a deal?"

"Almost," Eric remarked.

Ching said, "When we spoke initially, I was rather skeptical. But when I saw the documents, I thought it would be more likely to succeed than not. China needs more energy. Buying it has made my companies very dependant. I can sense a good deal." He looked at George. "I have confidence Eric and his team have really got something. I think it's like the woodcarving. With the adventurous voyage, spices and strong wood changed the world China knew. I see this as an adventurous voyage we're embarking on, and will return with treasures that will change China and the world. George, this chance is too good to pass. Take it."

George nodded and said, "If the science adds up when I review all the documents, I will."

Eric thought, *We have the platform. Now we need the tanker. We have enough financial resources to start. But do we have enough to finish it? I'll have to work out the cost in more detail soon with the team.*

With that, they adjourned for lunch.

CHAPTER 18

MOVING FORWARD

Katherine held onto her father's arm as they walked down the street with the rest of the team for supper. She glanced at her watch. It was already past midnight.

She noticed her father's watch, which he had worn for years. "Why do you still wear this? Can't you afford something better?"

"What's wrong with it? It's been with me for years. I hope it continues for many more."

"You should get a beautiful brand-name watch. A Rolex or at least a ceramic watch by Rado," she teased him.

"It's a perfectly made watch. I like my Casio. It tells the time and much more. It has become a part of me."

"Aw, you should pamper yourself a bit, Dad," Katherine continued. She knew he wouldn't buy a watch just for the brand. He always believed only in its worth. If not, there was no point to it except perhaps as something ornamental. She knew he tended to be scientific, always analyzing everything, weighing the pros and cons. Unlike her mother, who was spontaneous and loved to shop and had her "ornaments." She always wondered how they ever suited each other.

They had reached the small shop, about half a mile from the institute. They had come here quite often in the last few weeks. It had the best noodles in town.

As they waited for the food, Katherine observed those gathered with them: Stephen, Jonathan, Karim, and Jack.

Stephen summed up the night's work. "I think we're near the end of phase one. The science seems to check out. We've finished the designs. Soon we'll start building the turbines. I hope Eric has secured the platform to start modifications. Kim has already selected a site in Malaysia to begin phase two building test models before the actual manufacturing of the turbines and the other components for the final ocean test. You would know Lumut, wouldn't you, Alex?"

"Yes, of course I know Lumut. There's a naval base there."

"Kim has secured a piece of land suitable for us to use to develop phase two. The land is owned by a Malaysian tycoon who has business connections with Shi. They have an electricity production plant there. Kim thought it would be a good idea to site it there as a research facility adjunct to the power plant."

"To minimize suspicion?"

"Yes, and anyway, when we build the storage facility, it can also be used to store excess power from the power plant. Anyway, that's how Kim has sold the idea. So they do not know about the rest of Regenesis."

"Great," Alex said.

Jonathan said, "We haven't figured out how to transport everything to the ocean test site though. If we build the facility in Lumut and then dismantle and rebuild on the platform, it will add weeks or months to our schedule. While moving the facility, we won't be able to work. Anyway, at the moment, Kim thinks the site is suitable because it's near a port and transporting would be easier."

Stephen, deep in thought, added, "I agree. All of us have been thinking about it."

"Here come the noodles," Katherine said.

"Let's eat then," Stephen said. "With a full stomach, we'll think better!!"

They laughed and dug into their noodles.

Alex was looking out the window deep in thought as he ate. Katherine smiled, seeing her dad as a team member dressed so casually in a T-shirt and jeans, teaming up with men so much his junior. He looked like one of the team. So different from his usual formal self in the clinic.

As she glanced around, she noticed Stephen quickly changing his glance. He had obviously been observing her. *Is he into me?* she wondered.

Suddenly Alex turned to the team and said, "I've got it!"

They all looked at him as he pointed out the window with his chopsticks.

"See the trucks? The containers!"

"Huh?" Katherine remarked.

"We can use the containers. We build everything in the containers. We can combine a few. They can easily be dismantled, put on the trucks, and then put on a container ship. We can still continue our work while traveling to the ocean. Then we move the containers to the platform when we reach the final testing site."

A few moments passed as they appeared to absorb what he had said.

"That might just work," Jonathan said.

Stephen nodded in agreement. "Let's run that by Eric and Kim tomorrow morning," he said. "Looks like full stomachs really help!"

Everyone laughed.

The next morning, in Eric's office, the team gathered to report on their progress and to move onto phase two.

"Alex, looks like we've found the solution for the logistics of moving to the final phase from our land site in Lumut. Great idea," Eric said.

Being modest, Alex replied, "No, it was the noodles!"

The room was filled with laughter.

"On a serious note, we're now three months into Regenesis, and we've made good progress. Next week, Kim will go to the

Lumut site. Alex, you'll need to go along. Katherine, I think, you have already become part of the team. I'd like you to go with your father. We need a lawyer onboard. Contracts have to be drawn up. I know you're a good corporate business lawyer. Can I welcome you onboard?"

Katherine was momentarily speechless. "Of course. I'm so excited to be part of it. I'm thrilled." Her mind raced with excitement. She would now be part of Regenesis, and not just supporting her father. She was grinning from ear to ear.

CHAPTER 19

THIRTY YEARS TOO LONG

Eric slowly sipped his green tea from the small Japanese cup. He had frequented this little restaurant in Tokyo a few times. It was cozy, and he loved spending time here to think. He looked at his watch. It was still early. Ten more minutes to go. It seemed a bit too long for him. Eric felt uneasy.

The door opened, and Sukimi entered. She still had the radiant look he always admired. His body went numb and then tingled all over as he gathered his thoughts and waved to her. She saw him, smiled, and walked over. Eric's mind saw everything in slow motion. Sukimi's soft black hair flowed over her slim shoulders as she elegantly approached. She wore a beautiful, knee–length, flowing red dress that hugged her body. A thin gold chain with a small diamond pendant hung around her neck. She had a small smile and the glimmer in her eyes on her perfectly angled face that he remembered from thirty years ago. Eric felt a sharp pain in his chest, filled with emotions he had long suppressed.

"Hi, Eric," Sukimi said. "How are you?"

Her greeting broke his thoughts and he answered, "I'm fine. Still in one piece," trying to hide his emotions with a joke.

She smiled back and observed him from head to toe.

"You're still the same Eric—though the waistline has certainly increased. The same Eric," she joked.

119

"No, I *have* changed. See the balding? And my tummy," Eric said, holding his middle. "My triple chin, and ..." He pulled down his turtleneck collar, exposing the scar over his neck. "Things change people."

Sukimi hugged him at that point. He felt her heartbeat as they embraced. He felt the same thirty years later. His feelings for her ran so deep. Tears welled in his eyes. Sukimi's tears touched his neck as she laid her cheek against his shoulder. They held each other silently for several minutes, letting time pass as if to make up for the lost time.

"I wish we could have the years back," Eric said. "All these years, and I still think of you every day."

"The same," she replied as they sat down.

Eric wiped her tears and stared at her face. "I should have come to you."

"And you could be dead," she said. He knew what she meant. She had a proud family who would do anything to protect her dignity. For centuries, Chinese and Japanese have been enemies. To allow her to be involved with a Chinese "nobody" at that time could have spelled death.

"I should have come when I made it," Eric said regretfully.

"You know you couldn't. I was already engaged," Sukimi replied. "So let's talk about something else." She seemed to be trying to hold back her emotions.

"Okay. How's Hirato?"

"He's a good man. He's been there for me all these years. He showers me with love and gifts. Unfortunately, I couldn't bear him a child, but we have Yuko. She is such a pretty girl." She showed him a picture with Yuko and Hirato on her cell phone. "She's going to college soon."

Eric knew she had adopted Yuko when the girl was young. He had kept up with her through the Internet over the years.

"She is beautiful. I'm glad you are as happy as you seem in the picture."

"Are you happy, Eric?"

"Mei Lin has stolen my heart, as you did. She's been wonderful for me. She loves the kids and has taken care of me. Always been there for us. I can't ask the gods for more," Eric replied, now unconsciously touching his pendant, as if he was going to wish for something.

"I'm happy for you, Eric. You deserve it."

Eric loved to hear her voice. He had not heard it for so long. Her soft voice had a slightly high pitch and perfect articulation. It was music to him. He had wanted to see her, challenge the feelings that had surfaced after his crisis in the plane.

"So do let me know more about Regenesis. Thank you for sending the file by e-mail. It seems like an interesting project. But why, Eric, are you in it?"

"I don't know really. I just know I had to do it. It seemed predestined. There were so many coincidences that it seemed like it was planned," Eric replied, rubbing the pendant even more.

"I understand. I think I'll be able to help you with the tanker you require. I had discussed it with my father, and we're in. It will be interesting to transport hydrogen. However, we need to first test the theories regarding the storage tanks. Live tests before we modify the tanker. I estimate it will take about nine months to complete once we're ready."

"Thank you. I'll get Ms. Katherine, our lawyer, to draw up the contracts. She is actually Alex's daughter. I thought it would be best to keep things under wraps for now. She has already built a reputation for herself as a corporate lawyer."

"Don't worry. I'll keep everything secret. The big picture will not be revealed. As far as Hato Industries is concerned, this is purely a tanker project to transport hydrogen for fuel-cell technology and nothing else. It will be kept as secretive as possible."

They spent the rest of the evening catching on lost time and conversations about themselves and the project. Eric was happy he finally came.

That night, as he walked back to his hotel, he was smiling. He had accepted his feelings for her and Mei Lin. He loved both women. They were different, and the love he had for them was different. He had come to the conclusion to accept rather than try to suppress one love over the other or choose. He didn't feel the need to tell Mei Lin. Right or wrong, he comforted himself thinking that it was like his love for his children. He can love them all yet in different ways, as they were different people.

CHAPTER 20

SLEEPING WITH THE DEVIL OR DEVILS

Eric was alone again in his room at Shi's. The view on this cloudless night with the Taipei 101 Tower standing tall was magnificent, with the stars in the background. The project was now well into its sixth month. There were the usual hitches, but all were ironed out. They needed more investments. Regenesis was gathering steam and needed more money.

A knock on the door broke into his thoughts. "Come in," he answered. The door opened and his secretary showed George Anderson in.

Eric greeted him. "Welcome to Taiwan, George."

"I've been here so many times, I've lost count. It feels the same every time. The hospitality is unique."

"How was your flight?"

"Good. I slept all the way. We have another flight tomorrow. Hope it will be as comfortable."

"You really think we can trust the sheikh?" Eric asked. Over the past two weeks, he, Ching and George had been exploring options to raise funds for Regenesis. If they asked too many investors in, it could jeopardize the project. It would no longer be a secret. They needed one or two more investors who could come in with large funding. Between the three of them, they had already put aside more than two hundred million dollars. They needed another hundred million or so.

"I think he can be trusted. I've worked with him for years. He's sensible and knows that oil money will end soon in the near future. Rather than investing in stadiums and resorts and owing things in the rest of the world, he foresees the Middle East will only succeed if they can compete in alternate energy."

"I don't have a feel for this one, George."

"Trust me, he's good for us," George replied.

Eric's heart sank as he looked out the window and all he saw was sand and dunes. It was his first time traveling to the Middle East. They were in flight for more than eight hours now and would arrive soon. It looked very hot outside. At least he was dressed for the weather with his light shirt. He wasn't wearing his turtleneck and had a scarf over his neck instead.

George said, "We'll be there soon. Don't worry. I've been here more than a dozen times. Do you know the sheikh has a stable here with some of the best breeds in the world? Arabian horses are fast. He has raced them everywhere. Last year, his horse won the Australian Cup."

"Tell me more about him. Maybe then I'll be more reassured."

"He used to chain smoke. He had to suddenly stop. The poor fellow. His two cousins died on the same day to sudden heart attacks. He was spooked and saw the best cardiologist in London. Since then, he stopped smoking, started exercising, and instead now carries worry beads with him. He banned smoking in his palace. He told me since he had given up one of his greatest pleasures in life, his mind was now faster and he craved to expand his businesses and reach. Do you know he has bought over a port in New Guinea and has started a shipbuilding company there? New Guinea of all places. He had brought his wealth there, and the people there treat him like a god."

"So he craves for power and control." Eric said.

"Not really. I think he genuinely believes he can make a difference for them. Of course he's so used to being a king, he loves the royal treatment."

"Hmmm. Okay. Does he have any weaknesses then?"

"Women. He has many wives. But as far as I know, he has always made sure they are well looked after."

"Ha, we seem to have reached civilization," Eric said as he saw the sand dunes ending and a city appearing in the distance.

The sheikh greeted George. "How are you, my friend? And how is Kismet?"

"Fine, thank you, Your Highness. And Kismet is running faster than ever. I think I'll race her in the Kentucky Derby this year."

"Arabian horses are always fast. She'll win. You'll see," the sheikh replied.

"This is Eric Shi of Shi Corporation, Taiwan,"

"Greetings, Mr. Eric. George has told me a lot about you. I didn't know you were into alternate energy. How did you get involved?"

They were now sitting.

"Thank you, Your Highness. Let's just say a good friend convinced me it was a good idea."

"You mean Alex, the gentleman with the idea?"

Eric didn't reply but nodded.

"George, are you sure of this project? By the way, we talk freely here, Mr. Eric. I always like to meet out in the desert here in my tent. This way no prying eyes or ears," indicating he knew secrecy was very important.

"I think it's a good shot. It cheap for you—the investment, I mean. You and I have been looking into alternate energy. I think this one is too good to pass up."

"I had my team look through what you sent me. Don't worry. They're all sworn to secrecy. They tell me it's workable. But there are areas that may be difficult to achieve, like Meyer."

"I have the best people working on those points," Eric replied. "I think it can be overcome soon."

"Ha, there is confidence in the team," the sheikh said. "So have you seen my horses yet? You should get a chance to ride them today over the sand dunes."

"I don't ride," Eric replied. He wondered if the sheikh had already decided.

"Ha. You should. George, you should teach your friend here to ride. Maybe some other time, Mr. Eric. And yes, I've decided. I'll invest in it. My assistant will be in touch," the sheikh said.

On the way back in George's private jet, Eric remarked, "That was fast."

"He just wanted to see you. He thinks he can read people's minds. He usually makes up his mind pretty fast. He must have judged you well."

Eric was amused. It was the first time he had dealings with a sheikh.

Well, we came and got what we wanted, he thought.

*

"Yes, father," Andre said with some annoyance. This was his off night. He had just finished a job for his father in Thailand. It was his night to enjoy. Mr. Hyde's time.

"I know you're close to Katherine. Can you fix a meeting for me with her father in the next week or two?"

"Why the urgency? I didn't know you took an interest in Katherine."

"I don't care about your flings. I want Alex, her father. I have news he is involved with alternate energy. I want a piece of it," Vasilly explained with some irritation in his voice.

"Okay, I'll fix it up," he said and hung up on his father.

Andre had two girls in his room, both tied and gagged. One was already semiconscious. She was covered with candle wax. Her breasts were bleeding from bite marks. Turning his attention to her, he thought, *Ha, I think I'll continue with her and let the other watch.* He was enjoying seeing the terror in the other girl's eyes as he continued his vicious rape fantasy, trashing her from behind. Soon he would assault the other one. Maybe he would hang her up first. He continued to fantasize and would act it out the whole night.

A week later Andre was on his cell phone with Katherine, "Hi, Katherine, how is Lumut?"

"How do you know where I am? You stalking me?" Katherine remarked with annoyance and some surprise. He couldn't have known she was in Lumut.

"A little bird told me. I'm in Kuala Lumpur, actually. You know me. I like to move around. You free for lunch or something?"

Katherine knew something was up. No way he would call like that. "What is it, Andre? This isn't a social call, is it?"

"No. I heard you are into something and we want in."

Katherine was stunned. She was speechless. How did he know? She gathered her thoughts. Should she hang up?

"Hello, don't be frightened. I mean no harm."

"How and what do you know?" Katherine asked slowly.

"I'm sure you know my father. He knows everything. Can we meet?"

"I'll call you back," Katherine said and hung up fast. She had to think and she had to tell her father now. Alex was in the complex somewhere.

"Dad!" Katherine called out to him from far, half-running down the long corridor. "We have a problem! Andre called me."

"Ha. He is interested in you. Not to my liking though. We'll talk later. Eric is here and we're about to start the meeting. Come, let's go in."

"No, Dad. It's not like that. We're not into that. It's something else," she tried to explain.

"Never mind, tell me after the meeting." He ushered her into the room. The whole team was there. She had missed the opportunity to tell her father. She would need to wait until the meeting was over.

"Kim, where are we now?" Eric asked.

"A total of sixty containers have been set up now. We've stacked them up three levels. By putting the containers in a rectangular formation, we'll have a center area, which would be three levels high, about seventy feet long and thirty feet wide. This area would be the main area we'll use to test the turbine design. We can have a water tank about forty feet long and twenty feet wide and more than fifteen feet deep. I hope that's large enough. The computers, meeting rooms, and logistics are on level two. The living quarters and rooms are on the top floor. We even decided to use the containers to be corridors and stairs. This way it will take only a few days to dismantle and reassemble the pieces like Lego blocks. The ground floor will be storage, dining, and recreation. We'll be onboard for at least three months to get to the ocean site."

"Good. Then the work on the turbines can start. Karim, have you found the site we require?"

"We have two potential sites. One is off the coast of Scotland. Another is just off the Norwegian coast in international waters. I think the Norwegian coast is better. There are fewer weather problems and the seabed is smoother there, probably helpful if we need to anchor to the seabed."

"Good thought. And how is the storage facility going?" Eric asked.

Jonathan replied, "We've started building the initial two compartments. It will take a while before we're able to test. We'll be using live explosives, so it will take a bit of organization with the fire department and the energy plant management before we can start for safety reasons."

"Hope that will not be too long. What about the electrolysis and Meyer? Jack? Stephen?"

"We're working on it," was Jack's answer. He was not convincing.

"We've had problems and actually have not moved forward much. I'm going to see how I can help with that, Jack," Stephen answered.

"Let's hope we can get that part settled. It's the link to ensure it's financially viable. We have to have efficiency up to at least 70 percent," Eric replied. He had to up the pressure.

Eric had noticed Katherine was unsettled and seemed disinterested. She appeared to be dreaming. "Katherine, are you okay?"

Katherine was startled, "Yes, yes. I'm okay," she said, realizing everyone was looking at her.

Eric sensed something was up, "We can talk later."

Looking back to the group, he said, "I think we've done a fair bit. The platform is being modified as we speak. The tanker is awaiting our specifications after the tests with the chambers. They have started stripping the interior of the tanker to prepare to build the storage compartments in it. Well, that's it then. Let's get back to work."

Eric, Alex, and Katherine stayed on while the rest left.

"What's up, Katherine?" Eric asked.

"I had a call from Andre. Andre is the son of Vasilly Karpanof. You may know of him."

"Yes, he is big in the oil business. Also into investing in football clubs and investment banking. Third-richest man in Russia."

"Yes, that's him. Andre says they know of our project and want in."

Alex was stunned. Eric was more composed. He knew this could happen. The project was gathering steam. Many people were working on it at different locations. Anyone could have leaked, but to know the whole project, it would only be from a few.

Eric asked, "How much does he know?"

"I don't know. He wants to set up a meeting with my father to meet his."

Eric asked Alex, "What do you think?"

"I have no idea what to think, Eric. I'm stunned."

"I guess we've no choice in the matter. They already have some knowledge. Let's use the meeting to see what they know. Then we'll decide our next move," Eric said. He had been in the business so long to know not to be fearful or stunned. Corporate espionage was common. The competition these days was intense. He had to treat it as just another chess game.

The devil has arrived, Alex thought as he looked out the window from the second floor. A limousine had pulled up and Andre came out. He seemed to give a look around, before his father came out.

Vasilly was smoking a cigar and exhaled. He was a stout man, with a belly as big as Eric's. He wore a red suit with matching red shoes. *He seems to want the attention*, Alex thought.

Soon they were shaking hands in the meeting room at the Hilton. Alex glanced at his cell phone and touched it. In the notification bar, he identified the icon. He had to be sure it was on.

"What do you know of my idea?" Alex asked.

Andre quickly handed over a book to Alex. "Before we start, let me present you with this antique book I picked up in Oxford. It's more than a hundred years old. It depicts the voyage of Darwin to the Galapagos."

Obviously he wants to pacify me, Alex thought and said "Thank you. I'd prefer to get to the point. I'm already disappointed we're having this meeting."

"I assure you, it will be worth your time, Dr. Alex," Vasilly said as he exhaled smoke from his cigar.

Alex frowned, as he disliked the smoke he was producing, contaminating the air he was breathing. "Interesting that you are into clean energy yet you are puffing out smoke."

Vasilly, a little annoyed, extinguished his cigar.

Alex wanted to exert some control over the meeting, and he probably had done so.

Vasilly said, "I know you're going for deep-ocean current as alternate energy. I know you have Eric Shi as your main investor. I also know you're a doctor and certainly not an engineer. Your encounters so far with alternate energy are amateur, lobbying for your cause but not making it work. What I'm not sure is why Eric is so sure your idea will work. Have I got it correct so far?"

Alex didn't move a muscle. He was not going to reveal anything that Vasilly didn't know yet.

Vasilly continued, seemingly wanting to boast at what he knew. "I know you have already started testing in Lumut and have partnered with the Americans and Japanese. So it's time a Russian got into the picture."

Alex noticed he left out the Middle East connection and was suspicious of the omission. "So you know a lot. What else?"

"I also know you need more money. That is where I come in."

"Hmmm. What do you want in return?"

"Nothing much. Just some shares, as appropriate."

"What else?" Alex knew there had to be something this devil wanted.

"Nothing. I'm a generous man."

"You're a billionaire. You have businesses everywhere. You own the largest oil company in Russia. So why would you want to sabotage your oil company and invest in alternatives?"

"I know oil won't last forever. I want in on the future, even though I don't think it will happen for a while longer."

"You mean you don't want us to succeed."

"No, no. Of course we want you to succeed. I just like to sometimes bet on two horses when I don't know which will win," he said with a twinkle in his eye.

"Hmmm. We shall see," Alex replied.

"Well, I'm not giving you a choice. I don't think you know the situation. I want in and you cannot refuse. If you do, you won't like me."

Alex knew a threat when he heard it. Eric had warned him about Vasilly. He was alleged to have links with the Russian mafia.

"I'll take it back to Eric and the group for them to decide."

"I'm sure it will be a positive answer. If not, Andre will use a lot of persuasion."

Alex looked out the window and watched the two Russians depart in their limousine. He switched on his phone and turned off the audio recording.

The door opened and Eric came in with Kim.

"We heard the conversation clearly. Thanks, Alex," Eric said.

"What do you think? Do we have a choice here?" Alex asked.

"We don't. It's better the enemy is close. At least we can observe them as they observe us," Eric replied, annoyed.

"What do you know about Andre? The threat he made seems to indicate Andre is more than just his son or Katherine's friend."

"I'm sure Katherine is not aware. As far as I know, they met when Vasilly was using her firm for his contracts in the UK. I'm sorry."

"There's nothing to be sorry about. We never could have known. I'll get someone to check out Andre. I'm not comfortable with either of them."

"I'm glad we didn't bring Katherine along. She may have reacted with anger toward Andre."

"Persuade her to keep calm. She can help us keep an eye on him. The best way to keep tabs on Andre is if they keep in touch. But warn her I think he is dangerous. She should not meet him alone."

Alex nodded. He had not envisaged this problem. He would leave it to Eric, who was probably an expert in commercial espionage. He would have a long chat with his daughter tonight.

CHAPTER 21

TURBINE WOES

At Lumut, Stephen, Alex, and Jonathan were putting on the final touches to the turbines. They were satisfied looking at computer-generated 3D images on the giant projection screen. The design was unique. Two rows of gigantic cusps were lined at the left and right sides. The center was aerodynamically designed with the front tapering down like the front of a bullet train. Its width was sixty feet with the cusps closed and eighty feet when opened. Its length was a hundred feet and had a vertical height of thirty feet. Each cusp was twenty feet in diameter and ten feet deep. They were fixed on hinges to the sturdy track, which was in turn attached to gears that finally ended with the electricity generator that would convert motion or kinetic energy to electricity. The generator and gears were in the center part between the two lines of cusps. The front of the center part, which tapered, was made up of large glass panels, which make up the cockpit or bridge of the submersible. It also housed the sonar detectors that would sense sea creatures at least fifteen hundred feet away. This would give ample warning to close the cusps, shut down the turbines, and allow the creatures to glide past. Smaller creatures will just flow into the cusps, move with it, and get thrown out of the cusps at the end as they turn.

"It's beautiful. Almost like a spacecraft!" Katherine said as she walked in. The three of them had already been staring at the design for five minutes.

"It is, isn't it? I think we shall call them submersibles rather than just turbines. They're certainly more than turbines." Stephen said.

"We should be able to make the scale model within a few weeks and test it out." Jonathan said.

Alex replied, "I can't wait!"

Another month passed. The model was ready for testing. The submersible was hanging above the huge tank of water. Alex was filled with excitement once more. This was the first model test. Eric had told him not to get his hopes up. It was the first of many tests to be done. But the first is always the most exciting.

Katherine said, "You're just glowing with excitement. Haven't seen you grinning so widely for a while."

Alex just nodded, wanting to take in the moment.

With a splash, the submersible was in the water. Three cables held it from the top.

"Switch on the tide generator," Jonathan instructed. A hum erupted, and the sound of waves slowing increased as the water now flowed toward the submersible. It wobbled but seemed to be streaming along well. It was steady in the water.

"Let's open the cusps and let the turbines work," Jonathan said.

A soft muffled clang could be heard in the water. Through the see-through glass tank, they saw the submersible shaking left to right, starting to wobble up and down.

Alex held his daughter's hand more firmly, highlighting his anxiety.

Suddenly the whole submersible turned to the left, flipped over, and broke into pieces.

"Shut it down!" Jonathan yelled.

Alex's heart sank. His grip on Katherine's hand relaxed.

Katherine said, "Don't be sad, Dad. It's okay. It was only the first test."

Alex looked around. Everyone looked disappointed.

"When the cusps opened, it generated turbulence and caused the problem," Jonathan said. "We need to correct that."

The next two months of designing resulted in different models. The last came closest but lasted two minutes and then broke up.

"It's not only the turbulence. We need dampers in the design. The vibration from the cusps transmitting to the gears and generators is shaking the submersible apart. Look at the telemetry from the sensors inside the submersible." Stephen said. "Back to the drawing board."

Two more months passed.

Stephen explained the newest design to Katherine. "Okay. I think we're finally going to make it. The dampers are in place. They work like shock absorbers mounted in the engine of a car. The final link to the generator is modeled like the shaft of the car linking to the wheels. This way the vibrations are almost totally gone.

"We realized we were using an airplane design, which won't work in the sea. We solved it by mimicking the fish. We added fins to the model—back fin, two side fins, one large fin on top, and another below. Isn't that just a beauty?"

Katherine said, "You're smart."

"No—it was teamwork as usual," Stephen replied modestly.

"Who thought about the fish?" Katherine asked.

"Actually, Karim suggested it. Ha, a marine biologist. He even suggested we put joints in the fins as the fishes have fins that curve when they turn. It's actually a great idea and that lessens the turbulence. We had the top and bottom fins made into six pieces latched together with hinges. We may still modify that and use pliable material instead.

"Finally, to adjust all the fins simultaneously, we just couldn't do it manually. That's why the last model failed. This is where my expertise came in."

Katherine felt he was trying to impress her. He didn't need to. She was already very impressed, but she didn't mind the attention Stephen had given her.

"I've modified the latest robotics software we have at Shi and used the fastest octa-core processors to power the software. Ten processors to be precise, working in unison. It's awesome, isn't it?"

Katherine was getting a bit lost. "I think it's wonderful," she said, hiding her ignorance in computer science.

Stephen continued. "Ha. It'll be the world's first autopilot submersible. We test in a week. Your dad and Eric will be here then."

CHAPTER 22

SATISFACTION ALL AROUND

All were gathered. The submersible was being lowered. Katherine had taken the liberty to document all the events so far. She positioned herself in the corner of the room to ensure a good view of the audience and the model in the tank.

With a glance at Eric, who nodded in return, Jonathan said, "Let the test start. This will be the test of all tests."

The crew started the tidal generator. As with the other tests, it began well. The submersible moved a little. She could see the fins on the submersible moving in unison, steadying it.

Katherine kept her camera on the submersible recording the event as she looked around the room. Stephen was looking intently at the monitors in front of him. Alex's arms were folded, and he stood almost totally still, unblinking. Eric was in a chair, leaning forward on its edge, tightly holding the handles.

A muffled clang signified the opening of the cusps on both sides of the submersible. It wobbled and almost instantly stabilized itself. The fins were working. A minute passed. The submersible was stable, flowing in the current stream.

Katherine was getting excited, and her hands, holding the camera, shook. She looked up at the overhead monitors. The cusps were turning around about once every ten seconds. The gears had heightened the revolutions to a thousand per minute on the generator side.

She looked at Stephen as he nodded to Jonathan to move to the final part. With a turn of a switch, the generator kicked in, the clutch system slowly allowing the generator to pick up speed without any sudden jerks. All was done with Stephen's software. She smiled realizing his immense contribution to Regenesis. She realized her attraction to him and turned back to the submersible. She blushed as Stephen looked up toward her.

The monitors showed electricity was made, and the power reached acceptable levels. It was now twenty minutes into the test.

With a nod from Eric, Jonathan signaled the end to the crew. They took the generator offline, closed the cusps, and allowed the submersible to glide in the current. It looked so agile now without the turbulence. Katherine could see the elegance of it.

The wave generator stopped, and within a minute the water was still. Everyone seemed to hold his or her breath until Eric said, "Well done! We got it! The world's first working undersea submersible turbine."

Everyone clapped and hugged.

Katherine was filled with mixed emotions as Stephen hugged her. She didn't want him to let go. It felt so right.

The day didn't end there. That afternoon, the next test would be underway.

Kim led them to the other structure onsite. This was the storage facility for hydrogen. It was a one-story building.

Kim explained in detail to George, who had just arrived. He wanted to see the progress for himself and to be sure the platform he was supplying would fit the setup.

Kim said, "Don't be fooled. The complex is actually underground. There are three underground floors. The topmost is the command center. The hydrogen storage is in the middle. The lowest floor is for equipment storage and allows us to make sure there is no leakage from the tanks. This way we have access to all sides of the tanks.

"Let's take the elevator down."

As the elevator doors opened and they exited, she said, "This is the hydrogen storage level. We've made two prototype storage chambers. Inside each chamber is an inner chamber, which will store the liquid hydrogen. It's ten feet in length, five in width, and six in height. All around it is the outer chamber, which is six inches around the inner hydrogen chamber. We filled the second chamber with liquid nitrogen. The outer layer is reinforced with bombproof material, which utilizes non-Newtonian fluid, the same used in bomb vests the army uses to defuse bombs."

"Have you tested the model?" George asked.

"No, this is our first test today," Kim said. "We had to build the whole complex. That took a few months. We're now standing between the two prototype chambers. The dimensions we used were intentional, although these two are anchored down." Kim pointed to the chambers as she spoke. "They are sized so that each can be transported on a container truck."

"Ha," George remarked. "You folks do think of everything."

"Just pay attention to detail. This way we can cut the costs when we transport the hydrogen," Kim continued to explain. "Now let's get back up to the command center."

Katherine had seldom been in the complex. The last time she was here it was still pretty bare. Now the command center had video monitors to all areas in the complex. Staff manned at least five terminals.

"Please take your seats. We've put explosives in the compartments to test the prototypes. Firefighters are standing by behind those doors. For your safety, there are stairs up to the surface a floor away," Kim said with a smile.

Katherine could see Kim was confident. Katherine wasn't sure and had already checked the exit.

"Let's start. Jonathan, all yours," Kim said.

Jonathan nodded and signaled to a crew member. "On three. One, two, three."

An explosion occurred. Sensors went off instantly. The computer monitors showed a surge of data. Red lights flashed on many screens.

The video showing the two prototype chambers were the same with no changes. No smoke.

Jonathan explained. "The explosion was triggered inside the hydrogen chamber. We used a chemical bomb. I think it was successful. There was no chain reaction as there are no other gases in the chamber, so the chemical bomb burnt itself out.

"We're going to conduct another test. This time the explosive will be placed on the wall of the inner chamber. The bomb is powerful enough to blow open a steel door. Let's start. On three. One, two, three."

A powerful explosion again shook the complex. Alarms again went off. In a minute, most had been restored. No danger. The nitrogen mixed with hydrogen, but there was no chain reaction to cause a larger explosion.

"Looks like it worked. We won't test the outer chamber as that will only cause the nitrogen to leak. Any questions?" Kim asked.

Eric asked, "In case the explosion is large enough, and somehow one chamber explodes, how do we contain it?"

Jonathan explained. "That could happen. By having individual chambers, they are all protected on the outside by the reinforced outer shell. If that breaks, nitrogen leaks and it's very cold. It would be like a carbon dioxide fire extinguisher. The inner chamber should remain intact."

"That's interesting," George said. "Maybe we can consider that for our oil transportation."

Eric replied, "Maybe," and smiled.

Katherine was relieved they didn't need to evacuate. Another part had succeeded. She didn't film this part, only took a few pictures. She would get the video footage later from Stephen.

CHAPTER 23

TO THE OCEAN

"Jack, how are we doing?" Eric asked.

"We're progressing. At least we found out what cannot work," Jack replied, trying to be positive.

"We're behind schedule on this. What is the efficiency at the moment?"

"We're able to get 50 percent," Jack said.

Stephen interjected. "The team has tried hard. We realized that to test the frequency of voltage pulse and amperage is more difficult than we thought. We have some way more to go."

Eric said, "The whole feasibility will lie on its efficiency. If not, it's not financially viable today. Maybe in years to come. I can't stress the importance." Eric was more irritated than usual this trip. He came to see the transfer of the whole center to the ship. This was a vital part. It had been four months since the tests in Lumut and fourteen months since Regenesis was conceived. The midsized container ship had arrived at Lumut Port.

It would take a week to dismantle and another week to move the containers. Then reassembly would require a further week.

"Kim, how's the storage facility going?" Eric asked.

"It's good. We're finished with the twenty chambers for the complex here. I was in Nagoya last week. They have duplicated the

141

prototype in exact detail. The tanker should finish in another two
to three months."

"At least that part has gone well. We set sail in about another
two months. We have to continue to test Meyer's hypothesis onboard
then," Eric said.

When they left, he sat in his office on the third level. This container,
modified to be an office, had a nice large window, allowing the view
of the central range mountains. He felt calmer now. He had been
in teleconference the whole morning. There were problems with his
corporation. Income was muted as the world had started another
round of recession. That had put him in a bit of a fix. He had Shi
Corporation investing in Regenesis. He had managed to hide it under
the guise of the hydrogen storage plant. His personal status was not
too healthy either. He had invested heavily in pharmaceuticals and
pushed research in those companies where he had main control. The
investments had not yet yielded the expected benefits. Still, Shi was
in the black and not red like the many companies now reporting
their annual reports and forecasts.

The Middle Eastern and Russian connections were in a way a
blessing as funding continued from those sources. However, they
would demand more of a say in the project. He would try to stall
getting more financial injections from them and give Regenesis more
time to finish testing. If they had too much say, they could sabotage
the project.

The private detective he had asked to investigate Andre was
going to report to him today. His phone rang.

"Mr. Shi? Good morning," the man on the other end said.

"Eric speaking. Have you got the information?"

"Yes I have. I've been tracking him the past two weeks. He is a
ruthless person. My connections in Bangkok tell me he is his father's
hired gun. He is Vasilly's son born out of an indiscriminate affair
with a Thai bar girl when Vasilly was not yet rich. She died of a
heroin overdose. He took Andre in at age nine and groomed him.

"Andre has some dark secrets. He likes to beat up prostitutes before having them. Interpol has a file on him, but he is discreet and careful. All the killings he has done are very professional. All made to look like accidents, and without evidence linking him, except that he was in the same city at the time, which is circumstantial at best. Because he is Vasilly's son, they don't dare move on him unless they have concrete evidence."

"So you mean he is his father's assassin and right-hand man. And he is untouchable at the moment."

"Yes, you are correct. Shall I send the file to you?"

"Make sure it cannot be traced back to you. No one must know of your involvement. We do not want to spook them." Eric hung up. He took apart his phone and removed the sim card. He reinserted his usual sim card. He didn't want to be traced to the private investigator's firm.

He didn't share this with the team. He didn't want them distracted or fearful.

*

Angelina was back in Singapore. She was going to meet up with Arshad, her boyfriend, again. She had not seen him for weeks. The e-mails and Whatsapp conversations were marvelous. She was on cloud nine.

She strolled along Orchard Road hoping to pick out a beautiful dress for dinner. As she passed the corner, she thought she saw him and shouted, "Hi, handsome. Wait up!"

He disappeared around the next corner on a side road. She followed, wanting to meet him while at the same time wondering what he was up to. She turned the corner and walked a couple of feet, and suddenly she was attacked. Someone grabbed her from behind, and then an arm was around her neck, choking her. She was about to scream when a large piece of tape was slapped over her mouth. She was hooded and her hands were bound.

She felt two people hold her up and throw her into a vehicle. As they pulled away, she was thrown from side to side. She felt dizzier and dizzier. Then she passed out.

She opened her eyes. There was a sharp pain in her head. She couldn't focus her eyes for nearly a minute. Her hands were free. As the drowsiness faded, she gathered her thoughts and a panicked feeling overcame her. She quickly sat up. She was on a bed, and two Caucasian men in black suits stared at her.

"Who are you? What do you want? Don't you dare hurt me! My father will come after you, and you'll never escape him."

"We asked the questions here," the taller of the two said. He turned on the TV.

"Oh my God. You got me on video with my boyfriend. How low can you go?" She was staring at the video of herself making love. "What do you want, money?"

"On the contrary. Why did you associate yourself with a known terrorist? Do you know he's wanted in the United States and Europe? And you enjoy yourself with him. You're a terrorist now," one of them said.

The other said, "Your father cannot help you now. In fact he'd probably disown you if he found out. He is patriotic. But you already know that."

She nodded. *My boyfriend is a terrorist? He doesn't look or act like one,* she thought.

"Not convinced? I'll show you." The taller man changed the video to a slideshow. "This is him with another girl. They're in bed in this one. Here he is passing on information to another in his terrorist cell. This is him, traveling under another name. Look at the name on his badge. He was at a conference for tourism for the Middle East. Now that's him walking down the street. See the bulge behind him in his shirt? That's a gun he carries. Enough yet?"

"What do you want?" Angelina asked with a trembling voice.

"Relax. We're the good guys. We need your help. You continue to be with him. When it's time to act, we'll tell you. For now that's all."

"If you're the good guys, then I'm not going to see him anymore," she said, trying to be defiant. She had to try to get the upper hand.

"Well. Somehow the video and pictures will surface in public. Imagine the fallout. You, sleeping with the enemy. The shame your father will bear."

Angelina fell quiet. She couldn't let her father down. She couldn't walk away from this.

"I'm sure you can put on a good show," he remarked. "You act very well in the videos." He smiled cynically.

"Which agency are you with? How dare you? I'm an American citizen. You can't do this."

"We'd like to keep that our secret. I never said we're from America. You'll only need to know I'm Michael. I'll be your handler. If I call you and you ignore me, the video goes public. Is that understood?"

Angelina nodded, clearly knowing she was now their servant. She thought, *How can this be? A moment ago I was so happy. Now I'm being blackmailed and I can't do anything.*

Angelina's boyfriend walked in the room as she was being led out blindfolded with a hood over her head. He smiled and waited for her to leave.

After she left, he said, "She is so naïve. So easy to be conned. She really believed I was in love with her. What is the matter with girls these days? Wanting to love or be loved so much?"

Michael said, "Arshad, you are a Valentino. No one can resist you. Good work. Now she is totally under our control."

"What do you have planned for her?"

"For now, nothing. We want access to her father. She can spy on him for us. We'll slowly convince her. Tonight, you let her accidentally see your handgun. Leave some Arabic writing somewhere in the room. That will spook her."

He just smiled as he imagined how he would torture her mind while he made love to her that night. Probably, as time went on, he could even get her to give him her money. He just loved what he did. No female could refuse him. And these guys paid handsomely for his services.

CHAPTER 24

THE LAST PIECE OF THE PUZZLE

Onboard the container ship, *Lumut*, Stephen, Jack, and Jonathan were trying to find the correct frequency to pulse the voltage and amperage of the current for electrolysis.

"We've tried again and again. We're not able to get anywhere. I think Meyer's theory is a hoax. It cannot be done." Jack was giving up.

Jonathan said, "There must be something we've overlooked. There has to be."

"Stephen, I'm sorry, but I don't think I can do it," Jack said. "Even with more time, there isn't any way it will work."

Stephen could see they were reaching the burnout point. Everyone needed a break. He said, "We're now three months to our final destination. We really don't have the time. Let's get some rest and take a break. No work for all of us, including the crew. Tell everyone to take a break. Full twenty-four hours. Good night to you all."

After they left, he locked the door of his room and walked over to the corner. He pulled open a small panel and revealed a touchpad. He keyed in a code and the side panel revealed a hidden door, which opened.

Stephen entered the secret compartment, a small, cramped room of only four feet by six feet. Inside, Stephen had two super computers at his disposal. He glanced at his watch. It was already nine p.m. It would be about midnight on the other side, he thought. He sat in front of the two thirty-two-inch monitors and started a video link.

"Hi, Diana. Sorry to keep you waiting. How are you today?" Stephen smiled as he spoke.

"Never been better. Just having a bite waiting for you. So how are things on your side? Manage to solve the final puzzle? You guys have been at it for months."

"Yeah. No breakthrough."

"I know from your expression. You look tired, Stephen. Get some rest and you'll be fine. You are the genius, Stephen."

"Come on. You know who the genius is. You. Without your help, many things wouldn't happen. Without you, One-Kill wouldn't exist."

"Some truth in that. I did find the bug in your programming. Ha. What would you do without me?"

"We've been at this for months and just can't find the frequency. You know what we're doing. It's been a slow process, and we don't have much time. For it to be on time, we need the answers now," Stephen explained.

"Well, if you want my help, just say so, Stephen."

"I do need your help."

"I looked at the data you sent me. You really want my opinion?"

"Yes, yes, please," he said, tired of it all already.

"I think you should not do it manually. I've written a simple software to link up the sensors and detectors and then let the computer do the work. By manually adjusting the frequencies, you have more than a million permutations and possibilities.

"We change the voltage from let say 10 milivolts to 100 volts, at only 0.01 milivolts intervals. Then at each interval, we change the amperage by 0.01 amps, for let's say a range from 0.01 amps to 100 amps. That would give about ten to the power of twelfth permutations. Thus, if your sensors and detectors can be ultrasensitive and we give let's say one second per permutation, it will take about thirty years to complete."

Stephen sat up after listening to Diana. "Ha, thirty years. Great. I don't have thirty years!" Stephen was laughing now, but his mind was racing to solve the problem.

"But if my sensors are more sensitive and we do the tests in parallel, like use ten systems at a time, then we can possibly cut it down to days. I think I have to get the latest sensors for it. They should be able to detect in milliseconds. Then it will take weeks with some luck."

"Ha, the great Stephen is back on track. You always need me for the hard part," Diana was giggling and clearly enjoying herself teasing Stephen.

Stephen's mind raced. He could finish the program with Diana in days. "Help me with this, Diana. We'll get the program done together."

"I don't have anything else to do. It will be like old times," Diana replied.

"Yeah, like One-Kill and a few more we worked on. How are you really, Diana? I know you don't like me to ask but I have to."

"Same as usual. The pain is better today. My back aches a fair bit, so I work on my recliner more these days."

"You keeping your appointments with the neurologist and surgeon?" Stephen asked.

"What for? They've said for years they can't help me any further. Only pain medication. They have not seen a condition as severe as mine with the tumor encasing and infiltrating into the spinal cord. This tumor is not sensitive to any treatment."

"Are there more lumps appearing?"

"I don't know. They found about twenty the last time I had the scan five years ago. I don't want to know. Anyway, those on my skin don't cause any problems."

"Make sure you take the vitamins, especially the vitamin D and calcium. Remember what the doctors say."

"Yeah, yeah. I've got to go out more—which I don't, so I have to take the vitamin and calcium or else my bones will rot away!"

"You need to look after yourself better. And did you get the encrypted file I sent to you?"

"Yup. Got it. I'll break the code and see what's on it."

"Ha-ha," Stephen replied, knowing she wouldn't ever do that. She'd been his collaborator for years and had helped him with a lot of the programming he had done. "Did you check if the money was received?"

"I didn't bother, Stephen. I don't have much use for it. Already too much. Nice to have the money though," Diana replied.

"Work always must be paid. Check it please." Stephen had always rewarded her handsomely for her work. The amount was never discussed. He knew she did it because it challenged her and she wanted the challenges to help her continue to find a meaning to live. He had been sympathizing with her. She was nearly paralyzed from the waist down and had been in a wheelchair for a few years.

That night, Stephen felt a weight had been lifted off his shoulders. He finally found an option to move forward.

Three weeks passed with little activity. They just stared at the computer monitors as the computers were put to work to find the exact frequency. No breakthrough as of yet. The efficiency remained at 50 percent. There was a small spike a week ago to 60 percent. It wasn't enough.

Jack looked at his watch. It was four in the morning. Only he and another were working. They had taken shifts to monitor the computers. Just as he was about to doze off, the flat line slowly moved upward. He shook himself awake and continued to stare at the screen. It went up and up, now passing 70 percent. He froze. Not a muscle moved.

He stood up when it reached 75 percent. His hand was on the receiver of the phone. It started to plateau and held at 79 percent for a few seconds before dropping.

He felt numb all over. He could not speak. His partner for the night had noticed that he had stood up and asked, "Jack?"

That broke him out of the trance he had gone into. "Yes!" he shouted and jumped up and down, as if his football team had scored the final goal. He got on the phone, and when the other person picked up, he shouted, "Stephen, we got it. We got it! Seventy nine percent!"

*

Meanwhile, in London, Angelina was woken by her alarm clock. She was tired after a night out. She struggled out of bed and staggered to the bathroom. As she finished her bath, she got out and switched on her room lights. She was taken aback when she saw Michael sitting in the high-back chair, staring at her.

"What are you doing here?" she asked angrily, trying to cover her naked self with the towel.

"Come on. I've seen it all," he said, referring to the videos he had seen of her making love. "Nothing to hide. I heard your father is involved with a project with an Eastern group. What do you know of that?"

"Very little. Just that he is excited about the prospects. I'm not sure what it's all about."

"You've got your first assignment then. You'll go to your daddy and get on the project. You'll report to us everything about the project. Is that understood?" Michael said with a commanding voice.

"Yes," she replied timidly.

He handed her a phone. "This is a satellite phone. You'll call and update me every day. Is that understood?"

"Yes," Angelina said with sadness in her voice. "But I thought I was spying on the terrorist."

"Change of plans. We're going after the bigger fish. This Eastern connection is more of concern to us," he said as he stood up and walked out.

Angelina sat on her bed and started crying. At least the wait to hear from this man, Michael, ended. She was depressed now. She had to spy on her father. She really wasn't sure what she would do. She felt very much alone. No one could help her.

CHAPTER 25

THE FIRST OF ITS KIND

The following morning Angelina took a flight back to the United States. She had called her father and said she was coming home. She said she was homesick and needed him.

Angelina greeted her father at the airport. "Daddy, I'm so happy to see you."

"My sweetheart, are you okay?" George asked.

"No, not really," she replied, resting her chin on his shoulder. "I just broke up with my boyfriend." This was not too untrue. She was over her terrorist boyfriend.

"He hurt you? I'll get him if he did."

"No, he didn't. I don't want to talk about it, Daddy."

"Okay, sweetheart. It'll be okay."

Later, in the limousine, Angelina asked, "What are you up to these days, Daddy?"

"After so many mundane years in the oil business, I've joined a group that will go into alternate energy. It's more exciting. I'm going to be flying out end of the week to meet up with them somewhere in the Indian Ocean."

"In the Indian Ocean?"

"Yes. You see, the project is on a ship right now. It's sailing to the coast of Norway."

"Sounds exciting. Can I come along?"

"Sure, sweetheart. In fact, it'll be good for you. And I want you with me." George replied.

Angelina's stomach hardened and she felt nauseated. She had started spying on her father.

The next morning George took her daughter with him to the shipyard where his oil rig platforms were made.

"This will be the world's first alternate energy platform for sea-current energy harnessing. Do you know we called it Regenesis? The project I mean," George explained.

"Interesting name," Angelina replied.

George replied, pretending to lower his voice, "I want to keep it secret. We retained most of the oil platform but added a lot of other features. Look at the support beams. There's another platform. That's a floating platform. At the moment, there are four bays to anchor the turbines. See the building at the corner there? It will house the facility to convert electricity to hydrogen and oxygen. Hydrogen will be stored in special chambers there."

"That's clever," Angelina remarked. She was the spy who would leak the secret. She had to hold back her emotions.

"The other interesting part is we made the four supporting pillars to sit on moors, which are anchored to the seabed. The good news is by using ballasts to float the platform, it can separate from the anchored moors. It can be towed away to another place if bad weather occurs.

"Let me take you up to the top of the platform. We'll have to take the elevator at the bottom where the floating platform is."

With the whine of the winches, the elevator, made of a steel enclosure with steel netting at the sides, rose to the upper platform.

Angelina held onto her father's arm as they ascended, saying, "I didn't realize it was this high. I'll hang onto you."

"Sure, sweetheart. You haven't been on one of these before. Up top you'll be able to see a far distance as it's seventy feet high—or seven stories."

They reached the top and got onto the platform.

"This is large, Daddy. Huge!"

"It is, isn't it? It's almost a hundred feet wide in both directions. Let's get to the control room."

George opened the door. About ten people were inside watching the many monitors mounted on tables or hanging from the ceiling and walls. They were engrossed with fixing up the systems and testing them.

He said, "From here we'll be able to monitor the whole platform, including the floating platform and the turbines that will meet up with us in Norway."

He pointed to an open large area and said, "That will be the place the containers will be brought over to the platform from the container ship, which is now sailing on the Indian Ocean. That way we save some money and make it easier to continue the project once we rendezvous there. Rather than shipping equipment, we just move it over. See the huge cranes on this platform? Those cranes are present on all platforms to move equipment. They will serve us well out in the ocean."

George turned and walked to the other side of the room and pointed out to a building. "On the other corner, we have the ECHO complex. ECHO is short for electrohydrolysis. We'll be storing the hydrogen there in specially created chambers. The chambers are almost ready. There will be ten chambers inside the complex. The two containers from the ship which house the electrolysis tanks and equipment will be brought over and connected to the complex allowing the hydrogen to be pumped over to the chambers."

Angelina was amazed. She knew how important this was to her father, yet she was a spy. She felt quite unwell.

"You look pale, sweetheart. Are you okay? Sit down here."

"I'll be fine in a while. I think it's the height." Angelina lied and continued to ask, "When will the platform be taken to the rendezvous point?"

"Probably in a week or two. A long way to sail. See that ship over there? That's a special ship that will bring the whole platform over. That's how we always take the oil rigs around the world. We'll be flying out to the Indian Ocean and then to the ship in two days. Are you sure you'll be up to it?"

"I'll be fine. Just the ladies monthly thing." She had to give an excuse for her anxiety and fear. "I just need a nice cup of tea and a bit of rest."

At night, in her bed, fast asleep, she heard a phone ringing. It didn't sound like her usual ring tone. She suddenly realized it was the satellite phone. She was wide awake when she answered,

"Angelina, you should answer faster in the future. I was about to hang up and wonder if you had gone against us. I know you have met your father. Tell me his plans."

Angelina's heart sank and she felt miserable. She had no choice but to tell, him. "I went with him to the platform. They're planning to harness the sea currents for energy. The energy will be converted to electricity and then hydrogen. I'm not good at science."

"When and where will the live tests be?"

"I don't know. All I know is the ship is in the Indian Ocean and we'll go there in two days. Dad said something about the coast of Norway, I think."

"At least you got us some useful information. I'll be in touch again."

He hung up, and Angelina was left alone in her room, feeling horrible. She was crying softly now. She had betrayed her father, yet she had to prevent a scandal that could be his downfall.

CHAPTER 26

THE FLOATING RESEARCH SHIP

Angelina looked outside the window of the helicopter. The pilot had pointed out the container ship in the distance. As they neared, she saw containers stacked in an unusual manner in a rectangle formation and a center area, which had containers only on two layers.

They landed on the helipad at the end of the ship.

Stephen greeted them as they alighted the helicopter. "Welcome to the *Lumut*."

George said, "My daughter, Angelina."

"Glad to meet you, Angelina. Welcome aboard."

"Thank you. The *Lumut* is the name of this ship?"

"Yes it is. We decided to name it Lumut after the port where we fitted the ship. Thought it would sound nice. The tanker is *Nagoya*, again named after the place they're sailing from."

"Ha. Nice," Angelina remarked. "Hey, it can't be!" as she saw Katherine a distance away.

Stephen turned to see what Angelina was seeing and said, "That's Katherine Liang. Do you know her?"

"Actually yes. We're friends. How come she is here?"

"Katherine!" Stephen yelled as they walked toward her.

"Angelina! It can't be you, can it?" Katherine asked.

The two of them ran towards each other and hugged.

"Ha, you two are friends. Such a coincidence. Alex's daughter and mine are friends! Small world, isn't it?" George remarked.

"What are you doing here, Angelina?"

"I just followed my dad. He said he was coming here, and I tagged along for the week."

"My, my. Glad to see you here. I'll show you and your father around with Stephen. I'm very excited, as we've got all the pieces done and the only thing left is to connect them all together. Regenesis is becoming real."

Stephen and Katherine showed the Andersons around the maze of containers, which housed everything they needed for the project.

Later, when the two were alone, Katherine said, "I'm really glad to see you. We've not met for ages now. How are you? And your boyfriend?"

Angelina's mood immediately changed when Katherine mentioned her boyfriend.

"What is it, Angelina?"

"We broke up," she said, trying to hide her secret. "It's nothing."

"Oh. I'm sorry," Katherine said and hugged her tight. "It'll be fine."

"Tell me. How come you're here?" Angelina asked.

"Remember I mentioned that I was going to Taiwan with my dad so I could spend some time with him? Well, that was the trip that sort of started it all. My dad had this idea that he could have a chance to make alternate energy work. Eric thought it was possible, so we're all here now. So, George is your father. I should have known as both of you are Andersons."

Angelina nodded in agreement, as Katherine continued. "But Andre and his father are in this too."

"Andre?"

"Yes. He and his dad muscled their way into the project. I'm a bit suspicious of it all. I don't trust his father."

"Oh. What a coincidence. All three of us are in this with our fathers. Almost sounds impossible." Angelina was really wondering how this was possible. Fate?

She would not only betray her father but also her good friend and father. She felt even worse. She must be strong for now while she decided what to do next.

*

In Japan, Eric and Alex just arrived with Kim at the shipyard of the Hato family business. They were driven by limousine and pulled up at the entrance.

"That's a pretty long ride. I can't wait to see the submersibles." Alex remarked as he emerged from the limousine.

Eric smiled and said, "In time. Let's meet our host."

They were led into a large conference room. A short moment later the door opened and Sukimi entered.

"Meet Alex, Sukimi." Eric greeted her.

"My pleasure, Ms. Sukimi. I heard so much about you and your company. My thanks for believing in Regenesis."

"The honor is mine. I wouldn't have it any other way. I think Regenesis is just what the world needs now. Anything Eric goes into, I'll trust." Sukimi replied.

"You're being modest, Sukimi," Eric said.

Alex couldn't help noticing that Eric was suddenly quite talkative and seemed a notch happier.

"Let me show all of you around," Sukimi said, moving out of the door together with her team. "It's a short walk to the tanker."

As they turned the corner, the *Nagoya* stood proudly in dry dock.

"This is the *Nagoya*, a midsize tanker. We stripped the inside and made six levels. Each level can house thirty chambers. They are made exactly as the chambers in Lumut. There is a gap of three feet between the chambers. Piping connects them, and all are monitored from the bridge. Let's take the elevator to the top."

They ascended to the ship. "Come through this door, and we'll go inside the hull."

Soon they were standing inside the hull. Sukimi said, "This corridor, as you can see, is lined with chambers on both sides. We can monitor each and every chamber. Safety has always been on everyone's mind when it comes to hydrogen transportation. I hope with the design of the chambers, we've achieved the level of safety we need. Come, let's proceed down the corridor and to the ship's engines. I have something exciting to show you. This is what we've hidden so far and is not part of Regenesis but can be."

Her crew opened the door to the engines. They all went through. "This is the first fuel-cell engine in the world to power a ship." She pointed to a large rectangular-shaped object in the middle of the room. A few pipes were connected at one end. On the other were two large cables.

"The pipes feed the hydrogen and purified oxygen into the fuel cell. From that, the electricity generated will be channeled by these cables to the electric motors here." Sukimi pointed to the electric motors mounted at the stern of the ship. "We'll have clean energy. No pollution. The very first of its kind."

Alex could see Kim and Eric were both grinning and seemed content with what they were seeing. Although all of this was interesting, Alex was really dying to see the submersibles.

"Time to see the most important part of the project," she said as she led them up the stairs on to the cargo deck. "Open the doors," she said as she pointed to the roof.

With a whining sound, the huge doors opened. The sunlight flooded in, and they could see the two objects appearing. Sukimi didn't say a word.

Alex was speechless. He just stared in awe at the submersibles, which were slowly revealed by the sunlight as the roof retracted. They just needed some time to admire what they were seeing.

"Their names are Yin and Yang," Sukimi finally said.

"Yin and Yang?" Alex asked.

"Didn't Eric tell you? We decided to christen them as that. For good luck."

The two submersibles were immaculate. They had been completed to the very detail like the models they tested in *Lumut*. They shone in the sunlight and could pass as spacecraft. The tapering fronts with closed cusps on both sides and a glass cockpit in the center made this a unique design.

"As you are aware, we have added fuel-cell electric engines at the back, hidden by the large panels. When the horizontal panels open, the engines should be able to power up to about ten knots. This way the submersible can actually propel itself away in bad weather. You can see it's gleaming in the light. We've coated it with an interesting material that Karim and his team came up with. It's an organic gel that sticks perfectly to the hull. That should reduce the friction and increase stability. Karim managed to make it synthetically but it mimics the slimy layer on fish. Needless to say, the material we used for the hull developed by Jonathan and his team is an alloy that should withstand a few tons and should be fine until sixty-five hundred feet deep. That should be safe enough. At the moment, we're targeting a depth of about one thousand feet only."

Alex smiled as he felt the immense satisfaction of seeing things coming together. He looked at Eric. He also seemed happy. Kim was listening intently. Alex's mind drifted, reflecting the journey of the last few months, which resulted in the achievements so far. *We're almost there,* he thought.

That night, Eric was alone with Sukimi in the hotel restaurant in a private room.

"More tea?" Eric asked.

"Yes, please," Sukimi replied. "What is on your mind, Eric?"

"I'm not sure if I've taken on more than I can handle."

"What do you mean?"

"This Regenesis thing is becoming too big. Financially it's becoming a nightmare. Now the Russians, Middle Easterners, Chinese, and Americans are in on it. The Japanese too. I'm not sure if everyone is following the same agenda. I fear there are other motives involved with some of them."

"Why do you think that?"

"I received a call an hour ago. My chief of security detected a breach in security in Shi. Somehow our server was hacked and files relating to Regenesis have been copied. They only got the schematics for the chambers. Luckily the submersible and turbine designs were stored on another server. I've directed all files regarding Regenesis be transferred to a server that will be disconnected from the network. Things are getting a bit more dangerous. I fear for all of us."

"It's just files. Not bombs. Eric, you know as well as I do industrial espionage is about stealing the technology, not destroying anything. We're totally committed. We're already at the brink of a new dawn. We just have to go forward."

"I guess there is no other way." Eric said, slowly turning his teacup around, staring at the few small leaves at the bottom, almost as if hoping to be able to read the future.

Late at night, Eric waited until it was midnight and then chatted with Stephen at the prearranged time.

"I'm not sure how serious the breach of security is, Stephen, but I'm worried."

"I think we should be concerned. What do you want to do now, Eric?"

"I'm not sure. We can't stop. The investment is far too advanced. If we stop now, I don't think we could recover from it financially. We've passed the point of no return. If we fail, Shi will take a big hit. Should we still survive, I'd probably lose control of the company. We have another two months or so more to go."

"Then we have no choice but to go forward. I'll try to improve security on the ships and the platform. If we hire guards, it may attract more attention to Regenesis."

"I think we have to safeguard Regenesis. The designs and plans now appear to stand a good chance of succeeding. We've hidden that from all investors, including Ching, so far. They only know we're still researching on the ship. No one knows the submersibles are ready. As far as they know, only the model is going to be tested and our breakthrough with Meyer is still a secret. But now with the security breach, I'm afraid someone knows we're nearly there."

Stephen replied, "Yes. And the tanker and its storage chambers?"

Eric replied, "Luckily no. These files were only on your side and in Japan. I've asked Sukimi to lock down the files and take them off the servers. Anyway, the tanker and submersible are complete, and there is no further need for the designs to be exposed on the network."

Stephen said, "I think I'll set up an additional backup plan. We cannot be totally sure with security. What about our security?"

"That's difficult and my worry. If we get governments or other organizations involved, our secret will be out. And there is every likelihood they won't like our plans and will stall them or even shut us down. The climate with the recession looming with uncertainties ... those in power are likely to maintain the status quo if they have the upper hand."

"I agree. I think we may be a bit paranoid. Our project is very large and involves more than a thousand people. It's nearly impossible to sabotage all of us."

"I pray you're right. We're a bit stuck in this."

"I'll speak to the captain of the ship and increase security. And ask him to report anything out of the ordinary."

"You have a good night, Stephen."

"You too. I think everything will work out fine."

"Diana? You asleep?"

"Sort of," she said in a sleepy voice. She didn't expect Stephen to call her. "What's up?" she asked as she reached her computer and opened the video chat.

"We had a security breach and files have been copied."

"Oh! That's near impossible for your security protocols."

"It happened in Shi," Stephen replied.

"To beat your system, he has to be one hell of a hacker," Diana said, now fully awake. "That's serious. There aren't that many people who can possibly penetrate your systems."

"That's what I'm afraid of. This is becoming very serious. Eric just told me. Looks like there is a serious threat now. I need your help. No one knows you at the moment. Our link has been secured and encrypted. I'll send you copies of everything about Regenesis encrypted. You redirect them to anonymous accounts in different servers. I'll send you the decryption code separately as our usual arrangements. The next two months are crucial."

"I'll do everything on my part here. You'd better be careful, Stephen. Anything can happen. Do you think you should still go ahead with the final test phase?"

"We have no choice. No turning back now. Too much is at stake. Although Eric didn't admit it, he is financially in a bit of a mess. Too much of his personal wealth has been invested in this, and he doesn't want to ask for my financial help, although mine is certainly not even 10 percent of his."

"I understand. And from what I know of Regenesis, it's bigger than all of us."

CHAPTER 27

RENDEZVOUS

Alex, Stephen, and Katherine were on the top deck of the container ship. They could see the platform. This was the rendezvous. After months at sea, they arrived at the designated point, their final destination.

Katherine had gotten used to the sea life and was now enjoying her time onboard the ship. She wore shorts with a white tank top. She had on a pair of sandals, and her large sunglasses hid half her face. It was too windy for a hat. She had a large scarf tied over her hair, helping to block the sun from her neck and face.

She turned to her right and could see the tanker, *Nagoya*, in the distance. The *Nagoya* had caught up with them two weeks earlier. She had gone over with Stephen a week earlier by helicopter and had seen the magnificent Yin and Yang. She was impressed. It was like a science-fiction novel in the making.

She turned back and felt a sense of admiration for her father. Alex was keenly looking at the platform with a pair of binoculars. Her father was so unique and special. No one else would or can ever fill his shoes. She felt a kind of sadness as the project was nearing its end. Two weeks more and the final test would begin, and with that the end of a journey of nearly two years she and her father had made, a journey that brought them so much closer. Their years apart during her time at boarding school and studying had distanced them since she was twelve.

Her father was the doctor, the caring one, the amateur environmentalist who wanted to create a better world for all. His lifetime accumulation of work was going to be determined in the next two weeks.

She touched his arm, grabbed hold of it, and hugged him, saying, "I love you, Dad."

Alex stopped looking at the platform, seeming a bit startled, and touched her arm. He rubbed his face over her hair as her head rested on his shoulder. "Me too, always."

Another day and the test would begin. Eric, Kim, Sukimi, and the Andersons had arrived over the last two days.

"Eric, the Karponofs and his entourage are on their way over with the sheikh," Arsene Widderman said.

"Thanks, Arsene. And you've been a great help organizing the land base," Eric said.

"I wouldn't miss this. I must thank you for the opportunity. It was made easy as you already have the European headquarters here. I'm working from home," he said half-jokingly.

"Everything well on your end?"

"Yes, we have everything under control. I have direct control of the base here for the past few weeks. Being chief has its advantages. We have direct links with the platform established. Ten of our best security guards are on the platform, as you have requested. As far as the Norwegians are concerned, you all are testing a new oil platform. In fact a team went out with me to the platform a week ago. Good to have the oilrig equipment still there. They are satisfied."

Eric replied, "Yes, George had filled me in about that. Got to go. They've arrived."

Eric turned to the arriving guests. "Welcome, Mr. Karpanof and Andre." They had only met for the second time. He still felt a sense of insecurity when he was with them.

"Ah, yes, Eric. Please don't be so formal. Please call me Vassily."

Eric said, "Vassily it is. Come. My crew will show you to your quarters. Later they will show you around," he said with a tinge of annoyance in his voice. He would never trust him, and to call him by his first name nauseated him. First names were reserved for friends.

The first helicopter took off to base on the *Nagoya*. The second came in to land with the sheikh and his party.

Eric greeted the sheikh. "Your Highness."

The sheikh said, "Thank you, Eric. So nice to be onboard. And you must be Alex. I've only seen a picture of you. Finally we meet. Tomorrow will be your day and ours."

"Your Highness, thank you. I really hope so," Alex said.

Eric directed the reception crew to show the sheikh and his entourage their accommodations. "You must be tired after the long journey from the Middle East. We have your rooms ready. They are the best we can do on this container ship. When you're ready later, dinner will be served."

Eric believed he saw the senior Karpanof glance at the sheikh and the sheikh nod back. *They know each other and didn't mention it to me?* he thought. *That's really worrying.*

At dinner, the two of them didn't show any sign that they knew each other. The oil world isn't that big, and they were probably acquaintances.

They were already enjoying the main meal when Eric said, "Forgive my manners. I forgot to introduce you all. This is his Royal Highness, Sheikh Abdullah. Here are the Karpanofs. Vassily is the senior, and Andre is his son."

Vassily said, "The pleasure is mine, your Royal Highness."

The sheikh smiled and nodded in acknowledgement. At that moment, Eric realized they must know each other but wanted it to be kept a secret.

"So, Eric, we're here to witness the test of your models. How far has the project succeeded?" the sheikh asked.

"We haven't had any live tests yet. Tomorrow will be the first. As agreed, you investors will get to see the final result."

"And you think we'll succeed tomorrow?" Vassily asked.

Eric said, "I really don't know. We've tried to put the pieces together. The turbine possibly will work. We have a bit of a stability issue. The electrolysis is incomplete in its development and has not reached levels to be efficient enough to better the oil market. We'll get there soon."

"And yet the tankers and storage facilities on the platform are ready?" the sheikh said with some disbelief.

"Unfortunately, the different parts of the project were to run simultaneously regardless of the others. So, yes, the tanker and storage facility are ready." Eric tried to convince them, hiding the most important part about their success with Meyer's hypothesis.

"I see. Well, let's hope our investments will bear fruit when it all falls into place," George said.

With that, Alex said, "I propose a toast. To Eric: without him, his belief, and his complete dedication, Regenesis wouldn't even come close to what we've achieved."

"Hear, hear!" everyone added, and they toasted Eric. Then they toasted to success the following day.

It was going to be a long night for all. The research crew was going over the data. The main team working on the ECHO complex was on the platform fixing the final bits, connecting the two containers that housed the electrolysis equipment to the storage chambers in the storage facility on the platform. The containers were hauled over by crane and fixed on the platform. The turbines were already in the water, anchored to the floating platform for two days. Final checks were still being done that night.

Stephen was on the platform. He had run out of time trying to secure video feeds back to the *Lumut*. Somehow the equipment was faulty, and he could only receive feeds from the control room. It was already two in the morning.

"Stephen, are we good to go tomorrow morning?" Eric asked.

"No. I couldn't get most of the video feeds up. We have faulty equipment. How was dinner?"

"Dinner was challenging. I think the sheikh and Vassily have some secret between them. They're not letting on that they know each other."

"That doesn't sound too good."

"I invited them all for a reason. If they want to sabotage the project, they put themselves at risk. If they didn't come, I'd have canceled and rethought the plan."

"So you want to go ahead tomorrow? I doubt I'll get the video feeds fixed by tomorrow. We'll only be able to see the control room. I only have one more working feed. I think I'll put it on the outside to see the helipad and most of the buildings on the outside. That's the best I can do."

"Yes, we'll proceed. And thank you."

It wasn't only a long night for the crew. Vassily and Andre sneaked into the sheikh's room. "I know for sure Eric is lying. My sources already told us that the electrolysis research has been completed and the prototype has already been made. And tomorrow's live test is not a model but the actual turbines," the sheikh said.

Vassily said, "I knew he was not telling the truth but I came prepared." He looked toward his son. "We're prepared, yes?"

Andre nodded.

"So are we. If it's a success, we'll leave the platform to you. My two bodyguards here will secure the helicopter to return to this ship. We need the designs and data. My butler will see to that when we're away for the test. He will remain on this ship. I have someone on the tanker who knows what to do when the alarms sound. We have a few people already in place for action on this ship too."

At the other side of the top-floor accommodation containers, Katherine and Angelina were sharing a room. Both were having difficulty sleeping. Angelina was filled with mixed emotions. She had just spoken to Michael on her satellite phone an hour earlier. Her orders were to observe, and if the test succeeded, to immediately inform him. That was a simple order. But she knew there could be consequences.

"Katherine, are you awake?"

"I can't sleep. The excitement has gotten to me. I've put aside a good part of the last two years on this project. I even thought up the name. Now we're nearly there. And as all good things, it ends when we succeed. The journey we've embarked on ends. Of course the next phase starts, but I don't think my dad and I will be in it. Father has already taken a backseat the last few months. The experts were all doing their thing. Father was a bit disappointed that he couldn't contribute more."

"Your father has vision, Katherine. He has."

"And why can't you sleep? You always seem not to have worries and fall asleep so fast. What's your story?"

Angelina hesitated about a full minute, thinking of what to say.

"Angelina? You okay? Got over your boyfriend by now, haven't you?"

That nudged her to talk. "I ..."

"Come on, you can do it. Say it. Get it off your chest. I'm all ears. That's what friends are for, right?"

"I didn't break up with my boyfriend. He cheated on me."

"Huh? He cheated on you? He had another girl? Then good riddance. I'll shoot him for you if I can."

"No," she said, falling silent.

Katherine was now at her bedside, sitting on the floor, looking straight at her. "Don't cry. It'll be all right."

Angelina was very emotional. Tears flowed down her cheeks. "You don't understand. He's a terrorist."

"What? A terrorist?" Katherine said with utter disbelief.

"They got us on video in bed. They even got video and pictures of me asleep as he was awake cleaning his gun. How stupid I was. I'm sorry, Kat."

"Who are *they?*" Katherine asked in a puzzled voice.

"I'm not sure. I think they must be Americans. Either Secret Service or some intelligence agency or something like that. They threatened me with the videos. They said they would expose them to the public if I don't do what they say. I can't let my father be ruined because of me."

Angelina looked at Katherine's face. Her mouth hung open; her eyes were wide open. She seemed to be holding her breath in disbelief. "Katherine," she said in a soft voice, breaking Katherine's near-trance state.

"Why did you say sorry to me?" Katherine asked, seeming to grasp the seriousness of the issue.

"Because I've been asked to spy on this project," Angelina whispered.

"Oh," Katherine quietly replied, and they hugged each other silently.

Several minutes passed before they talked again.

"And what are you going to do, Angelina?"

"I report to my controller, Michael. I call him daily on this satellite phone. Our cell phones don't work in open sea."

"Only that?" Katherine asked.

"Yes, that's all. If the project succeeds, I'm to call him immediately."

"Are they the bad guys or good guys?" Katherine asked.

"I don't know. He was in a suit and spoke perfect American English. He looked government."

"Did he tell you why you are to spy on us?"

"No, he said I didn't need to know. I just need to do as he says."

"And why are you telling me this tonight?"

"I can't keep betraying you, your dad, or my dad anymore. Maybe I should tell him now."

"Hold on. Thank you. I'm annoyed, but I can see you have little choice. I believe you, Angelina. From the sound of it, they may be the good guys. Don't call when we succeed. We wait a while. I don't think he will do anything rash knowing the importance of this project. I think we'll have time, at least a few hours. We can then talk to my father first and see where we go from there."

"I'm so, so sorry."

"I think we'd better keep an eye on things. I know Andre and Vassily cannot be trusted. You keep an eye on Andre. I don't like the sheikh's bodyguards. I handled Vassily's corporate agreements before. I'm sure I've seen Sheikh Abdullah's name on them before. They can't possibly not know each other as they pretended at dinner. I think they're in some partnership here."

Neither of them slept that night, contemplating what they had to do the next morning.

Eric and Sukimi sat at the dining room, chatting until four in the morning. They had so much to talk about.

Sukimi could see Eric was still very much in love with her. She felt regret all this time. Eric was her love—her only love. Her husband was good to her. Her marriage had been arranged, a convenient one for both families. Here Eric and Sukimi chatted about life and each other's lives, not acknowledging their feelings for one another. She knew they had to keep their distance. But she truly enjoyed Eric's company. She wished she could have more opportunity like this to be with him.

"If wishes can come true, then I'd wish I was not from a rich family when I met you. Then we would be together," she finally said.

"Then I'd never have met you. You wouldn't be in Taiwan. We can't change fate," Eric replied.

Sukimi noticed Eric had unconsciously rubbed his jade pendant as he spoke.

He added, "We're here because of a series of events. Almost all of them had led from one to another. Do you believe in fate?"

"I do. Japanese believe in karma. All things happen for a reason."

"Then you understand why we're all here. Tomorrow, fate will deal its hand. I hope it will be a favorable one for us all."

Stephen took the helicopter back to the *Lumut* once daylight broke. It was five in the morning. It had been a long night. He would have a few hours to prepare on the ship before the test started. He headed straight to his room and entered his secret space. He spent another hour editing footage of videotape in his computer.

"Diana, you there?" Stephen called her on the video link.

"Hi, Stephen. Just grabbed a cup of tea—and a little something else," she said as she wheeled herself in front of the camera.

"You've got to cut down on the whisky, Diana."

"Aw, come on. I don't have the luxury of time. Let me enjoy the little life I have left."

"I'm sending you the final parts of Regenesis. Plus this last video file and an execute file. It's all encrypted. I'll give you the code later. If not, it'll time-activate and decode anyway in twelve hours."

"You're getting paranoid, Stephen. But I guess better safe than sorry."

"You are my savoir, Diana. Again, what would I do without you?"

"You owe me a nice dinner out when all this ends."

"That's a promise. You need to get out more."

"Not with the stares everyone gives me. No."

"As we planned, I need you for the next four to six hours."

"I have nothing to do. I'm awake and at your service."

"Okay. Got to go."

"You take care."

CHAPTER 28

THE FINAL DAY

Eric felt his shoulder being tapped from behind. He turned and saw a crew member behind him, trying to say something above the noise of the helicopter. They moved away and inside.

The crew member said, "There's a video call for you in the meeting room from Mr. Ching. Mr. Stephen transferred the call there."

"Okay, thank you," Eric said, wondering what Ching wanted. He had spoken to him just a week ago and he had declined to come. Ching never liked to leave China.

"Good morning. Or is it good evening?" Eric asked in greeting.

"Ah, there you are, Eric. I managed to catch you in time."

In time for what? Eric wondered.

"I just want to tell you that my feng shui master tells me the feng shui today isn't good. Do heed the feng shui, Eric. Good luck," Ching said with a stern voice but smiling face. Before Eric could reply, Ching disconnected.

Bad feng shui was a warning. Yet he was not telling the full truth. *Why indeed did he do that?* Eric wondered. Ching had never communicated with him like that before.

Another crew member came in and said, "The helicopter is ready, sir."

"I'll be there in a moment." He would need to think about what to do on the helicopter.

As the helicopter approached the platform, Angelina tugged on her father's sleeve and said in his ear, "That is a really beautiful sight. The platform and the floating platform. Are those the submersible turbines? They're shining in the sunlight."

"Yes, my sweetheart, they are. Yin and Yang. These Chinese are quite superstitious. That means harmony you know. The pair, I mean."

"Yes, Katherine explained the significance."

The helicopter landed on the helipad. The group was directed to the control room. The whole team except Stephen was already present when the Andersons and Eric walked in. The sheikh and Vassily were seated in the front row of the elevated gallery. Andre was standing at the back along with the sheikh's two bodyguards. Most of the team members, including Katherine, were seated in the second row. Kim and Jonathan were directing the operations and stood in front with the crew manning the systems. George and Eric took the other two front-row seats beside Alex.

Angelina sat next to Katherine. She felt the satellite phone in her pocket. Was this the cross she had to bear? *A few hours more and I'll know,* she thought.

Eric stood up when Kim nodded to him. "To all here, we're about to start. I hope we'll have a successful test. That's why we're here. Kim, all yours."

Kim signaled to the chief engineer to start. "Lower the submersible Yin."

They could see on the video feed channel from the platform and another from the bridge of the submersible on the huge center monitors. With a few bubbles, the submersible was lowered by cable from the floating platform.

"See the cables attached to Yin? Two will bring electricity to the ECHO complex where electrolysis of water will take place and then hydrogen created and stored.

"The other three are anchoring cables. These cables run all the way to the seabed, which is about fifteen hundred feet deep. This is the shallowest part of the ocean floor at this region. We think the current would be strongest here as the seabed is shallow, compressing the current's energy. The submersible has ballasts, and it has flooded its ballasts to dive now," Kim explained. "We'll allow it to dive to one thousand feet." She pointed to another screen that showed the depth.

After a short while, it had reached its targeted depth.

Kim said, "Now we'll begin the test. Jonathan, ready?"

"Yes. Here we go," Jonathan said, pressing the button.

The first cusps on both sides opened.

"We can see the computer-generated image on the screen," he said, pointing to another side display. "You can see the cusps opening. They are turning and gathering speed. They close at the end and come back along the track to the front. The speed is increasing."

The revolutions showed on the screen reached fifty times per minute and stabilized there. Another counter next to it showed a thousand rounds per minute. "Do you see the other counter? That's the revolutions after the gear system.

"The submersible is showing some movements in the current. It's self-correcting with a sophisticated program, which makes alterations to the 'fins' in milliseconds, which allows it to be stable in the current. It has sonar to detect large sea creatures and will power down and automatically close all the cusps until they pass by."

After the cusps had been rotating for a minute, Kim said, "Time to test. May we all succeed."

Jonathan was now seated, and he pushed a lever forward. As he did, the submersible seemed to wobble and the anchoring cables became taunt. He continued to count, "It's 80 percent, 90 percent, 100 percent," and released his hold on the lever.

Kim said, "Please observe the other monitor. Jonathan has activated the generators, releasing the clutch and engaging the generators. Electricity is now passing up to ECHO. Look at the monitor. The hydrogen is produced from the electrolysis of purified water. The hydrogen is being channeled to the storage chambers. We'll fill one chamber. You can see the indicator here showing the hydrogen levels are rising in the chamber."

Angelina cast a glance around the room. Everyone was looking up at the monitors. She returned her focus to the screens as the hydrogen levels approached the 100 percent mark.

Kim said, "We're nearly there. One thousand gallons. And it has taken half an hour."

Eric started to clap and everyone joined in. "We've succeeded!" Everyone was shouting and cheering.

As they settled down, Jonathan had already taken the generators offline.

Kim said, "We have a successful test. Close the cusps and raise Yin, if you may, Jonathan."

Within ten minutes, Yin was nearing the surface.

Angelina again glanced around the room. In the excitement of the success, she had temporarily forgotten to keep an eye on Andre. Andre and the bodyguards were gone. She pulled on Katherine's arm and pointed toward the empty seats.

Katherine quickly turned around. She had also been distracted by the success of Regenesis. "Where are they?"

As Yin surfaced, another round of applause and cheering happened.

The two women headed for the door.

"Where do you think they went?" Angelina asked.

"I'd go to ECHO if I wanted to sabotage. Hydrogen would make a great bomb," Katherine remarked.

They ran across to the complex. They discovered the two guards unconscious on the floor. "I think they must be in the storage complex with the chambers," Katherine said, leading the way. They raced down the corridor and opened the door.

Andre heard the door open. He swiftly turned around as Katherine was almost on him with her small penknife. With hardly an effort, he disarmed her and cast her aside like a rag doll. Katherine hit her head on the chamber and fell unconscious.

Andre faced Angelina, who stopped in her tracks when he turned to her. With a quick swing of his arm, he slapped her across the face. She fell down, stunned by the power of the slap.

Andre thought, *Time to have some quick fun. I've always wanted to have you, and here you are.* He grabbed her hair, pushed her forward on the large pipe. He was aroused by her incapacitation. He pulled down her trousers and panties in one go and was ready to enter her. He had his large hand around her neck, choking her. He could feel her struggling and slowly going limp. Just as he was to penetrate her, the door again swung open with a bang. This only made him angry as he was interrupted. He threw Angelina away like a dead animal and turned to the door. He was now enraged, not being able to continue.

Katherine woke as the door banged shut. She opened her eyes. She saw Angelina on the floor. She got up and rushed to her. "Angelina, wake up!" she said as she felt her pulse. The pulse was still there. She could hear commotion outside.

Angelina stirred and then in a jerk woke up. She jumped up. Katherine started to feel a lump in her throat and her whole body trembled as she realized there were plastic explosives in the chamber and along the pipes. They could explode any moment. She looked at Angelina, and as if they had read each other's mind, they raced to the door.

They tried to open the door by turning the large wheel. It wouldn't budge. They banged and cried for help. They tried the door again. Suddenly it loosened, and it opened. They found Sukimi lying in a pool of blood, her penknife stuck in the right side of her torso. She was in pain.

"What happened?" Katherine asked as she knelt down and held her.

"I saw both of you leave and followed. Andre rushed out, pushed me aside. Then I heard your cries and I reached out and pulled away the bar," she said with anxiety, wincing in pain. Blood oozed from the wound.

Katherine's instinct was to pull out the knife. She stopped herself as she was to do that. She had second thoughts. Possibly it was better to leave it there to secure the wound. She tore away her sleeve and used it to apply pressure to the wound.

"Damn Andre, he must have stabbed her with my knife and locked us in," Katherine said. She looked at the door and realized they had to close it. "Close the door, Angelina. Quickly. The bombs!"

Just as she turned the wheel to close, an explosion threw them to the floor. The door held fast. Alarms sounded and red lights in the corridor flashed.

Two guards came running to them.

"Help us. Take her to the helicopter now. Angelina, stay with her," Katherine instructed. *The worst has happened. I have to find Eric and Alex!* she thought as she ran back to the command center.

CHAPTER 29

SABOTAGE

In the command center, they were still in celebration mode when the explosion shook the platform. Alarms began going off. Alex thought, *Oh no, the hydrogen must have leaked and exploded!*

Eric said, "Kim, Jonathan, what's happened?"

"The alarms are coming from the ECHO complex. Something must have happened. The crew is running there now," Kim said, looking at the monitors around her. "Hey, that's Katherine running towards us!" she exclaimed as she saw Katherine on the video monitor.

The next moment, Katherine pushed open the door, looking anxious and out of breath. She said haltingly, "There, there ... is an explosion ... in ECHO ... bombs that Andre put ... Sukimi is injured ... she, she needs help ... Dad ..." She was trying to breathe as she spoke.

Alex got the message and quickly ran out. Eric felt a sudden fear overcoming him and also ran out, chasing Alex.

Kim shouted over the microphone, "This is an emergency. Code red! Fire in ECHO complex. Fire personnel to ECHO. Security to apprehend Andre Karpanof immediately!"

Almost simultaneously as she spoke, she heard the helicopter rotors picking up speed. Katherine looked around and asked, "Where is the sheikh and Vassily?"

"Oh no, they're getting into the helicopter," Kim cried as she saw them on the video monitor. "They're getting away!"

Katherine tried to radio the *Lumut*. "*Lumut*, can you hear me? *Lumut?*"

There was no reply.

Alex and Eric had reached the ECHO complex as the security guards carried Sukimi out.

"Put her down here!" Alex instructed. "I need to see how bad it is." Alex knelt over Sukimi and examined her. She was very pale as she had lost a vast amount of blood. The knife had twisted in her. Alex rummaged through the first-aid kit he had grabbed on the way and found bandages. He removed the cloth that was covering the wound. He packed the sides of the wound around the blade of the knife. He slowly pulled out the knife as he pushed the bandage in to halt the bleeding.

Sukimi groaned in pain.

"I'm sorry. I need to stop the bleeding. A short while, that's all," Alex said. He knew her liver must have been punctured. The blood was almost black, indicating it was from the liver. Alex did what he could to stop the bleeding. He knew he could do no more. She needed urgent hospital treatment with a blood transfusion and immediate surgery.

"We got to get her to the helicopter," Alex said.

"Sukimi, I'm here. Hold onto my hand. I'm here with you," Eric said. Tears rolled down his cheeks. He was a man in despair.

As they lifted Sukimi onto a stretcher, they heard the helicopter taking off. "What's going on?" Eric cried. He suddenly remembered Ching's warning. "Oh no, this is a disaster. We must have been sabotaged. Now we cannot get off the platform!"

At that moment Kim, who was still in the control room looking at the video feeds, realized that they were stranded. She radioed the *Nagoya*. "*Nagoya*, are you there? *Nagoya*, please answer!"

"This is the *Nagoya* captain. How can we help?"

"There has been an explosion. We've been sabotaged. Please send the helicopter here immediately as we have to evacuate."

"Roger that. We'll send the helicopter now."

A few moments later, Sukimi was on the helicopter with Eric, Alex, and Katherine back to the *Lumut*.

"Keep the pressure on," Alex instructed Katherine as he examined her. She was drifting in and out of consciousness.

Eric kept saying, "Stay with me. Stay with me. Don't sleep now!"

When they reached the ship, Alex instructed Katherine, "Run ahead to the infirmary and ask them to prepare oxygen and IV morphine. Also, get ready to insert two intravenous lines. We will follow behind as fast as we can."

When Sukimi reached the infirmary on a stretcher, the paramedics were on hand to immediately resuscitate her. Within minutes, she was more stable with oxygen and intravenous fluids running as fast as possible. The morphine helped to ease her pain.

Alex told Katherine and Angelina, "You two better see what's going on. I have to stay with Sukimi in the infirmary. Eric has to be here, too."

"Yes, we will. Come, Angelina, let's find them." Turning to the two guards with them, Katherine added, "Follow us. We need to find the saboteurs."

They hurried to the bridge of the ship as they would need to inform the captain and start a wide search.

"Oh no! Damn!" Katherine remarked as they reached the bridge.

The captain and the crew were all dead. Some were sprawled on the floor with pools of blood around them. The captain was in his chair with his head arched back motionless and blood dripping from his chest wound.

They were stunned. Katherine felt the world collapse around her. She was in despair and started to cry. This was too much for her.

Suddenly the ship was rocked as a loud explosion detonated. They were knocked off their feet.

Angelina cried, "Must be another bomb! It felt like it came from the stern of the ship. The engine?"

Katherine, having composed herself, said, "If they sabotage the ship, they must be heading for the helicopter again to get off. We've got to get to the helipad. Come on!" They ran to the helipad.

Katherine was filled with anger, no longer feeling fear. Fear seemed to have left her on the bridge. Rage took over. As they reached the helipad, they saw Karim, Jonathan, and Jack fighting with Andre, the sheikh, and one of the bodyguards. Vassily and another bodyguard were getting into the second helicopter farther away.

Looking around for something to use as a weapon as she ran toward the fight, Katherine remembered the large brooch pinned to her jacket. She took it off, leapt on Andre's back, flung one arm across his face, and stabbed hard with the brooch. She felt a spurt of liquid as the pin made contact. She had stabbed him in the eye.

Andre screamed in pain and released his grip on Karim. Karim, freed now, turned and kicked Andre in the midriff. Andre fell back and hit his head on the side of the helicopter. He did not rise.

Seeing what Katherine had done, Angelina tore off her stiletto-heeled boots. She held both of them in her hands and swung with great force at the sheikh's chest.

Her attack was unexpected. The sheikh's scream could be heard above the noise of the helicopter blades. In his chest were embedded the sharp ends of a pair of ladies lizard-skin boots. At that moment, Angelina was grateful she had big feet. Her larger-sized boots had made the impact she had hoped for.

His bodyguard turned instinctively as he heard the sheikh scream. Distracted for a moment, Jonathan and Jack jumped him and knocked him to the ground.

Katherine signaled for the helicopter pilot to take off. No one would get off until they had neutralized the threat.

When the helicopter took off, Katherine could see Vassily and the other bodyguard was onboard the second helicopter. Katherine lifted Andre's head, which was now covered in blood, and turned it to face Vassily. The man balked. Andre's head was a bloody mess, and one eye socket was an explosion of flesh and blood.

"Vassily, this is your son, Andre!" Katherine screamed as loud as she could.

Vassily took a step forward to go to his son. He was held back by the other bodyguard.

"It doesn't matter," the bodyguard shouted, "This ship will blow up soon. It's every man for himself now. We cannot fight them all." With the rotors already reaching speed, the bodyguard piloting the helicopter pulled back the lever, and the helicopter started lifting off. Many of the crew were now on deck and rushing toward the helicopters.

"Help me," Katherine yelled to Angelina as she ran toward a steel cable she saw lying on the deck close to Angelina. Angelina ran over, grabbed the end of the cable, and tossed it to Katherine. Katherine grabbed it and ran toward the helicopter. She just managed to grab the ski with one hand before the helicopter had lifted farther than her reach. With the other she wrapped the cable around the ski. She had to free the hand clinging to the ski to make a knot to secure the cable. She risked falling into the ocean. She wrapped her legs around the cable but felt herself slipping as she made the knot. Her weight on the knot made it tight and she clung to it until she felt a boot against her face.

Katherine looked up and saw Vassily's face.

"Bitch!" he shouted and then pushed his foot hard against Katherine's face. Katherine released her grip on the cable knot and fell twenty feet into the water with a splash. She disappeared from everyone's view as she slipped deep into the sea.

As the helicopter veered away, the cable became taut and the helicopter stopped moving. In a split second it dived toward the sea. The blades hit the cable. One broke. The helicopter was now spinning recklessly. The broken blade ruptured its fuel tank and it burst into flames. As it was about to hit the water, the helicopter exploded.

Alex had just reached the deck when the helicopter exploded. The force threw him back. As he got up, he saw Angelina rushing to the side of the ship. He ran to her.

As he reached her, she screamed, "Katherine is down there," pointing to the sea. Sudden fear overcame Alex, and then rage. No one harms his Katherine!

He climbed over the rails, looking out to sea where the debris of the helicopter was. He thought he saw Katherine. With one huge leap, he dived in. He must save Katherine. He gave no thought to his own well-being. Alex hit the water hard and started swimming. He didn't even feel the cold. The water temperature was almost freezing. Katherine had minutes or maybe seconds before she froze in that water and before thermal shock took over. Alex continued to swim as he scoured the waterline. She would be fighting to stay afloat if she were conscious. *Katherine will not give up so easily,* he thought.

Then Alex saw her head bob and her arms moving above the water. He swam relentlessly, totally focused on reaching her. It seemed everything he had learned about swimming, fear, and resolution was in preparation for this day. He would save her. The moment he reached her, Alex slipped his hand around his daughter's waist and raised her head and torso above the water.

"Daddy," she said weakly and then lost consciousness. Holding Katherine by the neck, keeping her afloat, Alex swam back as strong and fast as he could. After a minute, he was starting to tire. As hard as he tried, his kicks were weakening. He started to feel the cold. The adrenaline rush was nearing its end. He had to psych himself up to save his daughter. This was his greatest challenge. He would never give up. He had to continue no matter what.

He was very relieved when he saw a small-powered craft come towards him. It was an inflatable with Jonathan and Karim onboard. The craft pulled alongside them. They pulled Katherine onboard.

Alex pulled himself in. He said, "Start CPR." He wanted to do it himself but his body wouldn't respond. He was exhausted.

Karim started to resuscitate her with mouth-to-mouth respiration and chest compressions.

"Come on, Katherine, come on. You can do it," Alex said tearfully.

Soon they reached the ship.

Alex had regained some strength and managed to climb onboard. Katherine was hoisted up on a stretcher with ropes. Once on deck, Alex continued to give her mouth-to-mouth resuscitation while Karim continued chest compressions.

Suddenly Katherine coughed and started to breathe.

"Katherine, breathe. Breathe slowly." Alex held her wrist and felt her weak pulse. A sense of relief overcame him. He wept openly, holding her face as she woke. Sobbing, he said, "Warm her up with blankets. Keep the oxygen on. Take her to the infirmary."

Katherine whispered, "I'm okay. Just very tired."

Shivering, Alex got up and followed her, with blankets over him.

"What happened, Jonathan?" Alex asked as they rushed to the infirmary.

"They sabotaged the ECHO complex. It exploded and ruptured the outer chamber and the pipes. There was a fire, but as the nitrogen leaked out, freezing the flames, no further explosion happened. It's contained."

"On this ship, what happened?"

"The captain and bridge crew are dead. We think the bodyguards did that. The explosion came from the engine room. We're now without power."

Alex felt his anger rising. "How can this be? They were going to sacrifice themselves?"

"I think not. They were trying to escape on the helicopters. The first helicopter has returned to the *Nagoya*. Unfortunately we can't contact them as our radio is damaged beyond repair."

Alex said, "Hopefully that's the end of it."

CHAPTER 30

CHAOS AND DEATH

E ric and Stephen had planned that he would stay onboard the *Lumut* while the test was conducted. Someone should be on the ship in case of an emergency on the platform.

Stephen was looking at the monitors in his hidden compartment. He was stunned when he saw the video shake and then moments later Katherine running from ECHO to the command center. He witnessed the events there. He looked at the other monitors showing the *Lumut*. He saw the sheikh's butler in the research area rummaging through the room and trying to access the computers. *Damn, he's trying to steal our designs.*

Stephen grabbed his only weapon and ran to the research room. He rushed in and faced the butler. "Stop! Why are you doing this?"

Instead of answering, the butler drew out a knife and thrust forward at Stephen.

Stephen sidestepped him and shot him with his taser.

The butler shook violently for a few seconds and collapsed. Stephen made sure he was unconscious. He tied him to the table and ran back to his room.

We've been sabotaged. I have to get the word out! he thought as he ran. When he reached the hidden compartment, he saw on the monitors that the helicopters were ferrying people back to the ship.

"Diana, are you there? Diana?" Stephen said with panic in his voice.

"I'm here. What's wrong, Stephen? You look terrible."

"We've been sabotaged. Remember the files I sent you last night? The code is Regenesis, with a capital R. We may not have much time."

Stephen looked at the upper monitors as he saw activity in the infirmary. "That's Sukimi. Oh no. She looks injured. What's happening?" He enlarged the video and put the audio on. He could now see and hear everything in the infirmary.

"Eric, we've transfusion the two units of blood we keep for emergencies and are trying all we can. I don't know how much longer she can last," Alex said.

"Sukimi, don't give up." Eric said, not wanting to accept the situation. He just couldn't accept it. Just a moment ago everything was going well. Now Sukimi was near death and he felt so helpless.

Sukimi turned her hand and invited Eric to put his hand in hers. As he did so he stroked her hair.

"Thank you for everything and for Regenesis," she said, "I'm proud to have been a part of this. All of you have done something good for everyone trying to give hope to the world."

Eric whispered, "You'll be fine. You'll make it. I'm sure. Don't give up." His tears dripped on her hand.

Sukimi blinked for a moment and then continued. "Promise me you won't give up. Regenesis must succeed. Continue, please. I love you."

Eric was distraught. Barely able to find his voice, he bowed his head and said, "I love you too. I'll continue." He wasn't sure if Sukimi saw his nod, so he squeezed her hand.

Sukimi exhaled as if in acknowledgement and then her fingers went limp.

Eric dropped his head on her chest and just cried. He had lost her. Eric felt Alex's touch on his shoulder but didn't want to respond. He heard Alex say, "I'm so sorry."

Eric, with his face on her chest and his hand holding Sukimi's limp hand, shook his head as if dismissing Alex's words. He shook from the crying.

Stephen was stunned. Suddenly the ship shook violently as a loud explosion occurred. That brought Stephen back, and he said, "Diana, this is getting worse. Is the decryption working?"

"Almost there, Stephen."

"I'm sending you a video file now."

"A video. What do you want me to do with it?"

Before Stephen could answer, the power completely cut off. His monitors and computers stopped. He had lost all communications.

"I hope Diana will be able to finish the job. God help us all," Stephen thought aloud. There was nothing more he could do now. He would find the others and see how he could help.

Diana was staring at the black video frame on her computer. The file finished decoding, and she looked at the files. Only two files were present—a video file and an execute file. She clicked on the video file. The video played and Stephen appeared on the screen.

Stephen said, "Hi. If you are seeing this video file, it means something terrible has happened. As you know, the past two years working on Regenesis have been some of the most important years of my life. The live test must have succeeded. We may just have found a way to help solve the energy crisis of the world. Now that you have activated the file, it means we're in trouble. As we feared, someone has been spying on Regenesis. Remember, we can't trust anyone.

"So now you have to play your part. The video will reveal to the whole world at once what we've done. Our location will be pinpointed. Live satellite pictures of our location will be broadcast worldwide to every television and satellite channel that exists. The virus I've created will penetrate every communication system to do that. After the transmissions, the virus will self-destruct and not be usable again. I hope this video does its job. I hope someone will save us. Thank you and good luck. You are the best friend anyone can have."

She said a silent pray and clicked on the execute file. The file automatically connected to the Internet and seemed to send a video to more than a hundred Internet addresses simultaneously. She was deeply moved as she watched the video and heard Stephen's voice and felt warm tears on her cheeks. The worst they had feared had happened, but she could never have prepared for this moment. Suddenly she remembered Stephen's last words before the video chat disconnected. She looked for the video file and found it. She played it. It was the footage of the infirmary with Sukimi and Eric. She was crying uncontrollably when it ended. She recognized Eric Shi. It was a few minutes before she was in control of her emotions again. She grabbed the remote control and turned on her television. Stephen was on the TV. He looked worn out.

"Hi. I'm Stephen. I work for Mr. Eric Shi and the Shi Corporation. If you're seeing this video, it means we've succeeded and are in need of help. Over the past two years, we've embarked on a project we called Regenesis." The video showed footage of the project, from the Lumut facility and Hato Industries with the submersibles to the platform out in the ocean.

Stephen continued. "We started in Taiwan with the initial planning and then moved to the main research facility in Lumut, Malaysia. We've succeeded in making the first underwater turbines to generate energy from the deep-sea currents. The turbines have been made in Hato Industries in Japan. The turbines will generate electricity, which we'll convert to clean energy, hydrogen using an unconventional electrolysis process. We've also created a new way to store the hydrogen safely in transport and storage. We would like to share with the world our success. Unfortunately, if you are seeing this, we're probably in extreme danger. We need all the help we can get." A set of coordinates flashed on the screen. "We're here. Please respond quickly!" The video repeated every thirty seconds.

She suddenly realized the Japanese lady was Sukimi Hato of Hato Industries. She had been their spokesperson. She had charisma and should be easily recognized. Diana knew what Stephen wanted her to do with the video. He probably knew the video to the news channels wasn't enough to immediately alert anyone to the danger they were facing. This video would.

She typed away on her computer. She had to send it to all the news channels.

Back on the ship, the sheikh was ranting away although he was in pain. "Let me loose or I'll make sure no one lives. Release me immediately. I'm the prince. No one ties me up!"

Stephen was entering the room as the sheikh spoke. Alex and Eric were just a few steps in front of him. Suddenly Eric grabbed the sheikh by the collar and lifted him off the floor. Eric was large compared to the sheikh and looked like he could easily tossed the sheikh out a window.

"I'll kill you now if you say anything more!" Stephen and Alex rushed forward to hold back Eric.

Stephen said, "He's not worth it. We need to know what he means." Stephen coaxed Eric to let him go. "It's okay, Eric. He isn't going anywhere. He'll pay for his crimes."

Eric walked to a chair and sat down with his hands over his face.

"Alex, are you okay?" Stephen asked.

"Just about. Still feeling very cold. The blankets and changing into the jumpsuit has helped," Alex said. "Katherine is resting. She should be fine. Angelina is with her."

"Now what is it you want to tell us and threaten us with? You're not going anywhere," Stephen said to the sheikh as he sat in front of him, staring at him.

The sheikh said in a very irritated voice, "I demand to be released. There are drones on the way to destroy everything. They will be here within the hour. You cannot stop them. Only I can. My men have planted more bombs on the ship. They will explode at any time."

Everyone in the room started to voice their panic.

Stephen yelled, "Calm down everyone! Calm down!" He turned to the sheikh again and said, "You forget one thing. You're here with us. We all die together!"

The sheikh replied, "I can stop this! I can call them off, the planes!"

The room was silent for almost a minute. Suddenly the door opened and Angelina walked in. Alex looked at her enquiringly.

Angelina replied, "Katherine is fine, She is fully conscious and alert. She sent me to see what is going on."

Stephen replied, "The sheikh here is the problem. He wants us to let him go so he can call off the planes he has sent to destroy us. Isn't that right, Sheikh?"

Angelina felt sudden terror, as those present had a moment earlier. "Oh, God! What can I do?" Suddenly, she thought she may have the answer and took out her satellite phone. "Give me a few seconds, Stephen. I may be able to help."

She walked out of the room, calling Michael. "Michael, Michael, can you hear me!"

"Loud and clear. You're in a lot of trouble, right?"

"How do you know?

"I know everything."

"There are planes heading our way to destroy us. The sheikh is behind all this. We've captured him. The other saboteurs are dead or captured."

"I'll see what I can do and call you back," Michael replied.

Michael had been in teleconference with five other people when Angelina called. What she didn't know was Michael could hear and see everything from her phone. He could hear most of the conversation and see when she had her phone out of her pocket.

"What do you want me to do, sir?" Michael asked.

"I think it's out of our hands now. Have you seen the news channels?"

"No," he said as he switched on the television. "Oh," he replied as he saw Sukimi's last moments on the screen.

"I don't think we have any choice. We'll let events be. The decision is no longer in our hands."

"Yes, sir."

"Break all communications with Angelina. Don't reply. As far as they are concerned, we don't exist. Our other partners will take it from here."

"I understand," Michael said. He sent a message to the satellite phone.

Angelina stared at the phone when it suddenly fizzed with smoked and became warm. She felt the pain in her palm and let it fall. Suddenly it was in flames and disintegrated.

Stephen was at the door and had seen her on the phone. "Looks like it's also a dead end," Stephen said to Angelina, who was stunned. "Whoever that is won't be helping us."

Turning back to the room, Stephen asked, "Any ideas? If we give him his phone, he might actually call in the strike rather than stop it. Anyway, can he really stop it?"

"Of course I can," the sheikh shouted.

Eric felt a sudden rush of immense rage toward the sheikh. He rushed forward and punched him repeatedly in the face before anyone could stop him. The last punch floored the sheikh. He was bleeding from the mouth and a cut over his left eye. He was unconscious.

Everyone was stunned. The sheikh couldn't call off the planes if they were real. An atmosphere of total submission overcame the room. Everyone was down and silent.

Then they heard the familiar roar of planes slowing increasing in volume. They ran outside. A squadron of planes flew overhead and passed them. Stephen recognized the emblems on the planes as Norwegian.

Thank God. Thank you, Diana, he thought. *You did it!*

They changed formation, and two planes circled them. Two others circled the platform, and the last headed to the *Nagoya*.

Stephen waved to the planes. The others, a bit confused, followed him and waved. One of the planes gently fluttered its wings in reply.

Alex asked, "Stephen, what happened?"

"I think we're safe. I'll fill you in later."

Stephen returned to the room and sat next to Eric, "It's all okay. We're safe."

Eric sat with his face in his hands, tears dripping to the floor.

Stephen held him and kept hoping that being there with him would be enough to console Eric as he looked at the sheikh who was unconscious on the floor. Blood oozed from his mouth and cuts on his face and chest. His hands and legs were tied to the chair. He was a pale comparison to the godly figure he portrayed himself.

Stephen felt the adrenaline leaving him as he said a silent prayer. The gods had been kind today.

CHAPTER 31

WORLD NEWS

Stephen said, "It's been a long time waiting. They took us here very fast from the ship to shore and brought us to this room. I think it's been nearly an hour that we've been left here. What do you think they want with us?"

Alex answered, "I think they're waiting to hear from their superiors before they engage us. Since we have time, tell me what happened and how we were saved."

Stephen replied as all eyes were on him. "I managed to send out an emergency message before everything went dead on the ship from the explosion."

As he was about to continue, the door opened and a well-dressed, statuesque woman in her forties entered with a few others following. She seemed someone of authority as she spoke. "Who is the one who planned the interruption on our airwaves?"

Stephen raised his hand.

She looked at him and continued, "That was a bold decision. Are you aware of what you have done?"

Stephen nodded and said, "I guess we were saved and that's why we're here."

Alex opened his mouth as if to speak but the woman raised her hand to indicate he should stay silent.

"As we speak now, governments around the world are talking to each other. I'd assume that the United Nations would soon be convening an emergency meeting. It was a contingency plan, was it not?" she asked, looking intently at Stephen, who seemed to be the only one who understood what she was talking about.

"We've been monitoring your situation for a while now. We had not anticipated that you might shield your activities by altering satellite coordinates. If not for the coordinates you gave, we would have gone fifty miles to another oil rig platform. I think you have a lot of explaining to do. It was very clever of you to send the video message."

Everyone but Stephen looked confused.

The woman asked the room, "Do you know what I'm talking about?"

No one replied.

She switched on the television in the room and said, "This has been played so many times now that we're getting irritated. Some of the channels have been able to stop it. Others are having trouble."

All turned to the television. On CCN, the news commentator said on Breaking News, "The last six hours, many news channels in the world had been hacked and a video played. A group led by the Shi Corporation has apparently succeeded in generating clean energy from the deep sea. They have been sabotaged but saved by a global response led by the Norwegians. We have news that the group is now safe in Norway." Behind him, the screen was filled with Stephen's video message.

He continued. "We have Professor Daniels, head of strategic research from the University of Galwan, with us now. Professor, how do you assess the situation? Did the video message do its job mobilizing the global community?"

The professor replied, "Yes, I think it did, but the response wouldn't be as fast. The video clip of the poor lady, Ms. Hato, made it reliable and urgent."

"Dear viewers, the following scene has been censored to protect the individuals. Let's see the video."

As Sukimi and Eric's conversation came on with their faces censored, Eric turned to Stephen and said, "How could you? How can you be so cruel? That's Sukimi."

"I'm sorry, Eric. I truly am. I didn't think I had a choice. I didn't think we all had a choice."

The woman switched off the television, now realizing only Stephen had full knowledge of his actions. She asked, "They didn't know? Stephen, am I correct?"

"Yes, I haven't told them," Stephen said.

"I must admit we were not prepared for any one person onboard your ship to take any aggressive action. That was a bad oversight on our part." she said sternly. "Our prime minister instantly recognized the lady in the video as Ms. Hato. They had been business associates in the shipbuilding industry before he became prime minister. He immediately mobilized the air force and navy. My government has issued a statement to say we were aware of Regenesis and that we knew about a live test being conducted in international waters off our territorial waters, and therefore it was not within our jurisdiction. We understood the project to be a scientific endeavor. It's unfortunate that some of your associates or investors did not take into consideration the bigger picture."

"What happens now?" Alex asked.

"You must be Dr. Alex Liang. And you must be Mr. Eric Shi." Alex and Eric nodded. "You and Regenesis are big news now. I believe your test was successful. There will be many people who will want to speak to you, important and powerful people who make decisions that affect all our lives. You may even have affected the global balance of power. That is a huge feat for one relatively small scientific project funded entirely, if I understand correctly, by private individuals. For now we wait— or to be more precise, you wait. In the meantime, before I leave you in the hands of my team, please allow me to congratulate you on your achievement."

Her tone had not changed one bit through her entire speech, and the bedraggled members of Regenesis seated before her took a minute to react when her last sentence sank in.

Katherine gasped and buried her face in her hands. Alex reached out and put his arm around her. He too was stunned by what the woman had said. He looked at Eric, who looked like his world had collapsed, walked over, and hugged him.

Alex felt Eric's sorrow too. He now understood the loss of Sukimi was more than that of a close friend.

"I'm so sorry. She was so brave. We could not have foreseen what happened. It should not have happened," Alex who was close to tears himself, said. A thread of regret wound itself in his thoughts and he bit his lip. What else could he say? They could not go back in time. They could not undo what had been done. The price for success had been very high. *Too high,* he thought.

Eric didn't look up at all. He was staring at the floor, seemingly focused on the patterns of the carpet. Alex didn't know what words of comfort he could offer and just sat silently beside Eric. He wondered if Eric would blame him now for all the events of the day. After all, Regenesis began with him.

Alex looked around the room. Everyone was silent. Instead of feeling the joy of success, this day was deemed a tragedy for all. Everyone looked glum and depressed. They appeared deep in thought, possibly recalling the events of the day.

It was evening before they gathered again in a conference room. They had been debriefed and their statements recorded. Stephen set up a webcam so that those in Taipei and Lumut could watch and listen to what Alex had to say.

Alex said, "I'm sure all of you are aware of the day's events. I shall not go into the details. I can confirm that we've had a successful test, and Regenesis is a success. We were sabotaged by two of our investors. Fortunately, with Stephen's help, which you all are very much aware by seeing the news, we're safe. There will be much to do. For us here, it has been much more of a tragedy than any success.

For now, please refrain from giving any statements or even talking to anyone regarding Regenesis until we're sure with whom we're dealing. We certainly do not want another sabotage."

Alex turned to Eric and asked, "Eric, would you like to say anything?"

Eric nodded, stood in front of the video cam, and said, "Thank you for all your hard work, which has brought a successful test." Eric's voice was solemn. He sat down immediately after his short message with a total blank expression on his face.

Alex was silent for a moment and then continued on the video chat. "I don't really know where to begin to explain how I now feel. Katherine will confirm that I have, for many years, harbored a wish to do something of great value. My turbines were sketched when Katherine was still a teenager. That was all Regenesis was for many years: my notes, my drawings, and my dream. Without Eric and all of you, it would have stayed that—a dream. I now understand that it takes more than one person's wishes and hopes to make a dream come true. It takes faith, patience, determination, and a team of good minds. It has also taken courage. More courage than your contracts required and more courage than I could ever have imagined. I thank you all for making my dream come true. It's now also your achievement as much as it has been my dream. But the price we've paid has been far too high. There shouldn't be a tragedy."

At this point, Alex looked at Eric and continued. "We've lost a valued member of Regenesis and a good friend. Sukimi Hato, like the rest of you, put her faith in us. She also invested time and money, without which we wouldn't have most of our most important equipment. She opened doors for us that we would never have been able to do ourselves. We also lost many members of the crew, including the guards, the captain, and his bridge crew. My daughter, Katherine, risked her life to stop the sabotage, along with many of the team. If not for Stephen's presence of mind, we wouldn't be alive now. I'm still shivering from the knowledge that we were so close to death."

At this, Alex finally broke down and tears rolled down his cheeks. Only by articulating the words did the full impact of what had happened hit him. The enormity of the danger they had all faced was now laid bare before him.

Alex pulled himself together and continued. "I'll do everything in my power to ensure that Regenesis sees its full potential and becomes the success we dreamed of for the whole world."

With that, Alex sat. Everyone present nodded. It was not the time to celebrate but to be grateful they had survived what might have been a calamity. Quietly they shook each other's hands and congratulated each other. Some cried. It would prove to be a long, sleepless night for them.

In bed that night, Alex could not sleep. The events kept rolling over and over in his mind. He felt guilt, anger, despair, pity, and sadness. The starting point had been him. That had led to the death of Sukimi and some of the crew. The sacrifice had been just too high. Sooner or later, someone would have found a way to tap the energy. It didn't need to end in tragedy. He would live with the guilt forever.

Four days later, they left Norway to return to their countries and families. Alex returned to Penang. In the limousine, Alex looked at Katherine. Half of Katherine's face had turned a livid blue-black over the few days, but that mark had now subsided. She had cracked a couple of ribs and held her left side. He was very proud of her.

He asked her, "What do you think we should say to your mum?"

Katherine replied, "Hmmm. I don't really know. Guess sorry?"

Once home, Lai Peng opened the door and came almost running out. To Alex's surprise, she hugged him and then Katherine. Without any words, she held both of them and walked them inside. This was not the reception they had expected.

Lai Peng said, "I thought I'd lost both of you. Those few hours of not knowing what had happened was unbearable. My mind went berserk, and I could not stop crying. I've never felt so much fear before."

Turning to Alex, she said, "How could you bring Katherine to such a dangerous situation? Surely you must have known there would be danger. How could you endanger our only daughter?"

Before Alex could reply, she turned to Katherine. "I wanted to go to the airport to meet you, but I thought I'd collapse waiting for you two. I was so worried for you and Alex. Katherine, why didn't you let me know you were going on such a dangerous trip? I thought you went along to write on the project."

She turned back to Alex. "You finally got your dream but nearly lost your life and Katherine's. What were you thinking about? Certainly not me, right? You wouldn't have considered my feelings. Was it worth it, Alex?"

Both husband and daughter were speechless as they did not expect Lai Peng's response.

"Never mind. I'm so happy you two are safe and back with me. But you two must promise never to hide anything from me again. I have a right to know!" she insisted.

Alex and Katherine nodded, somewhat relieved.

Eric returned to Taiwan and spent the next week with his family. When Eric saw Mei Lin at the airport, he just went up to her and hugged her. No words were exchanged. Their children were also silent. They had all witnessed the events on the news. Back home, Eric was depressed and hardly wanted to talk. Over the week, he slept most of the time. Mei Lin held him for long periods.

Eric finally managed to force himself to speak about Sukimi. The pain in Mei Lin's eyes could not be ignored when he spoke of Sukimi. He told Mei Lin of the first woman he had ever loved and how she had given her life on the platform. He confessed to the long friendship and the lingering affection he felt for her and of Sukimi's loyalty.

"Are you asking me for forgiveness?" Mei Lin asked quietly as she sat close to her husband.

"I have no right to ask for that," he said.

Mei Lin could sense that her husband was ashamed that he had not told her about Sukimi. "She is dead now. She died in a terrible way. She died a heroine. Would I have done the same for you had I been in her shoes? Who can say? I don't know. I've never been tested. The people we love will always be part of our lives, Eric. I cannot ask you to forget your past. I know you love me and you are a good husband and a wonderful father. Now we go forward."

Mei Lin gave her husband a tender look of love mixed with a profound understanding of his pain. She herself had walked through fire since viewing the video. While it had wounded her deeply to see the depth of her husband's love for another woman, feeling that she too would die soon from her cancer made Mei Lin resolve to heal Eric. Before long, she felt, he would have another death to mourn and would have to be strong for the children.

Husband and wife held each other for a long time, seemingly understanding each other even more. Their marriage bond was now even stronger.

On returning to Taiwan Stephen went to see Diana as soon as he could. "I'm sorry I had to tell the others about you. You are not angry with me?" he asked penitently.

Diana studied Stephen's face. Something had changed in it. She could only imagine what stress he had been under and what fear he had experienced.

She shook her head kindly and smiled. "It was a good thing you did or I'd have been in a lot of trouble with the authorities. I think they may have tracked me down. I was careful but they can be very determined. I think Regenesis and Eric's clout have protected me. I should be arrested but no one came. I know I'm not a secret anymore." Diana said in that sage and calm way she always spoke.

"Always a guardian angel," replied Stephen, "My savior, our savior!"

"Don't talk rubbish. One day I'll ask you for a big favor and you won't be allowed to refuse me!" she replied, laughing. "Are you going to buy me lunch now and give me the blow-by-blow account?"

Stephen leapt to his feet, grabbed the arms of her wheelchair, and together they went in search of a good meal. They would continue to share a friendship many would envy.

A week later, Eric and Alex were seated in Eric's office in Taipei with a few members of the team. Before them on the large conference table were press reports and other important communications that had been coming in. Several governments were claiming credit for assisting and supporting Regenesis. The United Nations had gone public in acknowledging Regenesis, and an invitation was sent to Eric and Alex to address the Assembly. Some countries made claims that they too were funding research in similar technology. Public opinion was extremely complimentary and supportive, especially in countries that did not claim to be big powers. Many nongovernmental agencies had written to offer further know-how and support to promote this alternative form of energy around the globe.

"How are you?" Alex asked Eric as he ignored the documents on the conference table.

"Mei Lin and I had talked about a lot of things. I'm okay. I'll get over it," Eric replied. He seemed to want to get on with the business at hand. "Now that Regenesis had worked, Stephen, I want you to head the whole thing. Get anyone you need from our corporation or institute. George has assured me that repairs to the platform are almost complete. Make sure the patents are properly filed, and we'll ensure that we can have control over the whole thing.

"I'm taking a leave of absence to spend time with Mei Lin. The good doctor here probably needs to get back to his work in Penang. Right, Alex?" Without waiting for a reply, he continued. "I think the whole thing will take off on its own now. There are many interested parties." He pointed to the documents on the table. "Shi's shares are up, and so are many shares on all the boards. Banks are coming to us now to lend money without asking. Everyone seems to want in."

Turning to Stephen again and then Katherine, he said, "I'm sure you can handle this. Katherine, give Stephen a hand with the legalities. Thank you, everyone, for coming."

Eric left the room even before they could gather their thoughts. Eric had to leave. He was not going to show his emotions. He felt unstable, especially with Alex around. He could not stop himself blaming Alex for Sukimi's death. Maybe he would in years to come.

PART 3

A LIFE TO SAVE

CHAPTER 32

RECONCILIATION

A month passed, and Lai Peng received a call from Mei Lin, informing her they were coming to Penang for a holiday. She was coming a few days in advance, as Eric couldn't leave as yet.

When she told Alex about their holiday in Penang, Alex recollected his conversation with the Shis when they first met. Eric had mentioned that he had something he wanted to talk about when the time came. He wondered if they were coming over for reasons other than a holiday.

A week later, while Mei Lin and Lai Peng had gone to shop, Alex was again busy in his practice. As the last patient left his clinic, Alicia walked in.

"So how is the adventurer today? Still busy?"

"No. Finishing. You know. Nowadays, you are the famous oncologist here. I just work here," he replied jokingly.

Alicia put a file on his table and said, "I think you should have a look at this."

"This looks important."

"Yes. Not long after you started your sabbatical, which is what I call your adventure, what you'll read in this orange file arrived for you. I think you should read it before I go on any further," she said.

Alex was curious and opened the file. He read through the letters from Dr. Yue in Taiwan and Alicia's replies to him. As he pored over the documents, he realized this was the thing Eric and Mei Lin wanted to tell him when the time was right.

The last letter was dated just two weeks ago. It ended with Dr. Yue's summary: "Mei Lin's condition has again relapsed. Although the relapse is early and she would benefit from further therapy, she would likely have additional side effects. She has also been informed that the response is unlikely to be better than previous. She has made the decision to see you in Penang. She has requested privacy and feels that if treatment can be in Penang, her condition can remain private."

He was stunned. For at least a few minutes, neither spoke.

Finally Alex said, "I didn't expect this at all. It's just too much to be a coincidence. What are the chances that we met, go for an adventure of a lifetime, and then realize they actually wanted to see me professionally? My heart is very heavy. Eric just lost his close friend. His wife is sick with incurable cancer. And he is one of the richest men in his country.

"But it now all makes sense. One thing led to another. If they were not coming to Penang, we wouldn't have met on the plane. My idea wouldn't have seen daylight. No wonder Eric was in a rush to try to complete Regenesis. He must have felt he owed me. No wonder he had invested so heavily in cancer-related pharmaceutical companies. Now it all makes sense. He is doing all these things to save her."

Alicia replied, "He owes you? What do you mean?"

"Did I say that? Just a figure of speech," Alex didn't want to reveal the incident on the plane.

Alicia replied, "He really loves her. So what do you want to do?"

"Eric is arriving today. I guess I have to meet them. Eric has kept more to himself these days, and I've hardly chatted or communicated with him. Now I know why they are in Penang," Alex said.

When Alex got home, Lai Peng greeted him at the door. "I have something to tell you. I just got back from shopping with Mei Lin. I think she is not well."

"Do you know if she has seen a doctor? What has she told you?" Alex asked, struggling to hide his knowledge of her condition. He was still a doctor and had to respect Mei Lin's privacy.

"She has, but I think they have misdiagnosed her. Mei Lin has a persistent cough. She tells me she has tried everything from herbal remedies to medicines prescribed by her doctor. The cough is getting worse. The poor woman has lost a lot of weight and is looking tired all the time. I think she does not sleep well, and she certainly has no appetite. I've noticed this since she arrived." Lai Peng replied.

Alex looked at his wife with new eyes. Lai Peng had never before offered anything that sounded remotely like a medical comment, and now she was speaking with confidence. "Why are you telling me all this?" he asked kindly, for it pleased him to hear words of concern from Lai Peng.

"What? You think I have no heart? You think I don't care about anything except enjoying myself?" she retorted with a smile.

Alex lowered his eyes. He did not want her to see the affirmation of his unpleasant thoughts about her.

"This has not been an easy marriage, husband," Lai Peng continued. "You and I probably had different ideas of what marriage would do for us. I know you've been unhappy for a long time. I have too. We're on the same ship but in different corners of it."

Alex shifted in his chair. Lai Peng had dared to give voice to the deep unhappiness they had both felt for the better part of their marriage. He had never found the courage to do that. It was clear Lai Peng had more to say.

"When you and Katherine shut me out for two years, keeping the secret of Regenesis to yourselves, I did not know what to do. I knew only you had become even more remote. I thought I had lost my daughter and my husband. I sought consolation from my friends, and they told me that as long as I heard no rumors about another woman, you were not going to leave me."

Alex almost leapt from the chair, partly in guilt and partly in anger. He was horrified that the thought had crossed Lai Peng's mind.

"Stay seated," she said in an imperious voice. "I haven't finished."

Alex kept silent and resisted folding his arms, for he knew it would look hostile if he did.

"I did not think you were cheating on me. Whatever I did not like about your behavior, I knew you were not seeing another woman. I know you're not that kind of man. Maybe it was your principles, which you have always been unbending about, that helped me decide to marry you. I've always admired your principles, especially as a doctor." Lai Peng was silent for a moment, as if to gather strength.

"Your work and your daughter were always more important than I was. Everyone in Penang and in the whole country knows your name, know about your work as an oncologist. People travel from all over Asia to seek your help. I know all this. All my married life I've received respect because of your work. A long time ago it was because I was beautiful and wealthy, but for a long time now I've been known as Mrs. Liang, the oncologist's wife. You have made me very proud—jealous but proud," Lai Peng said, fiddling with the tablecloth.

Her words took Alex's breath away, and he could only mutter thank you before she continued.

"But when I saw that video and finally learned what you and Katherine had been doing all this time, my head almost exploded. My whole family nearly died out there, and I had to learn about it on the news. Thank goodness I had the TV on or I might have learned it from my friends. I don't think I'll ever forgive you for doing that to me, but I discovered something important that day."

Alex waited. The woman now talking to him was not who he had believed her to be. This was someone else, someone he could admire.

"I realized how important you are to me," she said with a choke in her voice, "I realized you had grown distant from me because I was, maybe, unreachable. Maybe looking outside more than inside. I felt ashamed that you did not share your great secret with me. That you only shared it with Katherine. I felt ashamed that she loved you more than I did, that she nearly died trying to save Regenesis for you. I felt ashamed for pushing my husband and daughter away so they only had each other to give them encouragement."

Lai Peng let her tears fall and ignored the handkerchief Alex offered her.

"Don't think I'm a stupid woman, Alex. I may not have appeared to care, but I've been a doctor's wife for too long not to be able to work a few things out for myself. Mei Lin is very ill. We've become good friends in the last few months. She is an example to me, and I'm not too proud to learn. Please help her."

With that, Lai Peng fell silent and wiped away the tears on her face with both hands.

Alex sat back in his chair. He wanted to reach for his wife and hold her close, but a habit of a lifetime prevented him from doing so. Instead, he put one hand out, and Lai Peng put a hand in his. He squeezed it.

"I'll try," he said and cleared his throat. His marriage, it seemed, had turned a corner for the better, but it had taken a crisis and near disaster to achieve that.

"Eric should have arrived in Penang by now," Lai Peng said as she looked at her watch. "But it's late. Maybe we can ask them over tomorrow. This afternoon, Mei Lin asked if you'll be free tomorrow. I think they plan to talk to you."

With a soft sigh of relief, Alex realized he didn't need to ask Mei Lin. The last letter from Dr. Yue clearly stated they would be seeing him or Alicia. He would need to keep it a secret until they met up with them.

"I'll call Mei Lin tomorrow morning. Can you see her tomorrow?" Lai Peng asked.

"Of course. My clinic hours are much lighter than they used to be. Anytime would be fine."

CHAPTER 33

A SECRET NO MORE

Eric and Mei Lin arrived at the Liangs in the late morning. Both wore solemn facial expressions as they walked in hand in hand.

Lai Peng greeted them as they entered. "Good morning."

Alex stood just behind her, and he smiled and nodded.

"Good morning to you too," Mei Lin said.

Eric didn't speak and just nodded in acknowledgement. It was so unlike Eric to be quiet.

As they sat in the living room and tea was served, Mei Lin asked, "Did you get Dr. Yue's letter?" She was so composed as she spoke.

Alex observed the Shis from the moment the entered. Eric was avoiding eye contact and seemed to be in thought most of the time. He and Mei Lin held hands throughout.

Alex said, "Yes I did. I only read it yesterday. Alicia showed me the letters from Dr. Yue to us."

Mei Lin said, "Then it's easier. I wanted Dr. Yue to inform you first so it would save me the pain of talking about my illness."

Alex turned to Lai Peng, who now seemed a bit confused. She probably wondered why Alex didn't say anything the night before. He said, "I'm sorry. I only knew hours before we talked. I was quite stunned when I read the letters. But without Mei Lin's permission, I couldn't talk about her illness. But I really appreciate that you realized Mei Lin was unwell. I really was so aloof and didn't realize anything."

He looked at Mei Lin as if to ask her permission to continue to brief his wife. She nodded.

"Mei Lin has lung cancer and has been on treatment for the last few years. Unfortunately the cancer has returned again. Dr. Yue is her oncologist in Taiwan. Mei Lin wishes to be in Penang to continue her care away from the limelight in Taiwan."

Turning to Mei Lin, Alex said, "I'm sorry I didn't realize you were ill. My obsession with Regenesis made me lose all my senses to things and people around. I should have realized and asked you or Eric sooner."

"You wouldn't have realized. I'm good at keeping secrets—right, Eric?" she asked with a sense of humor and a smile toward her husband, whose face was extremely glum. Eric nodded as a reply. "So would you be kind enough to be my doctor for the time I have left?"

Alex's eyes were now about to spill tears. He had to hold back. He fully admired Mei Lin. Even at this moment, she was composed and seemed to be a source of strength for her husband. While Eric seemed to be near his breaking point now, she was fully composed. She was obviously holding back her emotions and didn't let them show.

"Of course, I will. However, if you would allow me, I need Dr. Alicia's help. I fear my clinical skills have deteriorated in the last two to three years."

"I don't see a problem with that. Dr. Yue also thinks highly of her. But I wish to have full confidentiality. The last thing I want is publicity, as you know I value my family more than anything else. The last thing I need is the publicity to interfere with my family life. This is what has kept me going so far."

Alex turned to Lai Peng and said, "We have to keep this a total secret."

Lai Peng nodded and said, "Not a word will come from me."

Mei Lin said to her, "You are really the best friend one can have. You wanted Alex to see me because you realized I was unwell? I'm truly touched. Thank you." Tears rolled down Lai Peng's face. Alex handed her a tissue and held her hand.

Lai Peng said, "I'm so sorry. I wish I could do more for you. I'm ..." She was unable to continue as she sobbed for her close friend.

"Now, now. I'm fine. I've lived with this for many years now. Way longer that the doctors thought possible. And with Alex here, I have no fear," Mei Lin said.

Alex was even more amazed with Mei Lin. She was the ill one. Normally everyone else would have to console the patient. Now the patient was consoling her husband and friend. This didn't seem real. His admiration for her continued to another level. He felt the urge to go over and hold her shoulders or lay her head on his shoulder. He was speechless.

"What shall we do now, Alex?"

"I guess we could start with going over to the hospital and get you checked out," Alex replied.

"We could, but I'm okay today. Let's just have lunch and we'll be at your clinic first thing tomorrow morning. Eric just arrived, and I wish to spend some time today together," Mei Lin said.

"Okay. I'll arrange that," Alex said.

Lunch was indeed an awkward situation. Mei Lin led the conversations. She talked about everything but her illness. Surprisingly, they even laughed. Only Eric was still in his own thoughts most of the time.

In the limousine going back to their apartment, Mei Lin whispered to Eric while she held onto his arm, "A penny for your thoughts."

Eric didn't reply. Instead he embraced her with a bear hug. The last few hours had been difficult for him. He could not stop blaming Alex for Sukimi's death. Now he had to put his wife's life in Alex's hands. He couldn't lose her, he thought. But could he trust Alex? He'd caused him to lose Sukimi. The whole Regenesis was his mistake to trust Alex. He was not at all sure about Alex anymore. Throughout lunch, he didn't want to speak. If he did, he would probably start blaming Alex and questioned his judgment and sincerity. He didn't want to do that. He loved Mei Lin and wouldn't want to upset her. He hoped Mei Lin was right and Alex was the one who could help her. Meanwhile he would continue trying to accelerate the research and finding a cure for her through his investments in pharmaceutical companies.

The next morning Alicia and Alex were waiting for Mei Lin when she and Eric arrived. Lai Peng had insisted she accompany her and insisted on fetching them. Soon the Shis were in Alex's consultation suite waiting for the results of her tests.

Mei Lin looked at her husband, studying his expression. She knew he loved her very much and always looked out for her. Ever since the tragedy with Regenesis, he was different. He talked less and communicated less with her. She knew he was still in emotion pain.

She said, "It'll be fine. We've gone through this more than once. We'll be able to conquer it again." Deep inside she didn't really have the confidence anymore. "We have each other."

"I can't lose you. I just can't," Eric said with a trembling voice.

She felt his pain. In some ways, Eric was a boy when it came to emotions. He didn't find it easy when she was the focus. His emotions for her interfered with his judgment and objectivity.

At that moment, Alex opened the door and entered with Alicia. Mei Lin could see Lai Peng sitting outside alone.

Alex said, "We have the test results. Let's talk about your PET scan. The good news is, the amount of spread is not much. It is only in both lungs. There are no other sites that are involved we can see. But we cannot operate."

Mei Lin thought, *If that's the good news, what's the bad news?*

Almost as if Alex could read her thoughts, he said, "The bad news is we need to start chemotherapy. But chemotherapy is gentle these days. You'll generally feel normal. Your appetite may reduce, but vomiting almost always doesn't occur. A bit of nausea is possible. The intravenous medication we use is called Alimta. We usually combine it with cisplatin, another drug, to make it more effective. It stands a good chance to work for you."

Mei Lin and Eric did not look surprised. Alex realized they probably had already heard this from Dr. Yue.

"The other possibly good news is that another medication called Afatinib is almost available. We should be able to get it soon."

Eric asked, "How soon?"

"In a couple of months. It's almost US approved. Once it's approved, we should be able to get it outside a trial."

Shortly after, Alex and Alicia left the room. Alex had asked them to think it over.

Mei Lin gave a sigh and said, "We've been through this. Somehow it's just as difficult as the last. It's as if you know you have to push the button to open the door. But you don't know what's on the other side. You have opened so many doors before going into rooms and places, but when you don't know what to fully expect, there is always apprehension. Eric, we should just go for it and hope for the best; whatever is on the other side is okay."

Eric was not so sure. He could see the faith Mei Lin had for Alex. To him, if it were not Alex, the decision would be simple. Maybe he should suggest Alicia be her doctor. But Mei Lin seemed to only have faith in Alex, and he knew that with cancer, you have to have faith. Without hope, your whole mental and emotional state would fall apart. He had seen how Mei Lin reacted before when she'd had a relapse.

With a heavy heart, Eric replied, "If that's what you want, okay."

Mei Lin replied, "It should be what we want. I understand you've been under much emotional pressure since Regenesis. But you have to move on. I'll be here for you and want to be here for you. This is the only way I know how. Alex gives me the confidence to carry on as you have given me these years. Alicia will also look out for me. We need to do this."

Eric tried to smile as he looked into her eyes. Her eyes were glistering as tears swelled. He had to be strong and even stronger for her now. "Let's do it then. I'll be at your side forever. The kids need you all the more. We always have hope. I'm sure my investments will pay off soon and we'll find the cure. The best of the best are working toward it."

"I thought I had lost you on the airplane," she said quietly as she stroked her husband's hair. "Then I thought I had lost you when I watched the terrible video, but you survived both, so I'll try. Somehow the gods are still watching over us. Alex once saved your life and he will save mine." She stroked her crucifix as she spoke.

Eric could only nod. He didn't want her to see his loss of faith in Alex. It would be revealed in his voice. With the decision made, the couple held each other tightly, feeling the warmth from each other and the warm tears slowly rolling down their cheeks.

CHAPTER 34

AN ILLNESS WITHOUT A CURE

Alicia said, "How did the meeting go in Singapore? Anything new we can use?" They were sitting in the small lounge behind their consultation suites.

Alex sipped his coffee and replied, "There are many interesting things coming. The trials for targeting the immune response to lung cancer have started. But I think it will be a while before we can get some of it. There are clinical trials. They are all at the moment for later-stage illness. Vaccine trials have all failed after so much money invested." He gave a sigh. "I don't think there are any major breakthroughs. But we should get Mei Lin on the trial once she worsens again."

Alex had his hands over his face. He has been thinking of every possible way to try to improve Mei Lin's treatment. He felt lost. It's been two months since he and Alicia had taken over Mei Lin's care.

He rubbed his eyes. "At the moment, we give her the best possible and hope in the near future a breakthrough comes."

Alicia replied as she sat beside him, a cup of tea in hand, "You have already caught up with the research and literature on lung cancer. I think you know more than I do. I'm confident the great Alex will come up with something. You always have."

"You have more confidence in me than I have in myself. Alicia, it's really different this time."

"I understand. But there is only so much one can do."

Alex thought, *You don't know how I feel. My admiration for her has grown until it changed. Now I'm attracted to her. I think of her day and night. I need to think of how to find her a cure but instead I'm just daydreaming of her, smiling, talking, and caring. You wouldn't know.*

Alicia continued. "I can see you have taken a personal interest. It can cloud your judgment, you know? But of course you know. She is some lady. Controlled and so elegant."

Alex wondered if Alicia had read his thoughts. "She is, isn't she?"

"Hey, I know you so well, you know? Fifteen years and counting. That's how long I've known you, Alex. A word of advice. Concentrate on her illness, and everything should work out."

The nurse came in and said, "Dr. Moy, the patient is ready for you in your room."

"Sorry, got to work a bit. We'll talk more later," she said and left.

Alex lay back on the comfortable sofa chair and stretched out. His bones ached and muscles strained. A few soft "cracks" could be heard as he stretched. *I'm certainly getting old,* he thought. *Interesting advice from Alicia. Maybe she's right.* Alex continued in his own thoughts for the next twenty minutes.

"Come, let's let up a bit," Alicia said as she shook him awake from his thoughts. He was half-asleep. "We'll go into my room."

As he walked with Alicia, he asked, "So what do you have in mind?"

"Ah, it's time to just let it all go for a while," she said as she walked into her room. She opened the lowest drawer on the desk and took out a bottle of whiskey. "I've been keeping it for an occasion. It's vintage by now."

"What is there to celebrate?" Alex asked.

"Not to celebrate, but an occasion where we need to let it all go and drink and forget it all. Mei Lin is doing well with her chemo. The Alimta is working great. She has improved. Her weight had gone up. Let's relax for tonight. Just you and me drink away the blues. You deserve it. You are saving the world with your green technology. We've succeeded in helping Mei Lin. We have time. One day off won't matter."

"I suppose you're right. Give me a big glass. Haven't had a drink for ages. Remind me to call the driver. I certainly won't be driving back tonight."

"Ha-ha. Agreed. Let's drink to all good things to come," she said, pouring a full glass for Alex. She passed it to him and they toasted the whisky away.

An hour later, with conversations about nothing, they were almost drunk. Certainly the alcohol had loosened them up. They laughed over silly things they had done together in the practice.

"Do you remember the broad Chinese lady who you got well when all didn't work for her? The one who went to Singapore and Kuala Lumpur seeking treatment before she came to you? Madam Tan, I think was her name," Alicia said.

"She was here this week and asked for you. Since you've been away, she asks for you every time she comes. You have an admirer."

"Ha. Yes, I remember. She is okay, isn't she?"

"She's fine. I think she had a crush on you. Every time she comes and sees you, she buys breakfast for all of us. Since you didn't see her, no more breakfast for us. There goes our free breakfast. She told my nurse you are handsome. Look like a film star!"

"Yeah. I worry the way she looks at me sometimes. Anyway, thanks for looking after her."

"What made you give her Megace when she had failed three lines for chemotherapy for her ovarian cancer?"

"Ah, well. I'm old, as you know. Before established chemotherapy, we gave it to almost every patient. Although it worked only in a handful of patients, it was still worth a shot."

"Old is gold then! A toast to the old man," she said laughingly. "By the way, the whiskey is from her. She came wanting to give it to you. Instead she had to see me. So I got the whiskey!"

Alex smiled and they laughed together. The alcohol was working.

Alex thought, *Yeah. Old is gold. If it's meant to be you, you'll respond to treatment,* and he reflected on how he had treated her. Suddenly a thought came to his mind. An idea. He needed to think it through. He wouldn't say a word yet to Alicia.

The next morning, he had a hangover. A splitting headache. It was noon before he was sober. Luckily it was the weekend and he didn't need to work. As he sobered, he remembered the flash idea he'd had the night before.

The idea was simple. New researchers and new doctors have not known about medicine and research in the past. Many useful agents may have been overlooked and not gone into commercial development. In the past, agents were generally tested individually. They were sometimes combined empirically without much science behind it, as with most old medications, the exact mechanisms how they worked were not well known. He would look back at all the chemicals and drugs that had been looked at in the last sixty years. They should not leave any stone unturned to find the answer. They needed to combine them to improve the chances for a successful treatment. Instead of looking at where the current research was heading, he would need to look at old research and come up with something new.

His quest for some patients had been successful in the past, like with Madam Tan. Maybe he would hit the lottery again with Mei Lin. He couldn't lose Mei Lin. But he would need help. He would spend the weekend thinking over his idea and putting it on paper. He would then seek help.

The following morning Alex called Stephen, "Good morning, Stephen. How is everything with Regenesis?"

Stephen replied, "The further testing is successful and we've sent the first shipment of hydrogen to Lumut in Malaysia. Everything is going smoothly. By the end of the year, we'll be in full production. The second and third platform with the submersibles are being built as we speak."

"And Katherine?"

"She's fine. She's in the Hague right now, negotiating contracts with many countries. I think she is having the time of her life. Angelina is with her. She should be back in Taipei in two days.

"That's great. Stephen, there's an urgent matter I need to speak to you about."

"You sound serious, Alex. How can I be of help?"

"I can't discuss it on the phone. Maybe when Katherine is back, you can come to Penang with her." Alex felt he could not tell Stephen about Mei Lin over the phone. He had to see him. "Or I can fly over the coming weekend."

"No need. Katherine actually planned to return to Penang this weekend. I shall come along. I hope it's nothing too serious. We'll talk then when Katherine and I arrive in Penang this weekend."

"Thank you, Stephen," Alex replied. He trusted Stephen. He needed his technological and computer-hacking skills. Alex needed someone he could trust in research. He knew who he wanted.

He placed his next call. "Felix Cardune? Hi. This is Alex."

"Hi. This is a first. Didn't expect to hear from you. Chatted with you in Singapore. Didn't think you would call so soon."

"Well, good friend, I may have good news for you. Since Attis Pharmaceuticals retrenched you, I have the chance to get your help with something I have in mind."

"I'm all ears. I have nothing on my plate. Attis really did me in. I didn't expect to be sacked. Downsizing was their excuse. Sales bad, retrench the scientist. Madness. So what have you got in mind?"

"Well, I need someone who knows the old tricks and has been in research longer than I've been. I'm working on a new theory. If I can count you in, I'll send you the ticket to Penang. We'll talk in Penang in private."

"Like I said, I don't have anything else to do. Feels strange you're looking for an old guy like me and not chasing someone young and energetic. We're now discarded as trash. Send the ticket and I'll be there. Hopefully this old man gets another shot at something great."

"Okay, then. My secretary will arrange it and we'll see you this weekend. Thanks for agreeing." Alex felt a little excitement in his veins again. He was starting on another energetic and out-of-the-box thinking endeavor.

Later that night over dinner, Alex said, "Lai Peng, I have something to tell you."

"I see you've been doing a lot of thinking. Finally I get to know," Lai Peng replied, putting down her utensils and turning to him to give him her full attention.

With a smile, Alex said, "I've come up with an idea, a theory, that I need to see through. It may help Mei Lin. It's a theory and nothing more at the moment."

"I'm all ears."

Alex explained his theory to her. He realized Lai Peng was listening intently, trying hard to understand everything he was explaining.

"So what do you think?" Alex asked.

Lai Peng said, "Well, if you want my frank opinion … if it can be done, I think only you can do it."

"Hmmm," Alex said. Lai Peng seemed to be very understanding. Both of them had really changed. "I do hope the theory can be realized."

"I hope so too. I'll be beside you all the way. This time I'll be at your side, not Katherine," she said with a smile.

Alex smiled back, taking the hint. He would keep it a secret from Katherine.

He needed to text Stephen to ask him to keep this secret from Katherine for now. He would have the week to research more on his theory or hunch. Hopefully it would all bear fruit. Alicia would have to run the clinics for now.

"We need money to do this. A lot of money if we move ahead."

Lai Peng replied, "Whatever it takes. It's fine with me." She walked over to Alex and hugged him from behind.

Alex felt the warmth and at the same time a sense of guilt as he harbored feelings for Mei Lin.

"How was your flight, Felix?" Alex asked as they left the limousine. "The driver will get your luggage. I see you came prepared for a long stay," Alex said as he saw at least six bags being unloaded.

Felix whispered, "I brought all my things. You know I got sacked. Melbourne is rather far for now."

"No problem at all. If you join me, you'll be here for some time. We'll talk business after dinner. Just keep the business part quiet until we have a chance to be alone."

"I shall not say a word about it. My word," Felix replied with a slight chuckle.

"Come and meet my family. This is Katherine, my daughter. Lai Peng, my wife. And this is Stephen, our very good friend." Alex introduced everyone as they walked into the living room.

Felix said, "Nice to meet you all. Sorry I'm late. My flight was delayed as usual. Bad weather."

Lai Peng said, "Welcome to our small home. Dinner is almost ready. You must be hungry."

"Small? This is nice. Very big," Felix replied. Everyone laughed.

Over dinner, the conversation switched to Regenesis.

Stephen said, "Regenesis is going into full production soon. We managed to tweak the system a bit more, and we're getting even better efficiency. Only 10 percent energy loss."

"That's amazing. Sure the figures are correct?" Alex asked.

"They are. The UN team collaborating with us estimates that in two years, 10 percent of the world's energy will come from us."

"Don't take them too seriously. They always come up with figures that fall short," Alex said.

Katherine replied, "I think it's a fair estimate. The meeting in Hague was good. Contracts were signed, and we're ready to form the first worldwide multinational company that will join us as partners. We hold 51 percent shares. The company holds the rest. Every country has been given the privilege to buy shares according to their GDP. We kept a minimum of some shares for all small countries. It wasn't easy to negotiate with so many countries. Stephen and I played hardball and stayed firm, a take-it-or-leave-it stance. Luckily it came through."

"Wow! Katherine the Great!!" her father said with a grin.

"Amazing story, Regenesis. And it continues to be," Felix said full of praise.

"My father started it all with his dream of a better world," Katherine replied. "A toast to Daddy!"

After they toasted, Alex said, "Felix here is quite an accomplished scientist. Someone I admire and aspire to be. Felix was instrumental in developing a whole new class of medicine for cancer treatment. He believed in and spent two years creating a molecule to target cancer cells. More precisely, leukemia. His breakthrough led to nearly half of all new medications that exist for cancer today. A toast to Felix!"

Alex raised his glass and they all toasted.

Felix said, "It wasn't as adventurous as Regenesis. Hard work. Lonely, hard work. But my mind sparkles when I see the molecules in my mind. It's so exciting. But my company didn't think so. This time, my research didn't bear fruit."

Alex said, "Sorry, mate. These days companies don't value their workers as they used to. Must be too much football as they say. Sack, hire, and sack and hire for instant success. But medicine is not football. It takes time, and research has its ups and downs. Too much share market response and the CEOs are just there to make sure of profits. Anyway, now you have time to spend with us."

Stephen raised his glass and said, "Let's toast to a better and fairer future."

After coffee and tea, Lai Peng asked to be excused and said to Katherine, "Follow me, Katherine. I have some dresses I'd like you to try on. We shall leave these gentlemen to their chat about life."

When they left, Alex said, "Thank you for coming on such short notice. I hope this will be worth your while, Felix. While brainstorming for ideas, I realized we might have overlooked many compounds or medicines that we could use to treat cancer. More specifically, lung cancer. What if this is true and the answers are already in front of us but discarded in the past? There are possibilities."

Felix said, "I'm sure many have gone down that road, Alex."

"I agree. But how far down the road have they gone? Over the week, I've tried to retrieve data on old medications and publications dating back to the 1950s. Research then was scanty and not really as scientific as it is today. I need you as a theoretical biochemist to help me plough through the data and start new tests."

Felix frowned. "It'll be like looking for a needle in a haystack. Chances are poor and near zero. But I think you already know that. Tell me more."

"Well, that's why I've asked Stephen here to come. He's the best computer software scientist around."

"Of course he is. That television thing you did was amazing," Felix said, acknowledging Stephen's role in saving Regenesis.

"So what's my role?" Stephen asked with a puzzled look.

"I need your help to write the software to run a program to test the chemicals we'll look at. There is now so much information that we can possibly do simulated tests on the computer. That will quicken the search."

"What program do you have in mind?"

"I was hoping you could create something like the gaming programs today. The landscape is set, yet it changes with the environment, with players interacting. Not one but many, just like Internet games. The landscape will be the inner works of the human cell. The players are the chemicals or compounds we introduce into the landscape and see how they interact," Alex answered.

By now, Felix was deep in thought. He said, "That's a first. It sounds logical. What time frame and what do you hope to achieve, Alex?"

"Maybe a year, give or take. I hope we can at least come up with some combination that can retard lung cancer. I know a cure is not going to be easy or even possible."

"Why now? Why are you pushing forward with this when there is absolutely nothing concrete at all about your idea?" Felix asked. Stephen was also looking at him with a worried and puzzled expression.

"If I tell you, you have to promise to keep it a total secret."

They both nodded.

"Mei Lin has lung cancer and has already failed many treatments." Alex knew he had broken his promise to her and Eric for total secrecy. He had to in order to help her.

Stephen was taken aback and looked shocked for a moment.

Alex continued to explain. "She's had lung cancer for five to six years now. As it is, her current treatment is working. But for how much longer? She has been under my care for the last few months.

"They do not want anyone to know. That's why she is having treatment in Penang and not Taiwan. She doesn't want you to know, Stephen."

Felix asked, "Who is she?"

Alex realized he had not introduced Mei Lin. "She is the wife of Mr. Eric Shi, the head of Shi Corporation."

Felix immediately connected the dots. "Eric Shi. *The* Eric Shi. Oh. I understand now. The Shi Corporation has been pouring money into the pharmaceuticals. There is a rumor that he wanted to take over and merge companies to gain further profits. It seems he has another agenda."

"Correct," Alex replied.

Felix asked, "Why don't you run the idea past him and start it all with the Shi Corporation?"

"Two reasons. One, I do not want their hopes to rise and then we fail. Two, I sense Eric no longer thinks he can trust me. He has kept his distance from me since Norway. So, approaching Eric with such an idea wouldn't be ideal."

Stephen said, "I've realized that too. Eric is not the same since Norway. We've just got to give him time. Airing Sukimi's death has also caused him to distance himself from me. I don't think he has forgiven me either."

Felix said, "So there seems to be a personal agenda. If you want to proceed, I have the time. I'll give it my best shot."

Alex said, "Thank you," and turned to Stephen with an enquiring look.

"Well, I can only try. To make such a program is not going to be easy at all."

"Let's take the next two weeks to brainstorm and research further before we put together a larger team," Alex said.

Both nodded in agreement.

When Felix had left to go to his room, Stephen continued to talk to Alex. "I'm quite sad now. I never imagined Mei Lin is so ill. This should not have happened to her. She's like my own mother. I'm not sure I can do this, Alex."

Alex said, "We have to be strong. That's the only way we can truly help her. Lai Peng knows what we're up to. At the moment, please don't mention this to Katherine. Lai Peng's request."

Stephen said, "I'll do whatever it takes to make her well. If money is needed, just tell me. I have much more than I'll ever need. When we move ahead, I'll form the team."

Alex realized he had said *when* instead of *if.* Stephen had fully committed.

"Well, there is more that you can do. You can help me access systems for the data we'll need. The pharmaceuticals, trial organizers, and medical publishers all keep information in private servers that we have to access. The information they hold will certainly help. That means we need to hack into the programs and systems. We don't have time to slowly ask permission from each and every one of them."

"That's never a problem for me. Consider it done."

"That's good. We need all the information we can get our hands on. Only then can Felix get to work. Hope you can work with him. That's settled then. And how are you and Katherine?" Alex asked, knowing they had been spending more time together. Katherine's chats with Alex had mentioned Stephen a lot.

"We're fine. I like her a lot."

Alex smiled and replied, "Keep her safe. I love her very much. Take care of her for me."

CHAPTER 35

A SEARCH BEGINS

Research is never easy. It was two months since the three of them met in Penang. Stephen had a team of software engineers and game programmers onboard. They were now working together in a remote location outside Taipei. The tons of information Felix had looked over had paid off with at least 60 percent of landscape programmed. The areas that were yet to be programmed appeared as black patches, almost like missing pieces of a jigsaw puzzle.

Felix had been true to his word and started to work tirelessly, up to twenty hours a day. He had gathered a small team of three scientists he knew. Two were recently retired and were excited to have one last chance to participate in possible groundbreaking research. He needed Joan, an African American coworker he'd worked with for ten years before he was sacked. It was hard to convince her to leave her job and join them. Money mattered, and she came aboard with a guarantee of five years' salary regardless of success, with another five-year salary bonus if they succeeded. She was one of the best brains in theoretical chemistry.

They were housed in a bungalow on the mainland that was owned by Lai Peng, a gift from her father when she married. They had to be sure Mei Lin and Eric continued to be unaware of their new project.

"How many compounds have we identified so far?" Alex asked.

Joan said, "About three hundred. Possibly a hundred can be brought forward. As we discussed, at least we know the targets much better than we did twenty years ago. I think we can get something out of this."

"And the landscape?" Alex asked.

"Stephen has been great. Much has been done, but I'm afraid we still have much to do," Felix said.

"How much longer do you think we'll need before we can start trying?" Alex asked.

Stephen replied through the conference video link, "If we can have the remaining data, it should be fast. And that depends on the data."

"Could we start running even if we cannot fully make the landscape?"

"Trickier. We could extrapolate, but it may not be as accurate as we want."

"Okay then. We wait to finish the landscape. Once ready, we'll run the tests as fast as we can."

"Alex, I think I have a suggestion to hasten things. It would also result in more accurate data to program the landscape," Felix said.

"What do you have in mind?" Alex asked.

"I think we need a good sample of the cancer," Felix said.

"That's easier said than done. Biopsy has its dangers. And I presume we would need adequate large samples," Alex answered.

"We had discussed this and think the best way is have the sample. And we can do a full genetic analysis of it. NexGen in America can help us do the genetic mapping of her cancer that we need. Felix has a good contact there. We'll be able to do more than the commercial side," Joan added.

"Let me see what I can do. I understand. The information you are using is from other lung cancer cell lines."

Felix said, "If we can, we'd like to try to make a cell line out of the cancer cells. Then we can easily test the compounds more accurately."

"That will take time. More than we have," Alex said.

"Not necessarily. My friends in Singapore will be able to create the cell lines in less than a month," Felix replied.

"All right, I understand. We'll need the sample from her. I'll see to that."

With Alicia present, Mei Lin's latest scan was shown on the screen in his consultation clinic. "Looks pretty good. Much of the tumor has shrunk about 30 percent. But those two areas seem worse. What do you think, Alicia?"

"I think she is stable and we continue her chemotherapy for now. She is doing well clinically and putting on weight. Her cough is almost gone. We do have the afatinib already here for her, but I'd only use it if she gets worse."

"I think we should re-biopsy her."

Surprised, Alicia asked, "Why? That would change our decision?"

"I think we should think toward her future. I read NexGen can sequence the genes and maybe help us guide her treatment."

"We've not used their services until now. I guess it may be useful. Cost certainly will not be an issue. But will Mei Lin want it?"

"If we recommend it together, I think she would. Are you with me?"

"Alex, I sense you're up to something and not telling me. You want to share?"

Alex had avoided telling Alicia so far. He would have to, as he needed her to persuade Mei Lin into a biopsy. "I guess I have no choice. Can't fool you."

"We've known each other long enough to know when one of us is hiding something. So?"

"I've started a small group to try to find new medications for her, and we need a sufficient sample of her tumor to proceed further."

"Sounds like you have to fill me in a lot," Alicia said as she sat down, seeking a long explanation.

When Alex finished explaining, Alicia said, "I'm amazed. You never give up, do you? I wonder where you get all your ideas. Wish I could think up some too."

Alex looked directly into her eyes and asked, "Are you with me on this?"

After a few seconds, she replied, "Of course. I'll persuade her to have the biopsy. If there's a chance it will help her, we should."

Lai Peng was out with Mei Lin shopping as they discussed her imminent biopsy. They had bought beautiful dresses and handbags.

While having tea in the complex, Lai Peng said, "You're looking better and better. How are you feeling?"

"Better, thank you. Today is a good day. Some days are not so good. Thank you for asking me out today. It feels great to get out."

"Shopping therapy is a girl's best friend," Lai Peng said and they laughed.

"I'll see Alicia and Alex tomorrow. The scan and blood results should be ready. Can you come with me? I didn't tell Eric. I didn't want him to rush over to come with me for the results."

"Of course I will," Lai Peng replied, reaching out to hold Mei Lin's hand. She could see Mei Lin had improved. Her color was back. She had put on some weight. Her skin tone was much better. She was also more relaxed and appeared happy. "I'm sure the results will be fine."

Two days later, in the radiology department, Eric was with Mei Lin and Alex. Eric said, "Are you sure the biopsies are necessary? I didn't hear that re-biopsies are essential."

"Alex and Alicia told me that they want more samples of my cancer to analyze the genes. They think doing the tests with NexGen may help me. I'm okay with the biopsies," Mei Lin reassured her husband.

"If that's what you want," Eric replied.

Mei Lin felt a touch of sadness that Eric didn't seem to be confident with her treatment in Penang. She would keep quiet for now. She wanted Eric to be with her. She squeezed his hand tight.

"They are ready for you now," the nurse said, guiding Mei Lin into the CT scan room for her biopsy.

Another two months passed. Alex sat with his team in the bungalow, video conferencing with Stephen in Taipei.

Stephen said, "We're nearly finished with the landscape. My team has started programming the individual compounds' characteristics. We should be able to do the first screening for the compounds in the next few weeks."

Felix said, "The biopsies were really helpful. Without them, the landscape would be different. We've narrowed down the list of compounds to about eighty now. The real clinical test will need to be done later. How are we going to do that?"

"I don't know actually. The list you showed me last week had at least 80 percent of compounds that had been tested in phase one trials. So we probably don't need to repeat those."

"I agree, but we still need to get the rest tested if the computer simulations are successful."

"I'll figure that one out later. Let's find those compounds."

With Christmas around the corner, and nearly ten months on chemotherapy, Mei Lin joined Lai Peng and Katherine for Christmas shopping. "These ornaments are so nice. We should get them for our tree," Katherine said.

"You didn't like to decorate the tree before," Lai Peng said teasingly. She knew why. "Want to impress Stephen?"

Katherine smiled.

Mei Lin started to laugh. Then she suddenly coughed and continued to cough.

"Are you okay?" Lai Peng asked.

She continued to cough and suddenly coughed out blood.

"Oh, no!" Lai Peng said. "Katherine, call Daddy now. We need to go to the hospital."

Lai Peng and Katherine helped Mei Lin to the limousine and they rushed to the hospital.

Outside the ER, Katherine asked her mother, "Did you know Mei Lin was sick?"

Lai Peng was crying and only nodded. She needed another minute before she could speak. "Yes, I knew. She has been unwell. She had recovered. I didn't expect her to be still sick."

"What is Mei Lin suffering from? An infection?"

"No. She has cancer. Lung cancer."

Katherine was taken aback and said, "Cancer? Are you sure?"

"She doesn't want anyone to know. Just don't say anything, please."

They sat waiting for news. They had wheeled her down for an urgent X-ray and scan after Alex had seen her.

Alex came out to meet them. "She's fine now. She's stopped bleeding. She'll be fine tonight. I'm admitting her. Katherine knows?"

"I told her," Lai Peng said.

"It's okay. Katherine should know," Alex replied.

"How is Mei Lin?" Lai Peng asked.

"Her cancer has gotten worse than the last scan we did two months ago. We probably have to change her treatment."

"Why? Why did it have to happen now? It's Christmas. It's not supposed to happen like this."

Alex held Lai Peng and tried to comfort her. "Eric, their kids, and Stephen should be here in two days. I think she will be okay for discharge tomorrow."

Alex thought, *We're running out of time. The research has to bear fruit soon.*

He said, "Mei Lin has requested us not to tell Eric about her bleeding for now since she is okay now. So we have to respect her decision."

Christmas came and was over in a short time. The Shis had a quiet family dinner and enjoyed the company they offered each other. The kids were overjoyed with their visit to Penang. The Shis and the Liangs did not meet over Christmas.

Stephen spent precious time with Katherine. They left the day after Christmas to continue his work as he felt they now had little time left to find a solution.

"Eric, I want to go back to Taipei with you next week," Mei Lin said.

Eric replied, "Sure. Anything the matter?"

Mei Lin fell quiet for a while before saying, "The cancer has worsened again."

Eric said with some surprise, "When did this happen? How come Alex and Alicia didn't inform me? They should."

"I forbade them. I wanted a nice Christmas with you and the kids without any worries. Nothing happened. It's okay. In fact I think I feel better now on the new medication," she said while putting a hand on Eric's, trying to calm him down.

"What did they give you?"

"Afatinib. They have been keeping it in reserve in case my chemotherapy didn't work anymore. I have an appointment tomorrow with them."

"I'll go with you."

"That would be my wish. But please don't overreact. I'm okay. They have been very good to me. But I want to go back and visit my parents and yours with you next week. And not forgetting Stephen's mother. She is like family."

Eric said, "Nothing will happen to you. I'll make sure you have the very best treatment. I'll put in more investments and make things work."

"I already have the very best. But you know as well as I do these things have an end. It's just something I want to do." Mei Lin wiped Eric's tears away with her hands. "We'll be fine. You'll be fine."

CHAPTER 36

A TIME FOR RECONCILIATION

Eric said, "We're reaching Taipei," as he tapped her shoulder. The plane was about to land. Eric didn't sleep when he flew. And he ate much less and carefully chose what he ate. The fear of choking was still there.

Mei Lin stirred and touched his hand. He felt her hand and tears started streaming down his face. Deep inside he knew the reality. There were no new treatments of promise on the horizon. The new medication would keep things at bay for another few months at best. She could have more chemotherapy, but it would be more toxic and he was not sure she would be up for it. He couldn't bear the thought of losing her soon. He had two loves in his life. One had already departed. It was just too much to bear. He said a silent prayer as the plane prepared to land.

"Hello, Ma," Mei Lin said to Stephen's mother as she opened the door to their apartment. "So nice to see you after such a long while."

"I'm pleased to see you. Come in, come in."

Mei Lin and Eric entered the well-furnished, smallish apartment. Mei Lin always felt cozy in their apartment. Stephen's mother had refused to move when he found success. Instead, he had it well furnished as a consolation.

"I'll get Stephen. He just got back so late. I think it was four in the morning. I don't sleep so soundly as I age, you know?"

"Stephen, come and see who is here to visit us," she called as she knocked on his bedroom door.

A few moments later Stephen opened the door, looking weary, asking, "Who is it so early?"

"Come and see. And it's not early. It's lunchtime on Sunday," his mother said.

Stephen stumbled out to the small living room. He was a bit startled to see the Shis there.

Mei Lin said, "Good afternoon, Stephen. What are you up to staying up so late? I don't remember you liking to stay out drinking on a Saturday night."

Stephen replied, "Ah, no, no. Just working late. You look quite well, Mrs. Shi."

He looks a bit surprised, Mei Lin thought.

Mei Lin gave him a look and asked, "What are you working on?"

Stephen replied, "Ah, nothing. Nothing really. Just work."

Mei Lin sensed Stephen was hiding something. He was usually more vocal and chatty. She had not seen him for more than six months. He looked worn out and tired.

"I've got to get dressed. Please excuse me," Stephen said.

Mei Lin noticed he avoided eye contact with her..

They chatted away for thirty minutes before Stephen returned. He was now refreshed and appeared more composed.

Mei Lin smiled at him and asked, "How are things with you and Katherine?"

His mother chipped in before he could answer. "She was just over yesterday. They came in quite late and I made tea."

Stephen said, "We're fine. Thank you."

Eric said, "I hope the extra work you took on in my absence isn't working you so late."

"No, no. Not at all."

"Then it must be the dating," Eric tried to joke.

"No ... yes. Yes," Stephen replied.

Seems to be untruthful, Mei Lin thought.

After the Shis finished their tea and prepared to leave, Mei Lin whispered to Stephen, "You know?"

Stephen was taken aback and didn't reply.

"I'll call you later," she said.

Stephen just nodded.

In the limousine, Eric asked, "What was that about?"

"I'm not sure. I'll call Stephen later. He seemed rather withdrawn during the conversation. I think he knows I'm not well."

"I didn't tell him," Eric replied.

"Of course you didn't. But sometimes such a big secret tends to leak out."

"Maybe we should tell him and his mother."

"No. As I said, I don't want people to fuss over me when my time comes. I want to live life and not mourn it. We're going to your parents' place now. I shall ask Stephen tonight."

Later that evening, after dinner with Eric's parents, they were back in their residence. The children were with them and on the way back, both did not mention Stephen. Having seen the children to bed, and after she showered and felt refreshed, Mei Lin felt it was time to clear the air with Stephen.

"I think Stephen will be afraid to speak honestly if he thought you were listening, so please say nothing if you want to stay in the room when I make this call." Mei Lin said to Eric.

Eric frowned, appearing reluctant though he nodded in agreement.

"I think your emotions are clouding your good judgment when it comes to my health," Mei Lin said, squeezing her husband's hands. "I'll put the volume up on my phone so you can listen."

When Stephen answered the phone, Mei Lin said in Mandarin, which she knew made Stephen comfortable, "Hi, Stephen, I'm happy to have had a chance to see your mother again today. And I was happy to see you too."

"Same here," he replied.

"Now, Stephen, how much do you know?" Mei Lin asked, noticing Eric was sitting sullenly with his arms crossed.

"Well, I know you are not well. I know you have cancer and that you are receiving treatment."

"Who told you?" Mei Lin asked. She wanted to confirm her suspicions.

"No one, just rumors I've been hearing."

Mei Lin noticed the tone of his voice change.

"You're a poor liar. But why did he tell you? Alex knew we wanted complete privacy."

Stephen hesitated. Then he said, "Ahhh ... well, Alex needed my help. Something he couldn't do."

"What help? Just tell me straight. I need to know. Alex, Alicia, and Lai Peng have been good to me. I really need to know." Mei Lin could sense Stephen's hesitancy. She guessed he must have promised Alex not to tell. "He made you promise not to tell, didn't he?"

There was a rather long moment of silence before the reply came. "Alex embarked on an idea to find a possible cure for you. The last ten months have been a race against time to research and test his ideas. A team has been working for a while now."

Mei Lin certainly didn't expect this reply. She stared at Eric. Eric was startled and seemed to keep very still, as if expecting more unexpected news. Mei Lin's thoughts were racing. What was Alex doing to find a cure for her? He was supposed to look after her until her death, not try to find a cure. She had understood they were giving her every possible treatment available until none worked anymore. Neither Alex nor Alicia had hinted about any sort of new cure.

The short moment felt very long for Mei Lin as her thoughts continued to race. She was brought back to the present as Stephen continued to elaborate.

"Alex didn't want you or Eric to know as he felt the chances were very, very slim. More like none. I went along as we wanted to do anything and everything possible."

Mei Lin felt tears in her eyes. She was touched. She could not imagine what sacrifices her friends were making to help her. While Alex seemed to be mostly absent, having left much of the day-to-day care to Alicia, Lai Peng had been a constant friend who was always cheerful and full of gossip to entertain Mei Lin.

"Are you still there?" Stephen asked. Mei Lin had been silent for at least a minute.

"Yes, yes," she replied. "Thank you, Stephen. Thank you for telling me. Thank you for helping me. But why did Alex involve you? You're not a researcher or have knowledge about cancer."

"Alex wanted me to access information that would be out of bounds and write a program for him. It's complicated. I think I've already said too much," Stephen said.

Mei Lin thought, *Did he mean hacking into servers for information? That would be illegal.* She said to Stephen, "Oh, I hope you won't get into trouble. He shouldn't have asked you to do that, accessing restricted information."

"No, it's fine. I'm used to these things," Stephen said with a laugh.

She was filled with emotions and could not speak further. They were true friends. More than friends. More than she would ever expect from them.

"Are you okay? I'm sorry. Alex and I will keep trying. We won't give up." Stephen said.

"I'm fine. Just emotional. I'd better hang up now. Good night. Thank you for all you are doing." And with that she hung up.

Mei Lin looked at Eric as she cried. His face was as hard as a rock, for he was unable to make sense of what was happening. Neither could speak. They would get little sleep that night.

She pondering what Alex was up to and what his idea might be. They were due in Penang in three days. She was sure Eric would speak to Alex. She hoped he would face his feelings and keep an open mind. He needed to.

Mei Lin kept reflecting on Stephen's words and felt a sense of hope again. She wanted it all to be true. She wished Alex would be the one to find the cure. She prayed for the miracle that may be.

Three days later, the couple was in Penang and heading to the Liangs. They hardly spoke on the way. They just held hands. Mei Lin felt as if spring had arrived. Alex and Stephen had been doing something important all the while she had been in Penang. She wondered if Lai Peng knew. Thinking about it a little more, she thought she understood why Alex was looking increasingly worn out. The tidy and meticulously presented doctor had become increasingly disheveled. Exhaustion was etched in his face, and his stiff posture had given in to a slouch. Maybe, just maybe, she thought, it was not because he had grown despondent with the lack of success of the treatments she had undergone but it was because he had had too little sleep. Mei Lin felt a little excitement and hope. She could hardly wait to see Alex and Lai Peng to find out more.

She looked at Eric, who was deep in thought. She had three people who cared so much for her. Eric, Alex, and Stephen had sacrificed so much for her. Now she began to have faith again, the faith she had lost when she coughed blood during Christmas.

When they arrived, the maid and the driver greeted them and led them into the residence's living room. The maid excused herself, saying, "I'll inform Madam that you are here."

Moments later, Lai Peng greeted the couple. "Why didn't you call first? Alex is not in. Let's have some tea." She turned to the maid, "Fetch tea please with the nice cookies from the kitchen."

Mei Lin smiled and said, "Sorry we caught you by surprise. Eric and I would like to ask you a few questions."

Lai Peng turned and didn't look into Mei Lin's eyes. Mei Lin realized she had made her uncomfortable and she probably was involved. This was not her intention. She walked over and sat beside her and held her hands. "I know Alex and Stephen have been up to something to help me. I'm very grateful. But I think it's time I know. Don't you think I should know?"

Without looking up, Lai Peng said, "We didn't want to raise your hopes. You know Alex. He has crazy ideas. Sometimes it's something. Sometimes and many a time, it comes to nothing. We felt you should not know until we have something substantial."

Eric cut in and said, "So nothing near a breakthrough as yet?"

Mei Lin glanced at Eric and gave him a quick stare to indicate he should stop being antagonistic. She continued. "I'm already grateful that you all are trying so hard. Now I realize why you have been spending so much time with me. Did Alex ask you to? So that I'll be distracted and won't realize?"

"No, no. I wanted to be of help. He never asked me to do any such thing. I wanted you to feel happy and needed so you'll continue to hope and not be in despair. I believe positive thinking and positive energy will help. You know Alex. Always scientific. No evidence this and that work. I only want to help." She kept her gaze on her hands, which were held in Mei Lin's.

Mei Lin held her in her arms and hugged her. She hugged back. Mei Lin could feel the warmth from her friend. A friend indeed.

"When I got involved, I started feeling what Alex always felt for his patients. I've started to understand what it's like to be beside someone who is sick. Now I realize it's not easy. It has made me feel a lot more feelings than I had before. I've grown so fond of you and would do anything to help you."

"I know," Mei Lin replied and hugged her even tighter. She was looking at Eric, who was seated directly in front of her. Eric seemed a bit taken aback and embarrassed and appeared to avoid her gaze. She knew Eric felt the honesty, frankness, and warmth of Lai Peng's reply. He was also moved.

"Can you take us to Alex? Is he working on his theory or theories now?" Mei Lin asked.

"I suppose so since the secret is out," she replied. "Let me just get myself together and get my bag. Sorry, so sorry I'm emotional. You are the one who needs comforting. Not me."

An hour's ride in the Liangs' limousine and they arrived at the bungalow in the suburbs. "This property is our family's. We didn't have much use for it. Now, for the last few months, it has really been useful," Lai Peng explained.

The large bungalow was set in an enormous garden and screened from other properties by tall graceful trees. There were a few cars in the drive, but no noise came from the house and there was no one outside.

"What is Alex doing?" Eric asked as they walked to the main door.

"I'd better let Alex explain it himself. I don't understand all the science," Lai Peng said as she opened the front door. "Alex, Alex, we have company."

"Who is with you?" Alex asked as he walked out from the study. He looked up and stopped dead in his tracks.

Alex shook himself out of his little trance and said, "Lai Peng, how come you brought them here?"

"They know everything, Alex," she replied.

Mei Lin quickly said, "It's okay. We're very grateful for what you are trying to do. Really, I'm okay. It's okay for me to know. I want to know. I can handle it."

Eric held her hand. She gave Eric a nudge, signally him to say something.

"Yes, we're grateful. You should have let us know. Maybe I can help," Eric said unconvincingly.

"Please come into the living room. I'll try to explain," Alex said.

The next half-hour, together with the few scientists in the bungalow, Alex explained to the Shis his idea and the progress they had made to date. He explained how Stephen's help had been immense and about Stephen's team in Taipei. They were working together with the scientists here and communicating instantly over the Internet.

At that moment, Alex switched on the link and shortly after, Stephen was on screen teleconferencing with them.

"Hi, Alex. I see Eric and Mei Lin are with you. I guess you know now I leaked the secret. Sorry."

"No apology needed. I'm eternally grateful to all of you," Mei Lin said. She wondered why she was so composed at that moment and not overcome with emotion. Maybe she had been through so much with her illness, nothing surprised her anymore.

"So let me see if I've understood what you are doing. Your idea is to use already known compounds or medications to see if we can use them together to effect a treatment for Mei Lin. And, so far, you have narrowed down to about twenty compounds out of more than a hundred. Stephen has set up a computer program to test this, using theoretical chemistry and biology. Is that correct?" Eric concluded.

"Yes, you are absolutely right," Alex replied.

Mei Lin observed her husband's expression and actions throughout the discussion. She smiled. At last, Eric has gained his trust back with Alex and Stephen. That already was worth a lot. Eric seemed to have found new vigor and a new reason to push on.

"But everything is theoretical. No actual lab work has been done yet. Correct? I only see computers and servers and lots of paper here," Eric continued.

Over the link, Stephen replied, "Yes, unfortunately that is so."

Eric raised his hand and continued, "It's not unfortunate. It's fortunate that we came to know about this. I cannot let any possibility slip through my fingers. Any possibility that we can find a cure or even a workable treatment for her, we'll explore to the fullest. I think it's time we move beyond the computers."

Alex and the team were taken aback with Eric's response. They were not quite expecting this.

"I want all of you here to come over to my pharmaceutical companies and continue all the work immediately. Recruit anyone you need, and I'll make sure you have any resources you need."

There was silence in the room. Mei Lin went to Eric and held his hand. She whispered, "Thank you. I love you."

Lai Peng clasped her hands and remarked, "Thank goodness. Alex, please make everyone join Eric and continue."

"I don't think I need to convince anyone here," Alex remarked. Everyone nodded.

Joan said, "This is an opportunity of a lifetime for us. Of course we'll continue. When can we leave to go to your company? We need a real working place!"

Everyone laughed. The mood had changed from one of apprehension to one of hope and a sense of future achievement. Worried faces changed to smiles.

As they walked back to the limousine, Eric said to Alex, "Putting together this team and doing this work isn't cheap."

Lai Peng overheard and replied in her more bubbly way now, "We almost spent our last dollar already!" As soon as she said it, she stopped talking as if knowing she shouldn't have spoken.

Mei Lin said, "You have put all your money into this? How much has it cost?"

Alex quickly replied, "We can afford it. No worries."

"Now, now. Lai Peng, tell the truth."

"Well, not all. We did spend most of our savings. We have plenty in other things."

"Don't worry about the money part from now on. We need to get this off the ground and running in the shortest time. Money is no longer your issue. We're already in your debt," Eric said.

Mei Lin held Alex and Lai Peng and said to them with a big smile, "I'm blessed to have two wonderful friends I treasure as family."

CHAPTER 37

DISCOVERY

Within two weeks, the entire team from Penang was reassembled in Switzerland. They were now in the preclinical research laboratory wing of Alectran Pharmaceuticals. They were in luck, as the wing opened less than two months ago. Most of the wing was not yet utilized. That made the move much easier. At least another twenty scientists were recruited with promises of exorbitant salaries. Eric was wasting no time in moving things ahead.

Two months later, animal studies were almost complete.

"Where are we now?" Eric asked.

Felix, now the head of the research team, answered, "We've finished testing twenty compounds. Unfortunately, only four came through as successful. No significant toxicity and adequate effects observed. We think we need another molecule to enhance the effects we need. We'll need to make it. It doesn't exist yet. We were able to predict its structure based on the landscape Stephen and his team created."

Eric felt excited yet down as they needed more time to create the molecule. He asked, "How long do you think we'll need?"

"Hard to tell. Maybe a week or maybe a few months. But I've already engaged another two biochemists Joan recommended. With their help, I think it will be the fastest possible."

"When do you think we'll be able to use it for Mei Lin, Alex?"

"Another few months. Alicia tells me the latest test results for Mei Lin are good. The tumor is stable. We should have at least a few months to be ready," Alex said.

"I certainly have to hope so. I'll be flying back to Penang tomorrow. I'll leave all the research to you and Felix. Let me know the good news once there is any."

Another three months passed quickly. Progress had been made. "The final molecule is ready for testing. In Stephen's program, it's working. It should be a positive result tomorrow. The cell lines test should be ready tomorrow," Felix informed Eric via teleconferencing.

"Good. Keep up the good work. The visit to the doctor today wasn't as good as we expected. There is early progression of her illness again. I fear we have little time left. Please hasten the work as much as you can."

"We'll do our very best. The team has not taken any breaks for the last three months and are even working in shifts."

"I guess I cannot ask for more from you all. Let me know the results the soonest you can tomorrow. By the way, where is Alex?"

"I think he is in the library. Do you want me to get him to call you?"

"No need. I'll contact him later."

Alex was supposed to be in the library looking up some literature on his computer. He had Felix on the job. He could no longer offer any help. They were doing things way above his knowledge. He had to leave it to the scientists. Instead, he had been staring for a long while at a piece of paper he had kept for the past five years. He had forgotten about the notes he had written while in a blood cancer meeting in Australia. An idea he had at that moment. An idea he had forgotten until now. He found the single sheet of paper in the side pocket of his notebook bag two days ago. On the paper was written EBV virus—the Epstein-Barr virus. It was scribbled with arrows and lines and circles. He had written down an idea in note form. Over the past two days he had been recollecting his idea, adding to it, and wondering if it would work.

The EBV viral genome was already completely sequenced and published. The virus's method of entry into human cells was eluded, and the way the immune system responded to the EBV infection was already worked out. His preliminary research showed that over the past five years, much more had been discovered. The lecture he attended then was focused on how the EBV virus caused diseases and how it tried to hide from the immune system. He had thought that if modification could be made to the virus, it might infect cancer cells and kill them as it would in a normal infection, before the immune system kicks in and eliminates the virus. The past two days were spent developing the idea.

He had sent an invitation to two top virologists, including the one who had done recent research of the virus, to come for a meeting in Zurich. He had also asked two geneticists to come for the meeting. Alif Adam, an accomplished geneticist who helped complete the mapping its whole genome, was Alex's university friend. Tomorrow he would put forward his idea and see their reaction. Now he had to prepare the presentation about his idea.

In the meeting the next day, Dominic, the virologist asked, "You really think we can use the virus to kill cancer cells and achieve a cure?"

"I'm hoping it can be done, yes. I want to do that," Alex replied.

"Okay, you've got my attention and probably theirs," Dominic replied, pointing to the rest of the people gathered. "Please continue and show us your idea." His hand rubbed his stubby chin. This man of sixty years with vast knowledge was not going to just jump into the idea.

Alex said, "We need to identify a target on the surface of the cancer cells that we can use. I'm sure there are surface transfer molecules on the cell membrane that we can utilize. We already understand that the virus enters the cells latching onto the normal proteins on cells and then internalize to enter the cell. We'll need to change its gene so that it will attach to other protein molecules on the cancer cell surface. Then it will internalize into the cancer cells and replicate. The viruses will lyse the cancer cells, releasing the viruses to infect other cancer cells. This should continue until all the cancer cells are infected and destroyed."

"Why do you want to use the EBV virus?" Dominic asked.

"Well, it's a well-characterized virus. So we can exploit it easier as we know its genome."

"It will be easier said than done. Trying to find the correct molecule on the cancer cells and then reverse engineer the DNA and insert it into the genome sounds fictional," said Alif Adam.

"The good news is we've already sequenced the genome of the cancer we want to target. I'm hoping with your help we would be able to find the target easier," Alex said with some enthusiasm.

"Hmmm, workable and may even been thought about, if I'm not mistaken," said Dominic, who appeared unconvinced and now was ruffling his locks of gray hair. He stood up and continued. "It will take a lifetime of work."

"Well, I think the other reason I'm using the EBV virus is that it can stimulate an immune response. I hope that will hasten the killing of the cancer. The human genome project was stalled for years, more than fifteen years at least, until a group came together and got it done in one year. I think if the group is focused, with all resources made available to them, they should be able to get a breakthrough. So I do hope it will not be a lifetime of work."

"It will involve a fair bit of work, money, and time," said Karen, the other virologist present. "I've been involved with using a viral vector to insert genetic material into the cells, even cancer cells. But we actually make it sterile, preventing it from replicating. Here you actually want it to replicate. There can be a marked immune response that can be uncontrolled."

"I understand. I hope it wouldn't be so severe that we need to use steroids and other immunosuppressive medication to control the reaction. We can be prepared," Alex replied.

"It's possible. Sure the money and resources will be unlimited? Is there a particular patient we're doing this for?" Karen asked.

"Since you all have signed the confidentiality agreement, I'll tell you. Yes, it's for Mrs. Shi, Eric Shi's wife."

The room fell silent. It was indeed still a well kept secret.

"That's why the resources will be as unlimited as humanly possible. Financially, Eric will underwrite everything."

After another long silence, with much thinking done, Dominic asked, "When can we start? Tomorrow?" He smiled after stretching out and cracking his fingers. The rest nodded in agreement.

Karen said, "I'll need to finish up my work before I can come. A two-week period at least."

"I'm glad you have all come aboard. I'm very relieved." Alex said.

Alex thought, *I shall keep this quiet until the compounds have been tried in Mei Lin. The compounds are likely to work but will eventually fail as the cancer cells will find ways to be resistant. This viral method will have a real chance to cure her. Eric only needs to know at a later time.*

Felix and Joan looked over the test results and inspected the cell cultures again. They both wore worried expressions. The tests did not perform as they should have. The cells continued to live and grow. The cell cultures should all have died or at least stopped growing if they had been successful. These cell cultures were grown from Mei Lin's cancer.

"I have no further ideas," Felix said with his eyes closed, rubbing the bridge of his nose with his thumb and forefinger. He was tired. They were all tired. Months of work and now it just didn't work at the last phase.

"Me too," Joan said, "We have to recheck our initial data. There has to be something wrong with the last molecule. The other compounds, minoxycycline, tetrabenzene, pentamidine, and tretenoin should work. They are known to block the targets we selected. We need to check all the data again. Stephen, what do you think?"

Stephen said over the teleconferencing on Joan's android tablet, "We'll check all the data on our side. It will take a few days. We need to figure this out and see where we go from there. Have you all spoken to Alex? Maybe the visionary has a new thought." He was a bit sarcastic as they had pursued his ideas up to this point and had not succeeded.

Later that evening Alex sat with the team to brainstorm. "I'm sorry I was distracted with something else the last few days. You have my full attention now."

Karen said, "We've not succeeded at all with the cell cultures. The tests all failed. We think we got the last molecule wrong. It just didn't work. Stephen is going over the results."

"The target seems obvious from our theoretical data. I think we have to revisit the gene sequencing and the target on the cancer cells," Felix said.

Alex said, "I've looked at the test results and the data. I must admit I only understand parts. This is really beyond me. But we should possibly look at the molecule we created. We may have been trying to be too specific and trying too hard to make the molecule fit the target. Just a suggestion. Maybe we make mirror images, flip it, and see how those will work."

"Well, that is a thought. We were so sure that we didn't look at the isomers. That is an idea," Karen said with some tinge of excitement in her tone, as it could be a way forward after hitting a wall.

"We shall do that first thing in the morning. I shall tell Stephen to try to use the isomers in the program and see," Felix said. "Just maybe we'll get somewhere. How do you just come up with ideas, Alex?"

Alex smiled and didn't reply. He actually never really knew. The ideas and thoughts just popped into his head.

A week later, Felix and Joan were peeping at the cancer cell cultures. The first after three days, less than half the cells were present. Felix felt his pulse rising. They could have their breakthrough. They looked at the next culture. There were some cells present. Maybe a bit less than the first. With each culture, the dose of the five compounds were gradually increased. The next one they looked at for nearly a minute and then looked at each other. There were no visible cells at all. This was it. The breakthrough.

Felix suddenly laughed. Karen grinned from ear to ear. They hugged each other and jumped and danced together.

Hearing the commotion, the others all gathered. Felix shouted, "We did it!" They all joined in jumping and cheering.

Finally, after almost a year of intense research, the signs for success were there.

Felix called Eric and said, "We did it. We start the mice studies tomorrow. We should be ready in the next two weeks for human testing."

Eric said, "That's fantastic news. Please make haste. We don't have time anymore."

Eric was still awake in Penang. That morning the couple had seen Alicia. The news was not great. The cancer had started to be active again. Mei Lin had started to lose some weight. A mild cough recurred. He was worried. He felt quite helpless. All the investments for the past years into pharmaceuticals had to pay off now. There was no more time. He felt relieved after the phone call. There was real hope now.

Three weeks passed and Mei Lin was on her way to Zurich. Eric and Alicia were with her. Eric made sure everything would be taken care of when they flew. They were in a fully equipped private air ambulance jet. He would leave nothing to chance. Mei Lin was comfortable in the bed with oxygen on. She had not been too well for the past few weeks.

Alex was having the last meeting with the whole team. Stephen and his team in Taiwan were connected by teleconference. "We've come this far. There is no turning back. Are we satisfied that the four compounds will work? Or at least have a good chance of success?"

"We've checked and rechecked all the data. We think we're as ready as we can be without human trials," Felix replied.

Stephen replied, "My team is as certain as we can be. It should work. We can't see any problems at the moment."

Alex said, "There are always possibilities. Let's run a few scenarios where problems may occur and how we may overcome them. I don't like to be caught unaware."

"If you insist. We'll run further scenarios," Felix said.

"We almost always find problems in clinical research. We need to know if there are any serious reactions or interactions. We need to formulate some contingency plans if it occurs," Alex explained.

"Without human trials, we cannot be at all certain," Joan remarked, "and we don't have the time."

"No, we don't," Alex said. "Mei Lin doesn't have much time anymore. She will be the human trial. I think we look up similar molecules that have been used in human studies and look for class effects or side effects. The four compounds are known. The last we synthesized. So we look for class effect. We need to consider interactions, especially with the medications she is currently on. We have no time or chance to allow washout of her current medications. That will take one to two weeks."

"Okay, Alex. I understand. We'll run every possible scenario in the next two days," Felix said. "Stephen, you can try to see what scenarios you can run."

"We'll do that," Stephen said.

Alex said, "We'll use a phase one trial design to start giving her the medications. We'll start at 70 percent of the dose and then increase to 100 percent, one by one, if there are no problems. This will take at least one week to achieve. Mei Lin should be arriving in Zurich tomorrow. We'll have one day to get her prepared. We'll start her trial in two days. Please let me know if there is anything that we come up with."

"We sure will if we find any problems," said Joan.

"We'll adjourn then if there is nothing else to discuss," Alex said.

With that, the meeting was over and the scientists and researchers went back to work overtime to ensure Mei Lin's survival.

"Are you all set for the first oral medication?" Alex asked Mei Lin.

"Alicia has prepared me for today. I'm ready."

"Are you confident she'll be fine?" Eric asked with a hint of doubt in his voice.

"As sure as we all can be. There can be things we've not anticipated," Alex replied.

"Come on, Eric. I'm prepared. I have nothing else to do. It will be fine," Mei Lin said, with a small smile, through the oxygen mask she was using, which muffled her voice. She was lying in bed with monitoring devices hooked up to her.

Alex observed her calmness, which reminded him why he had grown so fond of her. Lai Peng was beside her holding her other hand. Lai Peng gave Alex a glance and smiled as he looked to her, almost as if asking her permission to start.

"These are the three tablets you have to take," Alex said, passing the trial medication to her. Without any hesitancy, she swallowed the tablets with a glass of water. That marked the start of the trial that could very well save her—or kill her.

Days passed, and each phase was uneventful. Finally, the last medication was to be given. This had to be given by injection. With steady hands, Alicia administered the medication intravenously with Alex looking on. It worked and had no side effects in the mice study.

It will be fine, Alex thought.

They waited for more than an hour, and there was no reaction. The following day, Alicia again gave her the medication at a higher dose. Initially she was fine. An hour later, her breathing was a bit labored.

"What's happening?" Eric asked with some anxiety.

"She may be having a mild reaction. This is not unusual," Alicia replied.

Alex was listening to her lungs and frowning. "She has some wheeze. Let's give her some steroids, hydrocortisone 100 mg and give her a nebulizer."

The nurse quickly prepared the medications, and within minutes, she was given the medications. Her breathing eased after another few minutes.

An hour later, Alex explained. "The last medication caused a mild reaction. I think it's because her cancer is mainly in her lungs. We'll change the schedule and give smaller quantities more frequently."

The following days the trial progressed smoothly. "Nothing seemed to have happened. Are you sure the medication is working?" Eric asked as Alicia checked on her.

"We don't expect anything to happen in the beginning. It takes time. This is new and not the usual chemotherapy that kills cells. It works by blocking the cancer cells and they stop dividing and growing. If successful, we should see no further growth and then in weeks or months, regression. It's like the earlier medication she took, Tarceva, Iressa and Afatinib."

"It's so distressing to wait," Eric said impatiently.

"I'm fine. So far, so good. I'm certainly not worse. It's two weeks now. It will be fine," Mei Lin said.

Alex was observing the scene from the back of the room. Eric really was in love with Mei Lin. He had not left her side and had slept with her in the room. They had their meals together. Alex envied him. She was the lady every man would want to have as his wife, he thought.

Alex shook himself out of his thoughts as Mei Lin turned to him and asked, "Isn't that what we expect, Alex?"

"Yes, ah yes. By another few weeks, we should know. I'm very happy with the progress. Very minimal side effects. The blood tests so far have been satisfactory."

"You look worn out, Alex," Mei Lin remarked, "I demand you take a break. Bring Lai Peng out to see Zurich and Switzerland. I'll be fine. Alicia is great. She knows what to do. Eric, tell Alex to go rest!"

"I will. I guess I've been neglecting Lai Peng too."

CHAPTER 38

THE ANSWER

Alex and Alicia looked carefully at the scans. Mei Lin had just finished her PET scan. It was six weeks since the start of the trial, and now was the defining moment of whether the medications worked. They had her scans from the previous tests side by side. They compared each slice of the scans. They looked at each other. They just smiled, probably too relieved to talk. Alex felt as if a weight had been lifted off his shoulders and all his energy drained. Alicia held his hands and shook them.

"Congratulations," she whispered.

He smiled back and just sat there staring at the scans.

Alicia said to him, "Let me talk to Eric and Mei Lin. You take your time here."

"Thank you. I just need some time. So much work. Finally we see success. I just want to savor the moment a bit longer."

"I know. I'll see to the Shis."

After Alicia left the room, Alex felt the pent-up emotions rise out of him and he cried. He'd had to hold back every emotion to be objective to succeed. There was no place for complacency or misjudgment that emotions could bring. It was nearly half an hour before he gathered himself, washed his face, and felt better.

That part was over but another would start. More serious and deadly if he was wrong. He was so tired. Somehow he would have to find the strength to continue.

A week later, with the whole team gathered, Eric addressed them. "I'm very grateful for the work. Thank you. Now Mei Lin can continue to live. She is feeling better. To be off the oxygen for the past few days was really good for her. Her cough has almost disappeared. She is really getting well. The whole team here has been great. It's a real honor to have you all work on this. I hope you all can stay on and do further research. And, as promised, you all shall be rewarded for your efforts."

They clapped and were all smiles.

"We did it for the science. Money is good though," Felix remarked in his usual casual way.

They all laughed.

As the team streamed out of the meeting room, Alex gently pulled Eric's sleeve and said, "I need to discuss something with you." Eric gave him a puzzled look. "Can you join me in the other room?"

Eric nodded and followed.

As they entered, Alex introduced the virologists and geneticists gathered.

Eric remarked, "I didn't know you had them working with us." He looked surprised.

Alex said, "They've been part of the team. However, they've been working on something else."

Eric replied, "You do like to keep secrets, don't you?," sounding annoyed.

"I've been spending time to find something better or an alternative should the four compounds fail," Alex said. "The treatment Mei Lin is receiving now will not work forever. It's the nature for cancers to continue to evolve and develop resistance. That is the essence of cancer. Mutations continues unless we can totally eradicate the cells or at least get them to a level where the body can take care of them."

Eric said, "I sense another far-fetched idea. I sense a vaccine in the making. Vaccine studies are ongoing. The PD-1 trails on immunotherapy are progressing well. So I understand geneticists being involved. But virologists? Immunologist certainly I understand. But virologist?"

Dominic replied, "That is the genius of the idea. The idea is unique. We've worked out the idea and have put together a workable model now."

Alex said, "I had thought of the idea years ago and actually forgot about it until a few months ago, when I saw my notes. The idea is simple. We infect the cancer cells with the virus. The virus kills the cancer cells but not other human cells."

Eric said, "Is that even possible?"

"I only conceived the idea. The team here worked it out. I shall let them explain," Alex replied.

Dominic cleared his throat to start a long explanation. He switched on the projector and got his presentation started.

"We're using the EBV virus. It's a common virus, and scientists have already mapped its entire genome and understand most of its function. The EBV virus is unique. It only infects certain cells in our body, the mucosal cells in the nose and the T cells in our blood. It does not affect the brain or nerves or red cells. It's known that the EBV virus enters the cells by recognizing a protein on the cell surface. It's like a door that the EBV virus opens with a key and enters. So if the door is not there in other cells, it cannot enter and infect the cells.

"We've managed to identify a protein in Mei Lin's cancer called aquaprotein 1A. This is a door we can use. It has mutated and is different from normal cells. We think we can design a protein key that can bind to the door and allow entry into the cancer cells. We'll reverse-engineer the genes to produce the protein. We'll then insert it into the EBV virus genome, replacing the gene that code for the key protein that EBV uses to enter human cells. That way, the EBV virus will only infect the cancer cells."

Alex sensed Eric was a bit awed by the idea. He said, "The whole process sounds unreal and is certainly difficult. But we've already got the building blocks. We have the virus and identified the protein we need to make use of. The rest is possible.

"Yes, the technology for everything we need is already there. Inserting genes. Reverse engineer the gene to code the protein. All have been done for other reasons. We're confident it will work. But major investments or collaborations with others will be needed."

Eric replied, "It's a big undertaking. I see where we're heading here. Can this work also for other lung cancers or other cancers besides Mei Lin's?"

Alex said, "Yes but not all. The mutated aquaprotein 1A is present in four out of ten lung cancer cell lines commercially available. We've tested it. So it will also be applicable to other patients. It would be worth an investment, and if successful, would translate to a possible cure for many."

Eric said nothing for at least a minute, seemingly deep in thought. Alex could guess he was thoroughly considering the idea. He probably also knew Alex needed him to put in a huge investment to get it going.

Finally Eric said, "I sense possible success here. I'd give up everything I own to get Mei Lin well. We'll proceed. I'll look after the investment part."

"Alex, I assume Dominic here will be the lead scientist?" Alex nodded. Eric continued. "Dominic, get me the list of things and people you require. To hasten the development, I need a list of possible pharmaceuticals dealing with these. We may need to do quick deals to move things as fast as possible."

"The group led by biochemist and geneticist Craig Venter is the foremost in technology in gene insertion and coding." Dominic said.

"Then we'll need them to help us. Make the contacts. We'll move this as fast as we can. What estimate time frame do we have to get this ready for human trial?"

Dominic replied, "A year to a year and the half, probably."

Eric said, "We set a time frame for eighteen months then. We'll meet in three days. Thank you, everyone. It's been a real pleasure to meet all of you. Mei Lin and I have been through so much the last few years. I really hope this will bring the answer to our prayers."

As they left, Eric held Alex back. Eric said, "Why didn't you tell me this before?"

"I didn't want the whole team working on the four compounds distracted. Also, it's just an idea until we could identify the aquaprotein. Just don't want any false hope."

"I don't like surprises. You should have told me. Promise me no more surprises."

"Okay. I'll not hold back anymore."

"I need to know I can fully trust you again."

"Anything I do is for everyone's betterment. I'll keep you informed in future." Alex said. Alex was puzzled at Eric's response. Something didn't feel right.

Later that night, Eric could not sleep. He looked at Mei Lin fast asleep in the hospital bed. He was beside her holding her hand as he had for the past weeks when she slept. He had to keep the financial part from her. Now he had to make another big decision. He had committed to the new team to finance them at all cost. He knew the new treatment she was getting wouldn't last forever. The best estimates were two to three years at best. She would need something up the road. PD-1 was a new treatment, which was exciting, but again not a cure. And it worked only in a small portion of patients. Every current research seemed to lead to near cures but not full ones. They kept the cancer at bay for a while, years at best. Side effects were always there. Now Alex had another far-fetched but clearly possible idea. It could be the magic he had been waiting for to help Mei Lin.

But he was now facing financial difficulty. Shi Corporation was not as robust as it once was. Pouring in unlimited funding to research the past two years had led to his financial resources being depleted. He was nearly broke. He would need to liquidate much of his shares to continue. He would do anything to save Mei Lin. Losing Sukimi was like losing himself. Now he had found himself again. If it occurred again, he would be as good as dead emotionally and probably physically. He needed to sell his stakes in many companies and buy quickly into the other companies to hasten the research.

He didn't sleep at all that night. He just looked at Mei Lin sleeping and savored the time he'd had with her all these years.

Stephen and Katherine were getting closer as time went by. They were comfortable with each other and as announced themselves as engaged.

"How's Alex?" Stephen asked.

"My father is off doing some research again. He just can't stop. He said something about a viral theory but wouldn't elaborate. This time it seems he wants to do it without me or my mother. I guess he thinks we've had enough. And actually, we probably have. We cannot keep up with his pace. The pace he sets is ridiculous."

"Yes, he does, doesn't he? Eric and Mei Lin are back in Taiwan and going out again. I'm so glad we succeeded the way we did. Are you aware of anything out of the ordinary?"

"No, why do you ask?" Katherine replied.

"I sense something is going on. Eric has been quietly selling his shares in Shi Corporation and his sister companies. In fact he has sold nearly half the shares he had in the Swiss company where the whole research thing was. I can't understand it. He would stand to earn a lot when the research is completed and commercialized. It's almost a certainty."

"He has? Maybe he has given up the corporate world to be with Mei Lin. He is rich enough to do that, isn't he?"

"I guess so, but I sense something else. It's not like Eric to do this. If he did, he would have told me."

"Hmmm. I wonder if it has anything to do with my father again," Katherine said.

"I wonder," Stephen said. "Time to go."

They left the small café where they met a few times a week and returned to their offices.

Katherine was heading Regenesis Incorporated to sign another deal with another country for Regenesis.

Stephen was deep in thought when he walked back slowly to Shi Corporation. He knew Eric well. When Eric sold his shares, Stephen felt something was amiss. Selling when the value for Shi Corporation was at the brink of increasing with Regenesis really taking off. He took a chance and had been quietly buying up the shares Eric sold. He could be wrong, but something was up. Eric just wasn't telling. It had to be something to do with Mei Lin's illness again. He would wait until Eric was ready to tell him. At the moment, he could still afford to buy up what he had been selling. What was Eric doing with the money?

CHAPTER 39

THE ULTIMATE TEST

The modified EBV virus was finally ready. Alex and Dominic chatted on the way to the laboratory. "A year on and we've made it. It's very exciting working with the project. We hardly have a chance to do cutting-edge research like this anymore. Especially so focused and with no red tape," Dominic said.

"Yes, I agree. Let's hope it really works. Theory is one thing. Reality is another," Alex remarked as he opened the door.

"Are we ready to inject?" Dominic asked his staff who was standing by. They were outside the isolation chamber looking through the glass. "Let's begin then."

The staff that was in white full biological suits with oxygen masks opened a sealed container containing the virus. Slowly and carefully, the scientist piped out twenty microliters of the virus and injected it into a Petri dish with Mei Lin's cancer cells. She repeated the procedure five times. When finished, she turned around and showed the thumbs-up sign.

"That's it then. We wait for the next one week," Dominic said. "With the installed cameras and microscopes above the dishes, we can record the viral activity on the cells."

Alex wasn't as happy as he should be at the phase where the virus was ready. He was in thought. He had received a call from Alicia a day before. Mei Lin's latest assessment was not good. The cancer had started growing again. They were running out of time. If this phase worked, it would need further human testing, which would take months if not years.

"If this test succeeds, then what, Dominic?" Alex asked.

"Then we analyze the data and consider human trials."

"Are we worried the virus might mutate and then we have an epidemic of some kind?"

"Well, there is always that possibility. We've not seen the original EBV mutate much, so the risk should be small."

"But it exists, correct?"

"Yes, but small. We would do further research, like passing it into monkeys and other animals to see. It would take time. We could also stress it in the laboratory cultures to see if it mutates."

"Can we develop a vaccine against it?"

"No, that's in movies. Scientists have been trying to get a vaccine for EBV for more than ten years. No success. So not today."

"Can we somehow have a failsafe mechanism?" Alex asked.

"It's possible. We could put in a gene in it to make it susceptible to antivirals. It would take time."

"Let's look into that, shall we?"

"Okay. I agree we should."

"Without any failsafe measures, I don't think we can get human volunteers for testing it. We can't get any approvals from the relevant authorities for a trial." Alex sounded his fears.

"Agreed. That is if today's test actually works."

"I'm confident you and your team have made it work," Alex said with a grin.

A week later they were looking at the video recordings and images of the cell culture dishes with the virus.

Karen remarked, "All the cells seem to grow until the fourth day and then the numbers have decreased. Now all the dishes show less than 10 percent of the cells," she said, "I think we did it!" She pumped her arms up and down and did a little victory dance, to the amazement of the gathered crowd of researchers.

"We did it," Eric said in a whisper. He was suddenly filled with a sense of total relief. He had flown over to the facility here in Japan to witness it. The year waiting had been very distressing for him. He shook the hands of each researcher and left the room.

A moment later he was looking at himself in the mirror in the restroom. He had locked the door. He felt so tired. He saw his reflection. Stress had taken a toll. He had lost weight, which wasn't a bad thing though, he thought. But the sagging chin and under eye bags told the story of a stressful life he had led, especially in the last year. Tomorrow more stress would come his way. This time he really had no further idea what to do. He was backed into a corner.

Alex was woken by a call from Katherine the next day. "Good morning, Katherine. Something wrong? You wouldn't call me at this time."

"Dad, something's happened. I think you should turn on the TV news right now," she said quickly.

Alex put on his glasses and switched on the television in the room.

A petite Chinese lady was reporting outside the Shi Corporation. "We're standing outside the Shi Corporation. We've obtained information regarding the status of the corporation. It's alleged that Eric Shi has lost control of his company and is no longer a major player in Shi Corporation. He has no holding stake. Our sources also found out that Mr. Eric Shi's assets have greatly diminished. His worth is now a fraction of what he had a year ago. What has happened? Let's ask our analyst here in the studio."

The scene quickly changed to the studio with a middle-aged American sitting beside another commentator. "Professor Cummings, what do you think has happened?"

"It's unprecedented. I can only speculate. Is it gambling? Has he been extorted? Had a business deal gone sour and he had tried to cover it up? What we know is he is nearly broke. And I think it will get worse for him. I understand he has huge borrowings."

The commentator asked, "Where do you think all his money has gone? The amount seems too large for just gambling. But again who knows? We've heard rumors that he invested in health-related companies."

"Yes, it would seem so. He must have thought the health sector would boom. Especially when the Swiss company he previously owned discovered a new medicine for cancer. But it's still in the pipeline, developed with clinical trials and not earned any money yet. He sold the majority of his shares there. It doesn't really make much sense."

"We have little time left. One last question. Will Eric Shi survive this downturn?"

"This is massive. Honestly, I don't think he will recover. He was one of the richest men in Taiwan. After the Regenesis incident, he has been on a downhill spiral. Maybe he lost his edge."

"Thank you for coming here so early in the morning," the commentator said. "There it is. The Shi Corporation is no longer Eric Shi's. Will Eric Shi survive?"

A commercial then aired.

"Katherine, are you there?" He was stunned by the news.

"Yes, I am. Do you know what's happening?"

"I know what it is," Alex replied, "but I can't say. I need to talk to Eric."

"Dad, Stephen is here with me. He needs to tell you more."

"Hi, Alex. Actually we know you're up to something. Eric has been liquidating his assets, selling below-market price. He's been channeling money to Japan. And we know you're in Japan. Are you cooking up another thing again? We need to know."

There was silence as Alex digested what Stephen had said. He replied, "I have to come clean. Yes, I am. I know the treatment we had given Mei Lin won't work forever. At best, a few years. So we've continued to research. We're working on a viral theory.

That's why we needed another research center with different facilities and different people. The Japanese here in *Nagoya* have the best in biotechnology. The Japanese researchers here have been excellent and working tirelessly."

"That's what Katherine and I figured. We know what to do now. Katherine and I will go to Eric. He is on the plane right now from Japan. We'll meet him at the airport. Leave it to us. Continue with your work, Alex."

"Huh?" Alex replied, even more stunned.

"We'll sort out things on this end. Dad, don't worry. We'll take care of Eric. Trust us. It's time for the younger ones to help. I love you, Dad. Take care," Katherine said.

"Okay. I have my full trust in you, Katherine. Love you always," Alex replied.

His daughter was now taking responsibility. She really was her own person now. *How proud can a dad be of his daughter? Extremely,* he thought.

Lai Peng stirred in the sheets next to him. He turned toward her and ran his hand over her head. She'd been with him the last week and came over to give him moral support. With the news, he'd better ask her to return to Penang and help with Mei Lin. His mind was now working at an incredible pace again. The stakes had suddenly changed.

Time was running out for Mei Lin. Alicia had called Alex a week earlier and told him her cancer markers were on the rise. Mei Lin was still well, but a relapse was imminent. The virus was not ready and would not be for at least a year or more if they followed the rules. Eric was near-bankrupt as a result of another of Alex's grand ideas.

For things to work out, he needed the virus ready for Mei Lin in fewer than three months. In his mind, he was already hatching a plan. There was no other choice. He knew what needed to be done. If not, all would be lost. He had to call Alicia now and get her to be with Mei Lin. With Eric and Lai Peng not in Penang, Alicia was the only one he knew who could be with her at this extreme period. He would text Katherine to let her know and to ask Stephen to call Mei Lin to reassure her.

Back in Taiwan, Katherine and Stephen rushed to the airport to meet Eric.

Katherine said, "How will Eric react to the news? I hope he'll be as strong as he has been."

Stephen said, "I really don't know. Despite knowing him most of my life, at this juncture, I just don't know. He was devastated when Sukimi died. He blamed me and most of all, Alex. Somehow he gathered himself and worked tirelessly to make sure Mei Lin survived. He lost interest in business. Now that his world is crashing down again, I really don't know."

"I think he'll survive. Eric is a fighter, just like my dad but in a different way."

"There he is!" Stephen exclaimed as he saw Eric coming out of the arrivals. "Eric!"

Eric looked up as he wasn't expecting anyone to come. A crowd of reporters descended on him. "Is it true you are no longer in control of Shi Corporation? Mr. Shi, are you now bankrupt? Are you aware of the situation and the news? Why were you in Japan, Mr. Shi?" were the questions thrown at him.

He looked stunned and at the same time worn out. He didn't reply and just stared blankly at them.

Stephen saw his expression and saw the sadness in his eyes. *I need to do something,* he thought. He quickly rushed up and got between Eric and the reporters. "Now, let Mr. Shi rest. He just came back from a long trip in Japan. We'll issue a statement later at Shi Corporation. Be there this afternoon. Have some courtesy. We'll explain everything in the afternoon."

"The exchange will open in twenty minutes. The people have a right to know. Taiwanese need to know," shouted a reporter from the back.

"I assure you Shi Corporation is at the peak and it's still very much a Taiwanese company. Do not fear. There is no takeover. Eric is very much in control. We'll explain with a statement in the afternoon."

He whispered to Eric, "Come, follow us. Things will be fine," and led Eric aside.

Katherine held the crowd back with her hands and yelled, "For everyone's sake, please let the man have some peace. You forget so fast how Eric Shi has given renewable energy to the world and sacrificed so much. Let the man have peace until this afternoon!"

Security guards appeared and held the crowd back as the trio went to the waiting limousine.

Eric was silent in the limo. Stephen and Katherine didn't speak either. Eric was in his own thoughts. Stephen had never seen Eric so spent. Not even when Sukimi died. He was not emotional. In fact, he seemed devoid of emotion. He looked like a person without the will to live. No tears. Just a blank expression.

Finally Stephen said, "Eric, we can help if you let us. We heard the news and came straight to the airport. We can help."

After a moment, Eric said, "How can you help? I've done all I can. I've come so near to saving Mei Lin and at the last moment, we cannot continue. I have nothing left to give."

"Not if you let us help."

"How can you help this weary old man?"

"Katherine and I can. Eric, all your life you have been seeing to things and rarely ask for help. I understand it's personal and you want to go it alone. Different from Regenesis. But trust me, we're ready to help. In fact, we've got everything ready."

"What do you mean?" Eric asked. "The banks will be after me by afternoon and the creditors will come. I cannot hold them off anymore."

"We're not ignorant, Eric. Though you might think we are. We all still have control over Shi Corporation and most of the companies you own."

"How?" Eric sounded bewildered. He turned and looked directly into Stephen's eyes.

"Well, we've been buying up all your sales through a holding company Katherine and I created. So we still have control."

"How did you manage to do that? That's a lot of money."

"We do have some money. With our shares together with Alex's shares in Regenesis Incorporated, we have plenty as the share price has soared. Alex had given Katherine full control of his shares. He does not know."

"So you and Katherine now own Shi Corporation?"

"Yes, actually. We're holding it in trust for you. It's all yours if you'll allow us."

"Why would you do that?"

"Eric, it's time you give us younger ones some credit. We're always in debt to you. If not for you, I wouldn't be who I am. We're here for you as you have been for us. It's time for us to help. Give us that chance."

Eric said, "I have no words. Let me have a quiet moment."

The rest of the drive back to Shi Corporation was silent.

It was almost two in the afternoon. Eric was in his office. He had just called Stephen and Katherine to join him.

Eric said, "I've given everything you said a lot of thought. Stephen, I'm tired. I don't think I'd like to continue to manage Shi. I'd like you to take over. You have already by proxy for most of the time. I've been away too much already. I've made up my mind. We'll inform the public I quietly sold my shares to you through the holding company as not to frighten the public and make them lose confidence. I've always wanted you to succeed me in Shi. I've decided to spend more time with discovering new medicines with Alex as my partner."

Eric stared at the floor, "But I still need your help. I need you to help finish what Alex started. I can't do it anymore. You can. Please, for Lin."

Katherine was humbled by what she had witnessed. Eric, the infallible person, humbly asking for help from Stephen. It just sounded so unreal.

Stephen answered without a thought, "Of course. Mei Lin is my 'mother' and 'sister.' You never need to ask."

"Thank you," Eric said quietly. "I'll fly to Penang and be with Mei Lin tonight."

"Eric, the shares you sold have all nearly doubled in price. We'll stand surety for all your borrowings. We've double the capital to cover that. With our shares in Regenesis, we've triple that. Don't worry about anything. I'll speak to the board and give a press release. You still own the company in Japan. Alex can continue without a problem, and we'll inject new capital into that. Just leave everything to me."

CHAPTER 40

A DANGEROUS MOVE

Eric held Mei Lin as she woke up and coughed. A bit of blood was in her sputum. His heart was broken seeing Mei Lin ill again. They had been through so much. Mei Lin was getting tired of it all. She wanted it all to end. It was another two months since Shi Corporation exchanged hands.

Eric was relieved that he could be with Mei Lin. Deep inside he knew her time was running out. The virus was not ready for human testing. Not for another year at least. They had just started animal studies.

Mei Lin said, "Just hold me. It's so nice to have you hold me. Remember the first time we met? I always thought you were the one. Deep inside my heart I knew. You looked into my eyes that day and I just felt we connected."

"Yes. How can I forget? You were so sure of yourself. You had that sparkle. That little thing in you. I just cannot ever put it in words," Eric said with a smile as he recollected. Eric held her in his arms. He smelled her hair as he had a thousand or a million times. It always smelled fresh.

"Eric, promise me you'll keep strong when I'm no longer here. The kids need you."

"Shhhh. Don't ever say that. You cannot give up."

"I'm tired. You know I don't want any more chemotherapy. I cannot go through it again. The fear is unbearable. My body is weak. We've fought this battle now for almost ten years. I cannot go on. The kids have grown up. They should be fine. So will you."

"Have faith, please. The virus is almost ready," Eric said unconvincingly. Tears were streaming down his cheeks and onto her face.

"Liar. I know when you lie. The virus is not ready. Alex tried and tried but he is not God. God decides. I'm ready for him."

Eric didn't reply but just held her.

In Japan, Alex was staring at the containers that held the virus. They were going to test the second batch on animals in the morning. They had tested on the mice. Now the dogs and pigs were next. His heart always felt uneasy when it came to animal studies. But without them, there was no way to know if it was safe for humans.

It was already past midnight. Lai Peng was holding Alex by the waist, with her head on his chest.

"You don't need to do this, Alex. You just don't. Ask someone. Pay someone."

"You know I can't. I have to do this. It's my idea. So the risk has to be mine. I'll be fine," Alex said as his heart started to race. The adrenaline was mounting.

"The isolation medical chamber with all the equipment for Mei Lin's care has been ready since last week. Eric wanted to have it ready should the remote chance we succeed earlier with the animal trials occur. I'll be fine. We talked this over already. There's no turning back."

"I'll be here all the time, Alex. I won't leave."

The night before they had a long chat about what Alex wanted to do. Alex had said, "I once thought I was special but I'm an ordinary person, Lai Peng, but maybe I have this fire in me that compels me to take on challenges. When I was young, I found the challenge in the framework of medicine. Then I wanted more. I wanted to help more people in a bigger way. That led me to thinking about creating clean energy. Now it seems I've returned to saving one life but in the course of this challenge I may have found a way to save more."

Alex surprised himself with his thoughtful words. He had never before been able to be so succinct expressing his deepest thoughts. He also knew he had not told Lai Peng the entire truth. Mei Lin was precious to him, more precious than he would ever admit. To lose her would be a blow he might never recover from. That she was Eric's wife did not matter. That he could never have her as his own did not matter. It was the knowledge that he would never see her again or be in her presence that drove a stake through his heart. His marriage to Lai Peng had recovered and found new footing, and it was a good one—albeit without passion. She had changed and so had he. While they would never find the sort of love he had heard about but thought impossible, they were now mutually supportive and kind to each other. Mei Lin, on the other hand, had shown him the possibility of romantic love, and his heart could never shut that out now.

Alex kissed her and hugged her before he opened the isolation room with his passkey. Calmly, although his pulse raced, he removed two canisters with the virus and walked into the medical isolation chamber with Lai Peng behind him. He gently put the canisters on the table and turned to Lai Peng.

He hugged her again and whispered, "It's time."

She slowly stepped out. He knew she could watch through the thick glass panel. The door closed. Alex was alone in the chamber. He smiled at her and mouthed the words, "It's okay."

Alex opened the first canister and removed a vial. With a syringe, he aspirated the contents and injected it into his vein. Through the corner of his eye he saw Lai Peng closing her eyes.

The human test had begun. Alex was the subject.

"You must be crazy. How could you?" Dominic had said when he arrived at the lab in the morning. "Amir, Karen, tell him it's suicide. You don't do human trials until you're sure."

"Come on, Dominic. Don't exaggerate. It's been done. H. pylori was ingested by the researcher to prove a point. Syphilis, the same. Come on, it's not new."

"You shouldn't have done that. You just shouldn't." Dominic shook his head. His eyes were full of anger. "You're really mad!"

Alex said from the chamber, "Well, I have. We can't turn back. If I'm correct, nothing much should happen. I'll just get sick for a while and then I'll be well. That happened with the mice. So, no worries. Don't worry, I'll be fine. I have everything I need in here. Besides, if we don't do it now, we'll shut down when Mei Lin doesn't survive the next month. There's no more money and no more need as far as Eric is concerned. We'll stop."

Dominic slowly calmed down. He knew Alex was right. They would shut down, and he would not have the chance to see it through. This would be his crowning moment in research if they succeeded. He sat down quietly.

"You do know you'll be in there until we're sure you are safe to come out?" Karen asked.

"Of course. I certainly don't want the virus out in the public," Alex said. "I'll inject an extra dose every day."

A week passed. Alicia was now at the facility. Lai Peng had called her. She only trusted Alicia to look after Alex if he got sick.

"Are you feeling okay?" Alicia asked. "You look a bit tired."

"I just feel a bit of a chill. Nothing more," Alex said. "You shouldn't have come. Mei Lin needs your care."

"You crazy guy. I've never seen a more crazy doctor than you. How could you even conceive of such an idea and get Lai Peng to agree to let you do this? You know the stress you put her through? I came as soon as Lai Peng called. Our colleagues can take care of Mei Lin. You are now my responsibility." Alicia said, half-turning to Lai Peng beside her.

Alex coughed gently.

"Are you sure you're okay? I'm coming in." She turned to the staff next to her and asked, "Where are the biological suits?"

Two days passed and Alex was now running a high fever. He continued to cough. Alicia had hooked up a saline infusion for him. "Looks like you got what you deserve now!" she said, annoyed. "It's not easy to work in these suits," she said as she adjusted his saline drip.

"I guess so," Alex replied, not wanting to quarrel with her.

"You are running a high fever. Take these pills. They should help. Now get into bed," Alicia ordered. "I get to call the shots! You rest. I'll see you in the morning."

When morning arrived, Alicia checked his temperature. "Your fever has broken. How are you feeling?"

"Better, actually. My throat feels better. What do you think? How are the test results?"

"The viral level is going down. Your white cells have risen. Just maybe you've done it. Another week more and we can confirm."

"No time to waste. Call Penang. Ask Eric and Mei Lin to come," Alex replied. "By the time they arrive, we'll know the final results."

*

"I have to explain the risks to you, Mei Lin," Alex said as he sat on the side of her bed a week later. Eric was seated next to Mei Lin. Alicia and Lai Peng were present in the room. "There is a chance everything will go wrong, and you might become very ill."

"I could die, right?" Mei Lin replied. "I'm fed up with treatment, Alex. I just want it all to end quickly if nothing can be done. So if it kills me, it's fine. At least it won't drag on. I'm just very tired."

"Don't say that," Eric said.

"Eric, we've discussed this already. I'm ready."

"Alex, don't explain further. I leave it in your good hands." Mei Lin coughed a little. "My total trust is in you no matter what happens."

Alex nodded, understanding the feelings she was going through.

She said, "We proceed tomorrow then as planned. Thank you for all you and the team is doing for me."

While she talked, Alex cast his observing eyes over her. Mei Lin had lost a considerable amount of weight. She probably weighed only about ninety pounds. Her cheeks were sunken. She looked pale. Her breathing was labored as she talked. Her ankles were swollen. Her tummy was swollen. *Is it already too late?*, he thought. *Could she take the reaction that would certainly occur when the virus reacted with her cancer cells?*

Eric caught up with Alex after he left. "What are the chances, Alex?" Eric asked.

"Well, you know the details. The virus should be safe in a normal person. But with the cancer present, a more abrupt reaction might occur. I have a fever and some symptoms only as the virus was destroyed once my immune system kicked in. With the cancer present, the virus will attack the cancer, grow in number, and may cause more symptoms."

"So there is a reasonable chance?"

"Yes, I frankly think so," was Alex's reply. "I think she is right. She will not survive another month without any new treatment."

"If she goes ahead and things go very wrong, she won't have that, correct?"

"No she won't. But if we don't gamble, she won't make it past the month."

"I can't accept that. But I'll go along with her decision. I really hope you are correct. How long will it take for her to recover?" Eric asked.

"We estimated it will take up to three weeks."

"Three weeks. That's quite a while," Eric remarked.

"Yes, but it might be sooner. The shortest time is probably ten days," Alex replied.

She might die even earlier if the reaction is too severe and cannot be controlled, he thought. He wouldn't tell Eric. It would be too unkind.

Two days later, in the isolation chamber, Alicia was ready to administer the first dose of the virus. She said quietly to Mei Lin, "Are you ready?"

Mei Lin nodded. She checked the syringe and slowly emptied it into her IV line.

Outside the chamber, Katherine stood in the corner with Stephen holding her hand. She could see the whole procedure. She felt the tension in the room. No one spoke. Alex stood beside Eric. Katherine's mother had her head on Alex's shoulder, while clutching his arm. Mei Lin's children stood in front of Eric. He had his arms around them. They had arrived with her and Stephen the day before. Dominic and a few of the team were also in the room.

When Alicia finished, she continued to hold Mei Lin's hand and sat there for a long while. She seemed quite used to her suit now.

Katherine thought, *This is the point of no return,* and said a silent prayer.

Everyday seemed like a routine the next few days. Mei Lin's condition remained about the same. Her blood tests were stable.

Eric asked Alicia, "Is anything happening?"

"Nothing yet. We fully expected this. The virus we injected was a small amount. They should hunt down her cancer cells and infect them. They'll grow and when they reach a certain number, will destroy the cell and be released to infect other cancer cells. As time goes by, more and more cancer cells should be infected. When a critical number get infected and destroyed at the same time, the cellular material released will cause a reaction. We call that a cytokine storm. It may be gradual but could be sudden. We cannot tell."

"It's so frustrating waiting outside here. Can I go in? Please," Eric asked looking at his wife sleeping with oxygen into her nostrils. Her breathing was slightly labored. She looked peaceful sleeping; devoid of the tension she expressed when she was awake.

"I can't let you in," Alicia said through her microphone. Mei Lin was asleep. "You're not familiar with the protocols. We cannot risk you catching the virus."

Eric said with a tense voice and worried face, "The waiting is just too much. I need to hold her." Deep inside, Eric was full of worry. He was worried he wouldn't be with her and have the last chance to be touching her if she didn't make it. He didn't really have any confidence the virus would work.

"Think of your children, Eric. They need you to be strong. Go and see them. Hold onto them as you would hold her. They are her in many ways," Alicia said almost automatically.

Eric understood what she meant, but to him, Mei Lin was all that mattered. He didn't even think of the children. All he could think about was Mei Lin. He didn't even think of Sukimi anymore.

Eric felt Stephen's hand on his shoulder as he whispered, "Come, let me get you a drink. She is asleep and Alicia will see to her."

They slowly left for the dining room.

Eric had his elbows resting on the table with his hands covering his face when he spoke. "I ask myself time and again why all this has been happening. For the past few years we've been challenged in ways we could never have imagined. So few ups and so many disasters. I'm broke and broken now. Mei Lin is dying. Why us? It's just not fair."

Stephen replied, "I really don't know. But there is always hope. We all nearly died a few years ago. We got through that. We're here now. Maybe we should just be thankful for the little things."

"I'm spent, Stephen. I have no more energy. In many ways, I'm glad I'm broke now. I don't have to worry about money and the company. Maybe that's a blessing in itself."

Stephen said, "You're not broke. We're holding on to all you owned in trust for you."

Eric said, "If Mei Lin doesn't make it, nothing matters anymore. Death for me would be kind."

Stephen quickly replied, "Don't ever say things like that. We have to hope. Alex has not given up. Alicia has not given up. We all refuse to give up. Don't you dare give up, Eric."

"I'm so, so tired," Eric said as he fell asleep in the chair.

Stephen had his arm over Eric's shoulder. He realized Eric had dozed off sitting there. He had not slept for at least two days. He really pitied him. Less than a decade ago, Eric was the leader Stephen had admired and would follow him to the edge of the world. Now he was a broken man. He survived an ordeal and cheated death. Now he was emotionally drained. Financially ruined. One love of his life was gone. Another was seemingly going. How cruel can life be? Stephen shook his head and felt life had been very unfair to Eric.

"Eric, Eric!" Mei Lin called out, half-coughing as she tried to speak. Alicia and Alex were in the room. Alex held her down. She was getting delirious. She had been running a fever for two days. She was sweating and her respiration and pulse were erratic. "We need to calm her down. A small dose of Haloperidol."

"I'll prepare it," Alicia replied. A few minutes after Alicia had given her the medication, Mei Lin was calmer. She continued to mumble and move but was much less restless.

Alex said, "It's been ten days now. The reaction is getting worse. We need to act now, I think."

"I've just seen the blood results. The virus is rapidly increasing. I agree. It's increasing too fast. The viral antibodies are not increasing. We'll have to suppress the cytokine storm."

"I'll prepare the scheduled medications."

Alex glanced at the see-through glass. Eric was sitting with his hands in his face, hunched over his elbows. Stephen was pressing his hands against the glass as he watched. Katherine had her back to the glass, probably not wanting to witness how Mei Lin was reacting. *These few days are critical*, Alex thought.

Since the injection, Alex was composed, putting emotions aside to do the job as he always had for every one of his patients. He had to be strong for all of them, he thought. He had to be strong for Mei Lin.

Mei Lin lost consciousness a day later. She was near death. Her respiration was more labored. The fever was high, above one hundred four degrees. Her urine output was slowing. She was jaundiced. Her blood pressure was supported with medications to keep her going.

Alex sat quietly beside her. Alicia kept vigil in the corner of the room, monitoring her vital signs. Alex said a silent prayer. *Please don't take her. I need her. We all need her to continue for our sake. I know it's selfish, but we need her. Don't make it her time yet. Not her.*

Eric was crying softly in the observing room whilst holding onto his jade pendant. Lai Peng had her hands on his shoulders trying to comfort him. No one spoke. All were there keeping vigil. Hours passed and most were asleep in their chairs as the night dragged on. Only Alicia was awake. Even Alex, exhausted, had fallen asleep in the chair next to Mei Lin.

Alex fell off his chair with a loud thud. He woke up realizing he had fallen in his sleep. He quickly gathered his thoughts and looked at Mei Lin. She was awake and looking at him. His heart must have missed a beat. He was fully awake and he stared at her. She gave him a slight smile. He looked at Alicia. She was smiling too.

Alicia said, "I think the worst is over. Her fever broke an hour ago. She just regained consciousness. Her vitals are stabilizing."

Alex could not believe what he heard. "Am I dreaming?" he asked Alicia.

"No, you are not. She has indeed woken up."

Alex looked at Mei Lin again and without a thought, embraced her, feeling her warmth and hearing her soft heartbeat as he had his head on her chest. A minute passed before Alex realized what he was doing. He let Mei Lin go and saw Alicia's querying look.

"I'm just too happy," Alex said in a slightly embarrassed tone.

Mei Lin smiled at him and whispered some words he could not hear.

"Just rest, Mei Lin. Just rest. We'll be here," Alex said.

"I'll inform the rest," Alicia said, gesturing to the glass panel. Mei Lin now had a good chance of survival.

CHAPTER 41

A CONTINUED SECRET

Alex and Alicia walked into Mei Lin's room. Eric was in a chair beside her bed. Mei Lin seemed well and gave them a smile as they entered. The kids were all sitting on her bed. Stephen was in another chair with Katherine sitting on his lap. Lai Peng was standing beside them, chatting with Katherine.

"How are the results?" Mei Lin asked almost immediately.

Alex said, "I'll leave it to Alicia."

Alicia gave Alex a look before answering, "Alex, you should tell her. Well, Mei Lin, we have good news. Very good news. The spots on the liver are nearly gone. What remains appear inactive on the PET scan. The lung nodules are all smaller and many have disappeared. The bone lesions appear to be healing. It looks as if the cancer has melted away."

Mei Lin asked, "Are you sure?"

"We're as sure as we can be. The virus had destroyed the cancer cells. And your immune system had destroyed the virus after they had done their job. There is no evidence of the virus now after six weeks. That's why we've allowed you out of isolation in the last week."

Eric said, "It's a total success?"

Alicia continued, "We could say that, but to be sure you'll have to be checked for the next months and years to come."

"I feel fine now, Eric. I've put on at least two pounds over the week. I'm eating better than I have for months. I have no difficulty breathing. Of course it's a total success. Isn't it, Alex?"

Alex smiled and nodded.

Mei Lin smiled back and said, "We should celebrate! I'm back!"

The kids hugged her and everyone in the room laughed and hugged each other. Soon the elation ended.

Alicia said, "Let Mei Lin rest. Doctor's orders," and showed the way to the crowd. "I need to just give her a quick check."

Alicia gave the thumbs up after examining her and said, "I can't find anything wrong. You are 100 percent fit!"

"So when can I go home?"

"Oh, probably by the weekend, when you are strong enough. We'll want to run final tests before you go home. We'd better let you rest." With that, Alicia walked out. Alex was about to follow her out.

Mei Lin said, "Alex, I just want a word with you."

Alex turned and said, "Yes, Mrs. Shi?"

"Shut the door. I want a private word with you." Alex shut the door and walked toward her. Mei Lin gestured him to sit beside her.

Looking straight into his eyes, she asked, "Was I dreaming when I woke up from the coma? I remember you hugging me and had your head on my chest. You were wearing the protective suit. I wasn't dreaming, right?"

Alex didn't reply. From his expression, he seemed embarrassed.

"It's okay. I didn't understand why you risked your life to test the virus until then. I know now what it's like for Eric to know Sukimi. I'm very grateful. I felt the warmth when you held me that day. I'm eternally grateful for everything you have done and will always be in your debt."

Alex appeared to try to utter a word. Mei Lin continued. "It's okay. It will be our secret forever. Now I know how much you care for me. But I cannot say I totally share the same feelings."

Alex seemed to have gathered enough courage to say, "I have absolutely no ulterior motive. I want you and Eric to be happy and have each other, with your kids and family."

Mei Lin said, "I know. I'll always be there for you and Lai Peng. Your sacrifice has been immense, and I shall never be able to repay you in this lifetime."

Alex seemed more relaxed with Mei Lin's further explanation. He said, "I ask for nothing and expect nothing. I consider you and Eric family. Family will always watch out for each other no matter what."

Mei Lin reached out to Alex, and they hugged for a short while as she whispered, "Thank you. I know you love me."

Alex was a bit startled by her whisper.

She said, "But I shall always be Eric's wife."

Alex smiled with tears in his eyes as he said in a hushed whisper, "I know. I understand. I'd never dreamt of separating you and Eric."

With that Alex left, leaving Mei Lin to reflect on her own.

Mei Lin quietly slipped out of her room after a while. A moment later she was in the hospital chapel. She knelt down and prayed.

"Dear God, thank you for everything in my life. The long arduous journey over the last years has made me realize how small I am. Everything that has happened in the last ten years has a meaning. I understand now. There are so many people I've gotten to know. They all are very good people. They have all helped me without question. I understand the test Eric and I had to go through. I don't feel the anger or fear anymore. I feel much nearer to you now. I'll make the best of my life to help everyone around me and us. I'll be ready for you when the time comes. I'll always cherish the added years you have given me. Thank you for letting me be the vehicle to find a cure for a dreaded disease. I do hope the sacrifices of so many people will make cancer disappear soon. Thank you for showing us the way. Amen."

CHAPTER 42

REGENESIS: NEW BEGINNINGS

A year later, they all met up in Eric's apartment in Penang. The Paragon penthouse apartment overlooked the beach. The lights in the distance were from the mainland.

Alex, Eric, and Stephen were on the balcony enjoying the night breeze. "Did you see the news today? They're still planning another link to connect the mainland to the island. There are already two bridges. An underground tunnel link is to be made. Soon the traffic will come to a crawl in Penang. The small island cannot support so many cars. The traffic is already bad."

"Yeah, I heard from Katherine," Stephen said.

"Well, I thought since we need to reclaim land, why don't we just reclaim from both sides, the island and the mainland? Then we meet in the middle. No need for any long bridge. Just a short one."

Katherine interrupted them. "Dad, please don't come up with any more ideas. We cannot go on another one of your quests. No more, Dad!"

They all laughed. "Yes, Katherine. Ha. No more ideas. We'll leave it all to the younger ones."

Katherine continued, "We're about to start. Come on."

Soon, Mei Lin and Eric were standing in the middle of the spacious living room. Many of the team members of Regenesis and the teams of the other two projects were present.

"We'd like to thank everyone present for coming to celebrate Christmas with us. Each and every one have sacrificed time and effort for us. Great strides have been made and since Regenesis, the green energy movement has really taken off. Finally, the energy crisis might be coming to an end. We're eternally grateful to the teams that led to my wife being here tonight. In another few weeks, the virus will be ready to go into full clinical testing, and we're confident many patients will benefit," Eric said. Everyone applauded. "Now I shall let Mei Lin continue."

Mei Lin said, "Our family owes so much to all of you. Especially Alex, Stephen, and Lai Peng. Katherine too. You all are family. I thank God for giving me the chance to be here with all of you." She held her crucifix while she spoke. She looked toward them and clapped. Everyone joined in.

She continued. "Eric and I have decided that we shall take a backseat. He will retire from business, and we'll be spending our time supporting cancer research and green energy. We feel it's time the younger generation takes over. Now Stephen has an announcement to make."

Stephen stepped into the middle, saying, "Thank you. Katherine?" He reached out to Katherine.

Looking a bit puzzled, Katherine walked up to him. As she did, he knelt down and said a serious voice, "Katherine, you are the one and only in my life. I'll follow you until the end of the world. Will you marry me?" He held out a beautiful shining diamond ring.

Katherine was stunned. Shouts of *yes, yes* echoed in the room. Katherine was grinning, embarrassed but very happy.

Finally she said, "Yes."

Stephen got up and put the ring on her finger. They kissed and hugged as everyone yelled congratulations.

When everyone settled down, Mei Lin said, "There is another announcement to be made. Katherine, please."

Katherine said, "Oh. I'm so happy. And embarrassed. Stephen, I love you." She paused and then continued, "Those close to me know

I've been writing about Regenesis and my father's ideas for cancer cures. Tomorrow my book, *Regenesis: A New Dawn*, will be released."

Another round of applause and congratulations went around.

Katherine said, "I'd like to propose a toast. To Eric and Dad, who made everything possible. If not, my book would not exist and we all wouldn't have met. A toast!"

They all said, "To Eric and Alex!" and toasted with the champagne.

"I'd like to quote my father, whom I believed in without question from a young age and whom I'll always continue to believe in. He once asked, 'If you had an idea with a remote chance for success that would take many years of your time, what would you do?' Alex and Eric believed, took the chance, and we're here today. An idea with a remote chance, dreamed by a few, shared by many here today, has transformed the world. This is indeed Regenesis."

Printed in the United States
By Bookmasters

ABOUT THE AUTHOR

Dennis Quiles, a US military veteran, is director of global security services for one of the world's largest multinational corporations. A thirty-year veteran of the protection business, Quiles is an acknowledged professional in casino, hotel, and corporate security. He studied at the Antilles Detective Academy and holds a bachelor's degree in criminal justice and a master's degree in business administration from American Intercontinental University. A father of three, Quiles is happily married and enjoys writing, hiking, and spending time with his family.